T0063010

OLGA RODIONOVA

OLGA RODIONOVA

Deepak Shrivastava

PARTRIDGE
A Penguin Random House Company

To order additional copies of this book, contact
Partridge India
000 800 10062 62
orders.india@partridgepublishing.com

www.partridgepublishing.com/india

Contents

CHAPTER 1

Olga Sergiyevna Rodionova was a graceful and unforeseen lovely jasmine of thirteen due to her sterling demeanour. That princess like the celestial damsel was the biggest example of unexampled substantial reigning beauty with golden hair, amenity on her fairly Circean face, rosy cheeks, argent figure as charming as sandal, claret lips, inebriating sapphire like flighty eyes and had a beautiful pair of pinkish palms. She was the perfectly mercurial rosebud of nature or in other words, she had paradisiacal beauty in this blue planet. She was the second Juno in the world and every person after seeing that girl said that the finest sculptor of the universe had specially created her apart. Obviously she herself had the empire of very delicate body as jimp as flower. That ubiquitous blonde was the most Elysian angel of the Elysium.

There was an unfortunate incident in her life, her father had passed away and now she had no one besides her mother. Some other workers hospitalized her father but potential god could not save him then her mother brought her up carrying her responsibility.

Her father's name was Sergei Mikhailovich Rodionov. He was the above middle class person and worked in an oil factory as The General Manager. One-day oil firm accursedly caught fire and he was injured badly. He died in the hospital just before an operation.

That day was the absurd day for both, Olga and her mother. Listening to that heart-breaking news, their lives were shattered. They got a bolt from blue.

Olga's mother remembered the first thing; named Dr. Irina Ivanovna Rodionova, was the future of daughter and the next was sorrow of avulsion- a sharp tearing pain of affliction that shot her mind and body. She felt herself as a patient of paralysis. Obviously, her world had demolished. She put up hardly with this heart-broken sorrow only for her daughter.

At that tough time, a fatal wonder was she was in labour. It was the fourth month and had a responsibility of her health, her daughter, and her womb in prime concern but upset too in those days because she was not able to give father's lap to her post-humus child. She could not have done anything during pregnancy but despite this, she had made herself ready to do good efforts for purveying Olga.

Now the responsibility of Olga's future was on her shoulders. She was an intelligent, frank, pretty, incredible, and gentle woman of dinky looks with kind heart. She was sensible and righteous too. She knew all her duties and completed them responsibly. She had been providing her every essential commodity at correct interval of time after the death of her husband. She tried to do good efforts and never made her daughter to feel the pangs of father's love. After the death of husband, she loved Olga many times to more for she did not want tears in the eyes of her amiable duckling at any cost.

———◆———

Twenty two days had relapsed and in that sorrowful moment, Christmas had come. People were celebrating Christmas all over the world and they were passing through the moment of grief. Their lives were in dark as a dreadful and ominous night is without recreational assemblage of stars.

Everyone was celebrating Christmas but on that occasion, Olga had been weeping. Ocean of misery was rippling clearly in her pearls. She was praying to God for the peace of father's soul. Irina was also on the same page with worst condition. Maybe, Jesus had written a vile Christmas for both.

Friends and neighbours were trying to alleviate their distress. They were showing them full sympathy but sympathy was formality. However, fellow feelings show attachment of one person to another but the real definition of pain can be given by the person who suffers from scars or such type of a fatal condition like death. Neighbours cannot give anything more than sympathy.

Dr. Irina was feeling giddy after seeing the precarious condition of her daughter. She said while wiping her tears, "Don't weep, my dear. Nobody can make victory over destiny. Fate rules the world and what is allotted cannot be blotted."

In the evening, all who sat near them for condolence had returned gradually.

The tight link of alliance relation had broken and Irina accepted her loneliness quietly but Olga was not contented from this devastating turning point in her life.

Olga dropped off to sleep in mother's lap while weeping. Irina kept patting her hand slightly on her forehead whole night. Out of tranquillity made her sleepless.

———◆◆◆———

Gradually, they were moving towards the daily routine life. As the days rolled on, New Year celebration had started. Approximately, one month had passed but Olga could not forget the death of her father. That day she was gravely serious because she was feeling the absence of her father in her life. She was in the room stark alone. Although her mother tried to make her happy yet she could not. Irina was also in very deep sorrow but in front of her daughter, she did not want to show it and for Olga's happiness she prepared confectionary and bought some chocolates and fantastic gifts to cheer her up. However, Olga did not come out from the room till the evening. She was feeling bad after seeing children with their fathers from the casement. She had taken her father's death to heart and grieved that no friend came to meet her.

At five o' clock in the evening, one boy called her by name almost coming into her house. Now it was the time when Olga was literally happy because she knew that voice. It was the voice of her classmate; named Igor Anatolyevich Levin. It was the first moment of that day when Olga met any other person after mother.

"Dear, why are you looking so doughy? Come on, let us celebrate New Year feast." He said after giving her New Year card.

"You know everything for all that you are asking about?" She said seriously.

"My dear, I understand your anguish condition and I also know if I had been in your place, I would have reacted in this manner. You should forget the past and try to live in present. I can only say that don't make this great day as a grave day."

"I too have been trying to make her understand but she is not accepting it." Irina said.

"Oh! Good evening aunty." He said.

She said very good evening to him.

After wishing Irina, he said to Olga, "Get ready. Now we are going to enjoy ourselves New Year night while you didn't celebrate Christmas."

"No, Igor. I cannot. Please, try to…"

"Oh! Come on." He had said before she could finish her sentence.

"Olga, don't lose heart. Hurry up and let's celebrate this New Year heartily." Her mother said.

"Please, accept my proposal. I have come straight here to change your mood." Igor said.

Finally, Olga accepted his proposal after much fuss but her mother was happy at last that her daughter was then ready to make the last moment happily of that New Year. She was happy in the happiness of her child. She gave her two thousand roubles for New Year celebration.

She was ready in thirty minutes and both moved to market. The market was looking like a bride of Moscow but *Olga was looking like a very cute princess of Russia.* Igor wanted to enjoy every moment with *the beauty of The Most High* and wanted to forget the dark part of the life.

Igor was very happy because it was going to be the most wonderful day of his life. He had the company of *one highly descended beautiful girl who was in the flower of her age. Psyche of this era. He would often think that that girl was the combination of Juno, Hebe, Venus, and Psyche. Other side, he also thought that either they are beauty goddesses or Olga was the beauty goddess of all of them.*

He would often live in dilemma. In front of her cuteness, he ever felt something strange in his heart but he got success in controlling his emotional ebullition. He respected her beauty, and ever wanted to see *her tempting face.*

Soon they went to church and prayed to God. He saw tears in Olga's eyes and gently held her as Olga put her head on his shoulder and began to weep. She remembered father's lap and love. Igor was making her normal but she wept continuously. He understood her feeling but what he could have done extra besides giving her company.

He said, "Now, come on. Don't weep. I am with you. Why are you weeping? I ever see Olga a strong girl. Come on. Who will take care of your mummy if you do not take care of yourself?"

She put her head in his lap but could not give him any answer. He wiped her tears while consoling her. After a while, somehow she pulled herself go on up the Moscow river. They were mooching around along with the river but Olga was serious. Seeing her unhappy, he put a proposal of watching one show in the theatre. She accepted his proposal with unpleasant mind.

Igor was happy that Olga accepted his proposal and he reached the theatre with her for the show while he had no interest in the theatre. Only for changing the mood of Olga, he decided to go there. During the show, Olga could not control her laugh after hearing some humorous dialogues. Igor stuck his eyes on her face and said, "Thanks, God! At least, she laughs. My decision of watching the show works."

They came back home at seven thirty. They were even happy after seeing an incomplete comedy show and he also celebrated New Year with Irina.

Before going home, Igor said to Olga, "I hope you will not turn the pages of past. I know it is not so easy to forget but you are to do it. I couldn't celebrate Christmas on December 25, but I will celebrate our Orthodox Christmas on January 7, and New Year's Eve on January 13, with full of jolly mood with you."

"Okay."

He smiled and moved out from there with his driver after giving and taking wishes. His mother had sent the car to receive him.

Her vacation of two weeks had started. She started practice of figure skating with Igor. He was not only an intelligent student but also a good figure skating champion and had won many trophies related to this sport. His partnership with Olga won silver medal at state level. He was at home in Mathematics also.

Olga was not perfect in this sport that's why they lost their technical points but he had full satisfaction that she was with him otherwise he were a gold medallist.

During the vacation, Igor celebrated Orthodox Christmas with Olga and on thirteenth of January; he also celebrated New Year's Eve with her. But Olga was not happy. She had contrition of her father's absence but trying to show him happy.

Party started around 11 p.m. when Moscow-Kremlin bell rang twelve times. He fed her one morsel of carrot piece from the Russian salad and served her coffee after opening the doors and the windows of Olga's room to welcome in the New Year.

***

Russian Orthodox had come and there was no writ of provision for celebrating Russian Orthodox epiphany. It came but there was no end of continuity of sorrow. On that occasion, Olga was unhappy. Every feast was teasing her father's absence. Possibly, The Most High was playing with the emotions of '*The peerless beauty*' but Igor had been with her to ease her sorrows.

More than four months had gone by and Olga had literally forgotten her father's death but her mother understood the genre of present life without husband. She knew that how she would travel a long distance that would never have been pleasant without hubby.

Irina had been living in tension because she wanted one duenna for her beautiful ducky but she never reckoned on governess. She had read many misdeeds of Duenna in newspapers that's why she was very afraid. It was her thinking that Duenna mixes drugs powder in meal to kill the members of family for money. That was the reason; she had a problem to find someone reliable to take care of her daughter. She also knew that her most immediate problem would be the last stage of pregnancy so finally she decided to find out one governess for her daughter.

She remembered Katherine Vadimovna Perttunen and phoned her, "Hello! Mrs. Katherine. How are you?"

"I am fine. What about you?"

"Not so good."

"Why? Is anything wrong?"

"You know very well about my condition. Well, I want your help, my friend."

"Yes."

"I am sorry to bother you, *Katya* but I have an urgent need of a housekeeper. Could you help me?"

"I will see. Let me find her."

"Thanks," Irina said.

"I will update you after getting some information of a good housekeeper."

"Okay."

Katherine helped Irina in finding out a good housekeeper. She told her through phone that one governess would arrive after two days. Irina thanked her profusely.

Petera arrived after two days. She wished Irina having a bright smile.

"Sit down." She ordered.

"Thank you, madam."

"Okay. Do you know what you are to do?"

"Yes. Mrs. Katherine told me your problem."

"Actually, I want you only for taking care of my daughter. I will also help you in the kitchen work but I hope you will be honest in your responsibility."

"Don't worry, madam."

"Okay." Further she asked, "Your wages?"

"Hundred roubles a day."

"Okay. You can join us tomorrow."

"Yes, madam. I will."

Then she stepped back from there.

Next morning, Olga saw Petera and asked, "Mom, who is she?"

"She is your care taker, my dear." She answered.

"Thanks mom but you have her need. I am able to take care of myself." She moved to governess quickly and said, "I hope you will look after my mother too."

"Don't worry. I will take care both of you. It is my duty to satisfy you anyhow."

"You are right." Then she moved to the bathroom.

Petera packed the lunch box for Olga. Doubt bells were ringing in her mind that she would mix drugs in meal so Irina was also helping her in the kitchen work.

When Olga was ready to go to school, Irina gave her the lunch box.

She left the house for school after taking breakfast.

Olga came back home and called out her mother politely in a dreary way. "Mom."

There was no answer.

"Where are you, mom?"

Again, she heard no reply.

"Where can she be?" She asked herself. "I think she must be in the kitchen with governess."

She stepped towards the kitchen and then again called, "Mom."

Irina was helping Petera for preparing lunch but after hearing her drear voice, she turned towards her immediately. She found her long face and tears through her eyes. She asked pampering her, "What did happen to you?"

"Nothing. I am all right."

"I think you are telling me a lie."

"N...No."

"Don't hide. Tell me without any hesitation...Tell me, what happened?"

"Mom, it is nothing."

"Then why are you so sad? If I am right, you are scolded by teacher for the delay in depositing your tuition fees. Am I right or not?"

"Y...Yes...N...N...No. Yes. Yes mom."

She could not hide anymore and said, "Mom, twelve days of this month have over and you are not depositing my fee. Having been punished by my teacher, I felt insult today. It is the first time in my life when teacher could point out to me. If you cannot afford fees of the private school, you should have admitted me in the government school. It is unfair with me."

"Here money does not matter, my child. I could not deposit your fee because my health is not good enough. Please, sorry. I deposit your fee tomorrow. Your father wanted to see you in the army that's why he decided to get you provided manual work in lieu of arts and cooking. The Director of your school is a good friend of your father. He told him his wish and he provided you manual work. This is the only reason; we chose this school for you. In the government school, it was not possible."

"Oh, sorry!" She said.

"It's okay. Be easy. I will deposit your fee tomorrow."

"You promise." Olga said.

"Yes, I promise." Dr. Irina gave assent. "Now stop weeping and smile."

"If you don't deposit my fee, my teacher will not allow me to attend the classes. Again, I cannot bear insult further."

"Okay, my dear. Well, fresh up and take lunch."

Olga turned to the bathroom but she returned suddenly. Perhaps, she remembered something. She went near her; fondled her politely and said, "Mom how is your unknown?"

"Unknown?" Irina asked startlingly.

"I am asking about your coming child."

"My naughty girl."

"Mom, I am not a naughty girl. It is wrong."

"Okay. Okay. I am sorry. Well! Go and be ready for lunch."

"No, you tell me first; will a son come into being or a daughter?"

"What do you think? Be it a boy or a girl?" Smilingly, Irina asked.

"In my opinion a boy will come into being."

"No. It will be a girl."

"It's a bet that son will see the light."

"How do you know?"

"My conscience is telling me and conscience never tells a lie."

"Okay, my dear. Now, stop a barrage of questions. It is too much. I understand you want brother."

"Well, one question is left to ask. How many days are left?"

"I think one week is left in delivery."

"Only one week!" She exclaimed greatly while jumping. Possibly, she was thinking that a living toy would be awarded for playing. She was very felicitous after hearing.

"Mom, when and how will I accept the pregnancy?"

Petera smiled after hearing her imbecile question.

"Oh, God…What type of a girl you are, my dear! Well, you may go and make me free to prepare lunch for you." Irina said.

"Please, tell me."

"I say stop at all." She said rudely this time.

"Why are you not telling me? Tell me the answer of my question, please. I also want to be a mother like you."

She conceded defeat in front of her daughter's innocence and said politely, "I shall tell you after taking lunch."

Olga saw her eccentrically. Dr. Irina further stated, "Why are you seeing me like this, my sweetie?"

She said nothing but passed an ingenious smile and moved to the bathroom.

Olga did not know about the pregnancy otherwise she definitely asked her mother's condition and she did not talk about her own pregnancy. Another reason was that her mother did not show her pains of labour. Olga was unaware of her mother's Anti Partum Haemorrhage problem.

When Olga left the kitchen, Petera said, "Madam, I will deposit her fee."

"Thanks but I will deposit because I also want to meet The Director of her school."

"It will be risky, madam."

"I know but this work is on priority."

"You will have my company for your safety."

"Thanks."

———◆———

Olga was fresh. Petera had laid the table and then Olga took lunch with mom.

After taking food, Olga washed her hands and paxed; mother reciprocated warmly and then she walked into the room and fell on the bed. She had forgotten her question. Due to suffering from tiredness, she fell asleep for a nap in a minute but her mother was mentally disturbed and was in a highly strung state because it was the first time when her daughter was scolded by teacher not for depositing the tuition fees while she was never scolded by teacher for any mistake. Now, her tenet of dignity had broken off and she did not want to excuse herself.

This matter made her very tense because she had a lot of money but feebleness belonged to her. She had only roubles 'three hundred fifty' in her home at that time. She was not able to go to the bank to withdraw money due to extreme pain. She was muttering while thinking in tension sitting on the bed hard upon Olga.

The government provided solatium of roubles '200000' and the empty post of The General Manager to Irina but she refused the post. She was also the heir of her father's property but the problem was that who would receive money from the bank because she was not able to do heavy work and Olga was immature to do such type of a work properly. The big problem with Irina was that her counted kith and kin lived very far away from her and she was helpless in such a hard time.

She was thinking. *Why are Bolts from the blue to us? What was our blunder? If I was the defaulter, you should have given me the punishment. Tell me God, what is the fault of my innocent child? Why do you not think about my child? Oh, Creator! Tell me, what is thy legislation? I think you have a heart of stone only.*

She felt ache in her every joint while engrossing in thoughts and felt pain in her womb. She was unable to stable herself in this highly critical condition. She was worried because she had done promise to Olga and did not want to make her child hip again. Continuous thinking made her mind dormant and heart started pounding.

She found her heart pumping fast when she put her palm on her breast.

At last, after much thinking, she decided to go to the Bank next day. Olga was her first priority than severe pain. She thought that she would also be free to deposit money in the hospital after depositing her fee.

She slept beside her while thinking in tension. Almost about two hours had gone and time was five o' clock but both of them were fast asleep.

Around five p.m., someone rang the door bell. One minute had passed but door had not been opened. As Igor raised his hand second time to push the button, Petera opened the door.

Igor was astonished who she was.

Seeing his odd face expression, she said, "I am a housekeeper. Come in."

"Okay, where is Olga?"

"She is sleeping with her mother."

"Oh!"

"Sit here and wait! I tell her about you." She said while indicating him for sitting on the sofa.

"Okay."

———◆———

"Good evening, aunty. How are you?" He wished her when Irina came out from Olga's room.

"I am fine. What about you? I see you after a long time. Where were you?"

"I am also fine. Due to home work and studies, I could not come to meet you."

"Oh! You were busy in your studies."

"Yes but where is Olga?"

"She is sleeping in her room." Then she said to Petera, "Go up and awake her."

"Leave it. Don't bother. Let me awake her."

"Okay."

He went inside Olga's room and woke her up but she was sleeping as if she could not sleep at all the four-five nights. At last, without striking anything in his mind, he held her hand gently and yanked in his direction. Finally, she awoke and shook her head with yawning while rubbing her eyes.

"Hi! Olga."

"Oh! It is you." She said.

"Hey! How much do you sleep?"

"Sorry, I was very tired."

"Yes, I understand. Well, would you like to go to the restaurant with me?"

"Yes. Sure, please wait for me."

"Why?"

"Oh, stupid! At least, let me change my dress."

"Olga, it is not good. I am not stupid. I suggest you to eliminate superfluous words from your speech."

"Sorry." She said with drowned face.

"Hey! Do not take it to heart. Here is a lovely rose for you."

"Cool! How pretty it is!" Then she kissed him.

Olga turned towards the wash basin and he left her room. He sat on the stool which was kept inside the kitchen. Dr. Irina was preparing strawberry juice for them. He said, "Oh! Strawberry juice, I like it. Its taste is good."

"That's why I am preparing it for you." She said smilingly.

"How do you know about my choice?"

"Dear, I know about your every choice. After all, I taught you English for two years and hence I know you very inch. Olga also usually tells me about you."

"It is interesting and my pleasure."

After sudden moment, Irina said, "What about your studies?"

"Not bad."

"Why? Are you not doing your studies properly?"

"No. Performance of Wolf and Olga was outstanding but my performance was literally good." He said while bowing his head.

"Oh! That is the trouble but it is also your good performance."

"I know aunty but difference is much among us. I am on fourth place along with Ashley."

"Do not lose hope and try to concentrate on your studies. The more you study, the more grades you will get."

"You are right aunty. I think so."

"Igor! Would you like to make a point of this thing what I am going to make you make out?" She asked.

"Yes, please. Sure. Why not?"

"Lore is not an important factor in life. It is only for gaining the maturity and makes the mind sharp to solve out the aspects. It gives you standard to stand in front of the society and increases your confidence level. The very important factors are wisdom, talent, strength, and saving of time. If you use your wisdom properly, it is truly confirmed that you can make your dynasty while changing the destiny. Thus, start to develop wisdom with knowledge for solving or understanding the worldly behaviour. As you want to be a professional like a big business man, so you have need of your deep sagacity and if you want to survive properly in this world, develop your good aptitude."

"Yes, you are right aunty. My Father also says it. I will remember it."

"Then you have no need to worry."

"Yes. But…If I shall acquire first place, then?"

"You and Olga are equal and I never feel any difference between you two. You both of them are my children."

"Sorry aunty. It is not that but I want to know your opinion on this matter."

"Don't be serious. Take it, juice has prepared." She said giving him glass.

Igor took the glass and drank it in single breath. Irina called out Olga but she did not reply. Again, she shouted, "Olga."

"I am just coming mom. Please, wait." Olga said.

He said to Irina after taking juice, "She is changing her clothes."

"Oh!" She mumbled.

Soon as possible, Olga stood in front of her mother. "Good evening, mom."

"Good evening, my dear." She gave her a glass of strawberry juice while accepting her wish. Olga drank it immediately. She asked both, "Do you want more?"

"No mom."

"Yes. I want a little more." Igor said.

"Sure!"

She poured juice in his glass and took it after him.

When Irina was taking juice, he looked at Olga intently. *He saw Olga in a crimson frock with a mazarine coif on her head and in medium heel sandals. She made two braids and she was looking like Hebe of Heaven. This colour combination of frock with her white ethnicity was appearing either blood soaking white handkerchief or bunch of red roses put over the bed of cotton. It was very difficult to judge for Igor either she was blossoming in deep red colour or red colour was being blossomed by her. In this dress, that little doll was the centre of attraction. Her beauty rendered him breathlessly with astonishment. Realm of her beauty made him a worshipper of her beauty.*

Igor went near Olga and insisted on while putting hand around her waist, "Could you permit us to go to the restaurant?"

"Okay but I want one promise from your side."

"Promise!" They said despondently.

"Yes. You will not spend more than two hours."

"Yes." They gave concurrence together.

Irina opened a wardrobe, drew out three hundred roubles for giving her but Olga requested for more and then she gave her roubles twenty more.

"Thank you."

While moving towards the garage, she remembered that her cycle had punctured. She moved back to tell him, "Bad luck, we cannot go together."

"Why?"

"My cycle has punctured."

"Why are you taking tension? Whenever I am with you it means no problem with you."

"Great! Did you come with two bicycles?"

"What a common sense you have. Tell me, can any person ride two bicycles at a time?"

"No."

"Then how can I?"

"I do not know but how will we go there?"

"We both will go on a single cycle."

"Oh! Not a bad idea." Olga said.

They went to a pleasance and started spending time in luscious talking while taking a round of a park. At that time, there was a tawny gloaming. *That beauty of nature was dead less in front of queer beauty of Olga.* There in the park, Olga plucked a rose flower and gifted him.

"Thanks but it is an excellent return."

"No. It is not so. You gifted me a pink rose and I am giving you a white rose and both the roses have different meanings. Well! Remember it, I hate these words like sorry or thanks in friendship. No formality."

"Okay."

After sometime, they went to the restaurant. Igor took a hamburger and she took French Fries with coffee. He took some pieces of French fries from her packet. Although he wanted to pay the bill yet Olga insisted and paid. He could not stand before her obstinacy.

At the time of returning, she asked him, "Why were all gazing at me inside the restaurant?"

"*It is because you are such a beautiful girl who has no description. You have a svelte look.*"

She laughed madly as though she had been listened to any joke. She said rhythmically, "Am I a beautiful girl?"

"I am not joking. *You are an extremely comely rose bud. You are totally lithesome.*"

"What a buttering! What a great buttering!"

"I am not buttering. Tell me; are you not two times winner of The Fancy Dress contest at school level?"

"Yes."

"Now your answer is on the tip of your tongue."

"Mmm. Well! They were the fancy dress contests not a beauty contest and I am not a Miss Universe that's why I am not a beautiful girl."

"Oh, imprudent girl, *you have a reigning beauty and Miss Universe is a small fly in front of you. I believe one day you will be a Miss Universe.*"

"Great exaggeration!"

"Why do you not believe in me? *You are even better than Cinderella, Alice, Snow white, and Barbie doll. They are comical babes but your beauty is realistic.*"

"Why are you exciting on my beauty?"

"What do you mean?" He said while entangling.

"I mean what do you want to prove?"

She made his mouth shut for a moment but suddenly he said, "I know, girls want to hear the expatiatory annotation of their beauty from boys that's the way you are talking again and again about your beauty and want to know my views."

"No, you are absolutely wrong."

"Can you answer my question?"

"Yes. Ask."

"Why do many boys in our school try to woo you?"

"What a silly question it is! I don't have any answer and I hope you will not raise such type of a cheap question in future."

"Sorry! Well, who is your fast friend?"

"Why are you asking me when you know?"

"I want to listen to you."

"Wolf Kotzwinkle."

"He is not a good boy. Come what may, as I know, he always cheats you because he never wants to see you being a topper. He is using you, nothing else."

"Why do you feel jealous? How can you say so with confidence?"

"Only dogs feel jealous but I do not. I also don't know about him but after judging his habits, I feel he is fishy."

Some moments later, Olga said seriously, "He can be fishy for you but he is good for me while in the final semester I want to make him upset."

"Good. My best wishes are with you."

By heart, Igor also wanted to acquire the first place because Olga liked Wolf's intelligence that's why she loved him. He was sure in that matter because he knew that she spoke only with him and Kotzwinkle. It was because she loved the 'Masters' of any field especially in studies. She gave much importance to the quality of the education and she had good capital hand in it.

Igor never saw her with any other girl and boy in school as well as in the neighbourhood. Sometime, not generally, he saw Olga talking with Ashley Djamalovna Dementiva. She was also one of the good grade gainers after Olga among girls. He knew her nature very nearly.

On the way home, Igor stopped and parked the cycle in front of a Book House and he went inside the store without Olga.

A young woman clerk walked up to him and said, "May I help you, little master?"

"Yes. I want a good__ Do you have a book on Romance?"

She looked at him unusually. "R-O-M-A-N-C-E?"

He felt like an idiot for a moment but he said confidently, "Yes. I want a book on Romance."

"Which type of romance do you want? Is temptation, expectation, intrigue, intense, Medical romance, historical romance or others?"

"I want enchanted romance."

"What is your age, my dear?" Seeing his confidence, she asked.

"Thirteen."

"Okay. Have a look at this rack. You can see all kinds of romantic books here."

"Sorry. I do not want in the Russian Language. I want an English novel."

"Do you know how to speak English?"

"I have passable knowledge but my girlfriend knows it very well that's why I am purchasing it for her."

"Well, come with me."

"Yes." He followed her.

"Look here."

"Okay."

He selected one book 'FRIENDS AND LOVERS.'

"How much is your bill?" Igor asked.

She told him the price.

"Okay. Please, pack this one." Igor said while giving her money.

She packed it and gave him back.

"Thanks." He said.

"Welcome."

He returned that place where Olga was waiting for him. "Shall we go?"

"Obviously." She said. "Which book you bought?"

"I don't know." Igor answered.

"My dear friend, never buy any book out of judgment."

"You are absolutely right but I have estimated."

"You are such type of a puzzle which is really beyond description."

"It is interesting."

"Well, be quick. We have wasted lot of time." Olga alerted him.

"Yes. Yes. I shall have you dropping in twenty minutes."

Near about fifteen minutes, Igor stopped his cycle in front of her home and they kissed each other; then he gave her a gift.

"What is this?" She said after taking upon it.

"I do not know. When you open it, you will certainly know about it."

"I know it is a book."

"Obviously it is a book but what type of a book it is I cannot tell you. Well, I am too late to go home."

"I want to ask you something." Olga said.

"Yes."

"Why do you buy so many expensive gifts for me? You should not. I never pay you attention then why you do for me a lot of."

"Because you are my friend."

Now, Olga was silent but after some moments, she said, "Sorry, I should not have showed my rude behaviour."

"Hey! No sorry. I never mind. I was wrong there. I should not have asked such a baseless question."

"No. I was wrong. *Spaciba Bolshoi* (Big thanks)." She said.

"No need of thanks. Well, Bye." He said.

"Good bye."

As Olga turned, he called her out by name.

"Yes."

"Olga, after the exams are over, our two months vacation will start. I hope you will give me company in figure skating practice."

"Yes. Don't worry. I will practise hard with you and next time, we will win gold medal."

"Yes. Next time, we will hold the trophy of first place. Okay, bye and take care."

"You too."

She pulled the door and went inside after seeing him off where Irina was waiting. Quickly she stood in front of mother and passed a charming smile.

Her mother looked at her sternly but after seeing her naive face, she had a pity on her. She hugged her gently with kisses rubbing her hand slightly over her back.

"You are late." Irina said.

"Please, sorry. In future it will not be so."

"Okay but why are you so late?"

"Igor was purchasing a book. He gave me a gift also; I think it may be either a novel or a story book."

"Remove the packing." Irina ordered.

After removing the packing sheet, she put it inside the trash-bin. She found one book.

"My conjecture was true, mom." Olga said. "He gifted me a novel, name is 'Friends and Lovers' and author is Diana Palmer."

"Is it FRIENDS AND LOVERS?" Startlingly Irina asked and her face was red after hearing.

"Yes but what is the matter? Why do you ask me like this?" She asked.

"No, nothing."

"Even then…"

"Everything is fair."

"After all…"

"Stop at all. Keep quiet and leave me alone. I do not want arguments. The words I say mean it."

Olga felt some strange suspiciousness in her mother's behaviour. She wanted to perceive what secret matter her mother was hiding but she did not want to do any argument with her. She always obeyed her mother. In other words, it was her noble attribute. She placed the book on the table and moved towards her room.

Half an hour had gone by as the watch struck eight p.m., Dr. Irina called for Olga. She quickly came near her and said politely, "Why are you calling me, mom?"

"Dinner is ready. Take…"

"Mom, I am not feeling hungry." She cut in.

"Why?"

"You know I have taken fast food…have you had food?"

"Why do you perceive it?"

"I can understand you are angry with me. Please wait, I am coming after switching off the lights and then we will dine together."

Soon she returned and went to the washbasin to wash her hands and then they both took food together while watching the television show. They had finished their dinner. Olga did not want to leave the company of her mother but her examination was round the corner; she did not want to waste her time. Her aim was to defeat Wolf therefore she had increased her study hours as her exams were going to begin after two weeks.

Her mother wanted to make her busy with the television show. She was again disappointed. She thought, "Obviously, Igor loves my daughter very much. As I understand, his love is expanding its wings. Today he gave her this book and it shows he wants to make my daughter clear about friends and lovers; especially about love. It sharply means, my daughter loves someone else and she treats him a friend. It indicates that he wants to draw my daughter in his life. He loves her."

Nevertheless, Problem with Irina was that whether Olga knows anything about this burning matter or not. Now she was confirmed that her daughter treated him a friend and she had told him about her own love affair. "Yes. That is the reason he gave her this book." She muttered.

"How should I tell her that love relation is like a thin thread? It cannot bear tension and Igor is going to take a sharp banking on the curvy road of love. If Olga loves him, I have no problem otherwise this one-sided love can spoil his life." Shaking head she further thought, "I will have to know about it intently otherwise his life will relapse."

Passing time in thinking about that matter, she saw the watch which was striking eleven more. She could hardly stand up and kept that book on her bed. She found a rose flower on her bed and placed it in the vase that was on the study table of Olga. She was back in her room and lost in sound sleep after taking sleeping pills and pain killers.

Olga awoke early in the morning but her mother was sleeping. Having completed the routine work Olga sat for taking breakfast. She said to Petera, "Aunty, take care of my mother after my leaving for school and make her remember to take medicine."

"Okay, don't take tension. I will convey your message." Petera said.

She was about to finish her breakfast, then the door bell rang. On opening the door, she found Igor.

"You are here so early in the morning! What brings you here? Is some important work?"

"No."

"Then why?"

"Can I not come here to meet you early in the morning without any reason?"

"Yes. You can but…"

"Dear, how will you go to school without cycle? Your cycle is punctured and you forgot to get it repaired."

"Oh, yes! I forgot. Thanks but you should have to concentrate on your study. It is more important in your life than me."

"I come here to help you and you behave like an inspector with me."

"Sorry…Come in. I do not want to hurt you but being a good student you must think on my statement."

"Yes."

"Good. Would you like to have breakfast?"

"No, thanks but where is aunty?"

"She is sleeping. Do you want to talk to her?"

"Let her sleep…Is she all right?"

"I think she is all right. Please, wait. I am coming after wearing my uniform."

Twenty five minutes had rolled on but there was no hint of Olga's return. "What is going on with Olga? Why is she not coming?" Worriedly he mumbled.

Watch struck half past seven and classes would start at eight o' clock. Now his tension was increasing.

She went to propose him that we should go.

"Of course we are late. Were you wearing dress or buying it?"

"Sorry. Girls take more time than boys while changing the dresses."

Then she put her bag on her shoulders and moved to the gate with him.

Suddenly Igor said, "Olga, where is your lunch box?"

"It is inside my bag. Canteen is also long-lived."

"Even if, you will want to share my lunch then without any hesitation you can take it in the interval."

"Thanks but I feel that you do too much care."

"It is because I lo…I like you. After all, you are my fast friend."

Igor came with his chauffer but they were late from beginning. He ordered him to drop them at the school as soon as possible.

On the course of travel, Olga said, "Drive slowly."

"Don't worry. He is a trained driver." Igor defended.

Further Olga said nothing.

———————

Dr. Irina woke up. On the other side, they had the school on time but the assembly was over. Students of secondary classes were giving the attendance to their class teacher, named Anna Sergiyevna Rusanova. When Olga's roll number was announced, teacher said, "Did you deposit your fee?"

She grew with shame but gave answer politely, "Madam, today my mother will deposit fee?"

"Okay. I am giving you last chance because it is your first time. Otherwise, I will have to fine you and also mark absent in the attendance register."

"Sorry madam."

"Okay, have a seat."

———————

Irina was in agony but the matter of depositing Olga's fee was hammering in her mind. After taking breakfast, she took some anodyne, changed her clothes and combed her hair. Petera put the key in ignition and Irina took back seat of the car.

She ordered her to drive to the Bank. Petera followed her direction.

She withdrew money and turned towards Olga's school. Cashier helped her seeing her critical condition. Now, she had deposited Olga's fee.

Cashier said, "Sorry madam but why do you come here for depositing fee in this critical stage. You should take complete bed rest. This time isn't for doing hard work and it can create problems for your baby."

"I know but sometime some circumstances make us slave."

"Well! You know your personal problems very well but I can give you only right suggestion. You are doing wrong with your womb doing this."

"It does not mean you are wrong. I respect your suggestion."

Cashier passed smile and then she moved back. Now, she was free from one big burden but actually, her heart was weeping. She was not able to bear the integration of pain. Her pain failed the effect of pain-killer pills.

She met The Director for an important work and after that when she was moving downward through the stairs, she slipped her foot and had a narrow escape but after that incident her pain was multiplying. Petera delivered her from falling but her face blanched. She said, "You escaped being hurt."

She screamed out with the stringing pain. When she was on the half way, she said to Petera, "Hurry up. I am unable to bear the integration of immitigable pain so, please, drop me immediately at the Hospital."

She phoned doctor and quickly she had been admitted in emergency and she was under the care of nurses.

One doctor came inside to meet her, "How is your life, Dr. Irina."

"I am literally fine and you?"

"I too."

"Why?" She asked strangely.

"My patient is in trouble so how I can feel well."

"It is my pleasure, doctor." She said passing smile.

He checked her up properly. Now he was serious. He didn't say anything to Irina but after completing his work, he moved to his chamber. He said to one nurse, "She is suffering from APH and with prolepsis. She is also suffering from Anaemia and the case is much too critical. Both Mom and womb are in danger. It is very difficult to say about success in operation."

"Here, the important factor is we should not leave our hope even you are one of the best gynaecologists of Russia." Nurse said.

"Yes, you are absolutely right but if she had been obeying my instructions, her precarious condition could be good but she did not. Well! What can we do when she does not want to help herself? But she must."

Nurse could not give him any answer but she had been seeing tension in his face. He was thinking something sitting on the sofa.

Ten minutes later, nurse said, "Why are you taking too much tension for this patient? I never saw you in tension for any other patient before. Does she a very beautiful patient for this you have chagrin?"

He took a deep breath and said, "I know she is very beautiful but it is wrong to say like this. She had been my classmate and I would love her. It is not true to say that I used to love her but my love is still young for her but I could not express my love that's why being a good friend, I want to save her life. You don't know, her husband died four months ago and she lives with her daughter. I know her hard condition and think to marry her but I don't have courage to say so."

Nurse smiled and said, "That's why you did not marry and adopted one daughter."

"Yes. I love her so much. She is my love, my life, my soul, my peace and everything. She is above all. But it is not true that I did not marry. I was in reproductive age so I could not have adopted a girl. Thus, I made a consignment wife who belongs to Italy. After adopting a daughter, she left me because our agreement had completed."

"Then why are you not getting courage to propose her?"

"Leave it. It is not easy to bring forward this proposal because I know her answer. She will not accept my offer."

"Don't lose hope. You should at least try for this."

"Leave it."

"But why? She does in need of a partner and can agree to this proposal."

"No. Never. She prides of her marital status and still wearing her wedding ring on the right hand. I have to wait to see her when she will wear this wedding ring on her left hand otherwise my proposal can hurt her. She is still in love of Sergei."

"Make her understand that how will she care of her daughter?"

"She is self dependent and can easily. She is a million dollar woman but problem is that god never did justice with her."

"What does it mean?"

"Her mother died when she was six months old. Her father married to an American woman but her step mother could not take care of her. Actually, she used to admonish her. Her father did not like to see cruelty on her that's why he sent her to Russia for studies. Her mother wanted to acquire the property of billion roubles of her husband but the inheritor was Irina that's why she used to quarrel with her husband. Her father died in her bereavement but before taking the last breath he handed over her more than seventy percent of his property and rest amount to her step brother and her step mother. I don't know it is right or not but her first marriage was not successful and finally after giving divorce, she married with Sergei that's why I am confirmed that she will not marry with me. Since birth she faced many ups and downs that are why she feels herself accursed."

"Oh! Tell me what I can do in this matter for you. It will be my pleasure if you please let me help."

"Thanks but I will talk to her after the operation."

"As you wish." She said politely.

In her school, Olga was also upset and Igor tried to cheer her up but she was acting like a wild cat.

It was the period of Mathematics. Her teacher was teaching but Olga was attending her period absentmindedly. Wolf had also understood her mood but in front of teacher, he could not say anything.

Irina pushed the button of bell and one nurse came inside her room.

"Yes madam. Is any work?"

"Yes. Please, call in a doctor."

"Yes madam. Please, wait."

Soon enough, doctor came to meet her. "Is there any problem, Dr. Irina?"

"Yes. I want to give you a little trouble."

"Sure."

She told him about her daughter and requested to receive her from the school. Doctor gave her assent.

The last period of the school was going on and his personal assistant, Roman Abramovich Tikhinov had reached to receive her. The Director sent one peon to inform Olga and Roman told her everything clearly when she was in the room of The Director.

"Your name, please?" Olga asked after wishing The Director.

"Roman Tikhinov."

"Please, wait."

She made face in the direction of the Director and requested politely, "Sir, I want to confirm it. May I use your phone, please?"

"Intelligent girl, your mother sends me an application with him."

"Yes sir." Then she read the application. She was satisfied after seeing the signature of her mother. Without asking any question further, she left the school building with him after taking permission.

Seeing her slender beauty, the attribute of Roman was like a drunkard. He made his desire to drink the peg of that *brewery of comeliness. Obviously, she was an unripe rose bud.*

He was tolerating to control the emotions of passion but he could not. During travel, He felt ebb and flow in his passion and wanted to come in her contact. He was unable to tolerate that time. At last, he put hands on her shoulders and asked, "Have you taken lunch in recess?"

"Yes. I have had lunch."

At that time, he was working like a meretricious sheep. That lip service behaviour which he showed her was the way of starting to make a physical contact.

Olga asked, "Is my mother relatively good?"

He answered, "Not in a good condition but not so bad."

Listening to that statement, tears rolled down on her cheeks. Again she remembered her father's death because her father was also died in the hospital. She started praying for the good health of her mother. Roman wiped her tears and forgot the passion when he saw tears on her fairly guileless face. Then he felt, "One universal truth over the world is that there are two foolish facts which people are very dalliance of, first is infatuation on the beauty of girls, and second is sex or rape with girls for taking the blessedness of orgasm. It belongs to me because I am one such type of a person who is libidinous. Who gives me authority to destroy her virginity? Oh, God! I am an impious person, really impious but I repent for helping her whenever she will have bad time."

Innocent face of that girl could change his character, although character persists.

Chauffer applied brake right opposite to the hospital. Getting out from the car, they reached Irina's room. Olga found her mother in thinking. She was lost in nostalgia. It was the night of August month; Sergei was reading one volume lying on the bed. Olga had slept. Locking the door from inside, Irina came near him with an eager desire of second baby. She grabbed the book from his hand and started kissing him. She was fully bent upon to make that night very romantic. Surely, her passionate kisses were augmenting his heat of masculinity while making his heart melt.

She was in her birthday suit and put off his shirt lying over him and dropped down after waving it like a flag. Taking her in arms tightly he also rolled on the bed and started cupping and titillating her breast. She also wanted to parch in his heat. In response, she increased his vigour and could feel in his arms how muscular he was. He also stimulated her strange feeling to bring on sexual blessedness. They were feeling the bliss of burning of souls.

Olga ran her flabby fingers slightly on her forehead. Feeling warm touch she came in the real world from the land of romantic dreams. Roman had left the room.

"Hello Mom! How do you feel?"

"Fine, my dear." She said but actually, the deliciousness of her romantic feeling had been ruined.

"What were you thinking?"

"I was thinking about you." She told a lie. After all, how could she share private feelings with her?

"Oh! Really."

"Yes."

"How did it?"

"I lost my balance on stairs."

"Oh! You should get down the stairs carefully."

"Yes. I should have."

"Obviously. Well! Mom, I recall my question. You did not tell me when and how will I give birth to a baby like you?"

It was a tough question. Irina was confused. Nevertheless, she told, "After five years, you will give birth to a child."

"How?"

"I do not know."

"Don't you? You know. However, you are going to give birth to a child."

Irina was in distress and confused too. She was now fully obscured to tell something about it. She drowned in deep thinking and mumbled after a while, "It is odd to tell such things."

"What are you thinking, mom?"

"Nothing. Listen to me carefully."

"Yes."

"When girls cross the age of eighteen, they are able to accept the pregnancy. Before eighteen years, pregnancy can create some problems in the foetus of girls and to their children also because one child cannot foster a child and this age is only for playing, studying and enjoying the life but not for getting such type of responsibilities. However, we Russian girls follow either age fourteen or sixteen for marriage and it is legal in our country but eighteen is perfect age for marriage."

"Mom, without marriage no girl can accept the pregnancy?"

"All the girls are able. Marriage is a part of life in which male and female make one strong bond but actual thing is sex between the partners. After contact, women become pregnant."

"Here sex means? I read it on some forms and certificates to fill up."

Olga was being released arrows of questions and lines on her forehead were showing how much Irina was irritative to tell her daughter transparently. Hesitatingly she started, "It means mingling of souls."

"How is it possible to mingle souls? Do we have supernatural power for mingling souls after marriage?"

"Oh no! How can I make you understand?"

Olga saw her like an idiot.

"When male sperm meets with ovum of the woman, it creates pregnancy."

"What is ovum and semen? What are you saying mom? These words are beyond my mind. I am unable to understand them."

"Oh! Why are you not trying to understand it?" She said putting her palm on her forehead.

It was very tough task to her for telling it but in a moment, Olga said, "How can I understand these terminologies. I never read them before."

Irina was going to tell something then she saw doctor coming into her room. He was on the routine visit. Doctor asked, "In which matter are you talking? How are you feeling, Irina?"

"I am much better now."

"Hello Olga?"

"Uncle, I am fine."

Then Irina said, "Doctor, Please, give light to her about marriage institution. She wants to know about the pregnancy?"

"Are you suffering from insane asylum? Don't you know she is just a child?"

"I know doctor but she creates a very typical condition."

"She is not in ample declining years."

"No doctor. She is thirteen years old and in this age, you know, menses period starts and I want to prepare her to face the realities of sex life as well as sex diseases. You don't take tension. It is also in my one of the responsibilities. By the way, imparting of sex education is the simple way to make anyone mature."

"What a frank lady you are. Even then…"

"It is her wish to know it. She raised the question, doctor."

"Okay. As you wish." He said ruminatively.

Then suddenly Olga asked, "What is menses period?" In addition, she was all ears when doctor began to tell the sex theory to calm down her curiosity.

"Menses period means monthly discharge from the womb. Blood comes out in this period. The average menstrual cycle is of twenty eight days. Ordinarily bleeding lasts three to five days. If a girl does not start menstruation by sixteen, it is a matter of concern."

Flabbergasted Olga said, "Blood."

"Yes."

"Does it pain?" She said while frowning with wide eyes.

"Yes."

Olga asked many questions on this matter and one by one doctor cleared everything and she caught on.

Doctor came outside after checking her up mother.

"Are you satisfied now?" Dr. Irina asked.

"Happy but it is Greek to me." Olga said while passing a smile.

"Don't worry. You will know about it perfectly with time."

"Whatsoever will be the time but some factors like AIDS, Vaginismus, menses period, Clitoris, and venereal diseases scare me."

"Why do you worry? It should be imparted to you for knowledge sake and security point of view."

"Okay but tell me, who is quean and light-minded, mom? Doctor used these two words."

"They are prostitutes. Those women offer the use of her body to earn money for sexual intercourse with others." She further stated, "It is enough to you and now I want to tell you something."

"Yes, please."

"Can you live six-seven days without me?"

"No mom. What are you saying? How can it possible?"

"But it is compulsory. You will have to do it. Please, my dear."

"But why? I cannot live without you."

"I am admitted in the hospital for six days but I want to make you prepare about worldly behaviour thus I want your entrance into the outer world. You have to gain some practical tips regarding the life and the society for adjusting with every situation using aptitude. Olga, it is your quest how you can make yourself ready to face the behaviour of the world alone and in this matter I cannot help you. You have to prove me within six days how you can create coordination with the surroundings using wisdom and strength. I want to see how you can manage everything properly without my support."

"It is a tough task to do and I need your help. You have also my need."

"Here, nurses are for me but you are to do it as per your intelligence and I am fine here under the care of nurses."

"How can I leave you alone? You have…"

"Shut up. Don't pretext."

"But…"

"I can understand your feeling but here is no other aspect. Being an obsequious daughter, you ought to obey me and you are not in a level to argue with me."

Hopelessly she said okay while Irina did not want to take this risk but she forced her under compulsion. Besides it, there was no other way to make her prepare for worldliness.

For a long while, they kept sitting in mum position but suddenly Olga said, "May I live with someone?"

"With Igor."

"How do you know? But you are wrong."

"Then in which friend do you have interest to live?"

"Wolf Kotzwinkle."

"Kotzwinkle." She said startlingly.

"Yes."

"Will he come?"

"I cannot say."

"I think Igor is good for you and he lives not so far from our house."

"No mom."

"Why?"

"I love Kotzwinkle…I…I mean…I mean, I like him." She said lightly.

Irina smiled but suddenly she stopped. Perhaps she remembered something.

Her face was showing acute tension but suddenly she relaxed. Olga understood that her mother had listened to her mumbled voice but there was another matter in her mind. She was thinking about Igor because she had known her daughter's choice. Irina knew the side effects of love that's why in her mind; question of Igor's life was striking. She thought. *I was right. Olga does not love Igor.*

She asked, "If you love Wolf, so what is the role of Igor in your life?"

"I treat him a good friend but he cannot take the place of Wolf in my heart. I lo…I like him."

"Don't tell a lie. Be frank with me. Do you love him?"

"Yes mom but there is much limitation between you and me and it is not in manners."

"Who said it is out of manners. Remember it; I am not only your mother but also your good friend. It is the matter of your life that's why you will choose your partner for surviving the life mutually. I can help to make you alert from the wrong partner because bad one can spoil your life. In my views, love is not a crime and any lover is not a criminal. Well, can you tell me what love is?"

"Yes. Simply you love me and I love you."

"Dear, I want correct answer."

"I don't know mom. I read love has many idioms so this humble word has no definition."

"You are absolutely right but love means to understand the emotions and responsibilities of a partner giving him security till death. If any friend swears with partner for leading the life together and to keep for company whole life, establishes the relation of love."

"Okay."

"You told me you love Wolf."

"Right."

"Well, if Igor serves that proposal, then?"

"It is a typical condition. Both of them are my fast friends. I love Wolf because he is a topper. Come what may, I cannot leave him and you know I want intelligent people in my life. It is true, Igor helps me lot but he is not a topper. He is only a hard worker and hard workers are always donkeys."

"Can you leave Wolf when he will not be able to maintain his position in the class?"

"It is tough question but all by myself, I can do it."

"Why?"

"It is a question of my life. How can I survive with a failure person?"

Irina said after giving a slight slap on her cheek, "Dear, love is divine feeling means above every relation. It is eternal. Love wants sacrifice not selfishness. Your statements show how much selfish you are. It wants only sacredness and good mutual understanding, strong bond and empathy between the partners. Always judge person from his heart not from his work and smartness. Tell me, what does Russian proverb say?"

"Wait. Mm…yes. When you meet someone, you judge him by his clothes, when you leave him; you judge him by his heart."

"What I want to say, I have said. Now, ball is in your court."

"Mom."

"Yes, my dear."

"Igor helps me a lot means too much. He stands by me in every weal and woe. It means he loves me."

"My answer is yes. Nevertheless, you have to remember one thing- love means love it, not leave it."

"Mom, Igor is my fast friend, not my love and you know infatuation is not love."

"It is right. Truth is that he loves you more."

"How do you know?"

"Don't go in depth but remember it that who helps in adversity is a real friend. It will help you every time to read the character of people through at a glance."

"Yes. I will remember it."

"Does Wolf love you?"

"I do not know about it. In fact, I never asked him but I know only one thing that in studies, he treats me as his foe and generally in other circumstances he talks to me in a good manner but ever gives him preference first."

"In my views, he does not love you."

"Mom, Igor also says."

"Simple, Wolf does not understand your value that's why Igor tells you. Well! Are you ready to face the problems of the outer world without my help?"

"Yes." Hopelessly she said.

"Don't be hopeless. God will help you."

"Maybe…"

She said to Olga, "Please call in a doctor."

She did it. Doctor asked her condition while entering the room.

"I am better." She said but she requested him again to get her daughter dropped at home while giving her keys. Doctor called the assistant and handed over Olga again to Roman. He kept glancing at her while driving whereas Olga was thinking so many things sitting silently.

At her house, he said to Olga that whenever she would be in problem, she can call him immediately without any hesitation. He left after giving her his contact number and gave assent of his responsibility to her mother.

CHAPTER 2

She opened the main gate of the house and went inside to open all the windows and inner doors because she was feeling suffocated. Standing inside the room, she said, "It seems that home has not been cleaned today. Where is Petera?"

She phoned her then got a severe shock. Her mother gave her permanent leave. She was disappointed why her mother did it and left her totally alone.

She put the receiver on the phone and started to set all the things at their right places. Her home was untidy then she started doing up the rooms. When she was about to free from this work, the landline phone rang up. She picked up the phone. It was her mother's call. She asked, "Have you reached comfortably?"

"Yes but why did you refuse to Petera for coming here?"

"People who take support do not move forward. And then how my daughter can take recourse."

"I do not know why do you complicate the things? But it is not fair."

"Sorry but it is my responsibility to make you strong. Well! Take care." And then she disconnected the phone. Now she was satisfied that Olga reached safely.

But Olga was disappointed that her mother did not talk to her pleasantly. She was tired after doing the remaining part of the work. Being feeling hungry she went to the kitchen and drew out two eggs from the rack. She began trying to fix evening meal. At last, she had succeeded in the preparation of fluffy omelette.

Ten minutes later, Olga placed the plate of omelette on the table and sat down in the chair. She picked up a fork and completed it.

After taking omelette, she moved to bedroom but she got a glimpse of her image in the mirror and again she studied herself in it. She muttered, "I am looking like the girl who works in mine. Oh! Many dust particles have made a net with my hairs. How abhorring it is! It seems I am a house of spiders."

Then, changing her program, she walked into the bathroom and came out after taking bath in the towelling robe, leaving wet footprints on the carpets.

She found Wolf in her house. First time he reached there to meet her. It was also a coincident. At once, she astonished and strangely asked, "When did you come here? Why did you not ring the door bell?"

"I came just before a minute but door was open. Therefore, I…"

"After all, you should ring the door bell. Well! You have come first time in my home so you are welcome."

He did not answer and saw her from top to bottom. *She was looking like a little nymph who came out from the river after bathing.* He imagined drops as dew on the leaves of a rose bud. It appeared that the drops of water over her body were kissing her gently.

He had melted over her cute look and wanted to hug her. He went near to embrace her but Olga did not allow.

Today he felt one truth, "It is true, beauty really does not want jewelleries because flower does not need accessories."

He further said, *"You are looking like a beautiful mermaid."*

She shied. "Oh! Sorry, Wait. I am coming after wearing my dress."

"No need of it. You are perfect in this towel."

However, she ignored his odd wordings. By the way, she loved him very much so she moved from there without saying him anything harsh but he held her hand. She did not understand that her look was enchanting him.

"Let go my hand." She said.

He did not.

"Keep your hand off. Please Kotzwinkle. Don't vex me. Why are you teasing me?"

"I am not teasing you but I want to talk to you."

"But before talking let me wear my clothes."

He left her hand. Olga went into her room to change the clothes and came after wearing a frock to meet him but she did not find him in the room. She searched Wolf in guest room, drawing room, bedroom, and study but there was no sign of him. Perhaps he had gone. For a moment she thought she was dreaming.

"I think he has gone. Oh! How stupid a girl I am! I have lost my chance." She was thinking moving to study.

Two hour had spent; she heard the ring of door bell. For opening the door, she went there and found a teen-age vendor vis-à-vis.

"Who send it?"

"It was ordered by a lady, name is Irina."

"Okay." She said.

He gave a packet of food to her and moved back.

After seeing her beauty, he was out of control. Really, he had gone off his head. He started dreaming for making a date with her. Reaching her home, he rang the door bell again. Olga opened the door and said, "Yes."

He saw *her stunningly alluring blue eyes* intently and then he was more under in the influence of her unworldly beauty. He asked politely, "Could I ask your name, please?"

"Why?" Olga said while frowning.

"I want to do friendship with you. I find you very charming and feel drawn towards you."

"Shut up stupid. First see the difference between your age and mine. If you want to live rest of your life safely, go away quietly otherwise, something will happen wrong with you seriously. Lest it should be that I will have your tongue torn out. Keep out of my sight. Without wasting time, clear out of my house." She instructed him angrily.

Affection of that boy who was sixteen years old had vanished. She had marred his pleasure. He was out of hopes because Olga devastated his wish.

Without doing further arguments, he turned to the Hotel.

Night was stretching its arms slowly and slowly and stars were flickering in the sky. The darkness embraced the world below. It was the time of eleven o' clock and night was too dark, only the lights of her house were glimmering for tolerating the fear of darkness. She was afraid at that time because she never spent the night alone. She phoned Igor and told him about her hard situation. He persuaded for arriving at her home with father.

After the conversation with Olga, He told her condition to his parents. Being an ingenuous boy, he ever did help to others without selfishness. He had a convivial nature. He reached there within fifteen minutes and rang the door bell. Olga opened the door and found Igor with his father and body guards.

"Good evening uncle." She wished.

"Good evening."

"Please come in."

"Thanks. I have a flight so I have to go back for packing. Don't worry. Igor is here to give you company."

"Please wait." She requested.

Quickly she moved to the kitchen and came with two glasses of water and gave them respectfully.

"Thanks." They said simultaneously.

"It is my pleasure."

Now he had gone and Igor was with her. He felt strange feeling inside the heart and his hands were numbed. He was feeling himself one of the luckiest boys in the world because it was the great opportunity to him that he had a company of a cute angel while he knew that it had been a dream of many boys. However, other side he respected her that's why he did not want to feel such things what others used to feel.

"What are you thinking, Igor?"

"Nothing but I am trembling." He said anon coming from dream world.

"Why?"

"I don't know. Leave it…"

"Would you like to take something?"

"No."

Even then, she moved into the kitchen, came back with food packets, and took varieties of food with him.

During taking food Olga saw one satchel and said, "What is this?"

"In this valise, here is my uniform and books."

Now he was talking to her. After sometime Olga asked, "Where do you want to sleep?"

"I want to sleep in the guest room."

"But you are not my guest, dear." She flirted.

"Then where should I sleep?"

"In the guest room."

He passed a wide smile because he had understood that she wanted to read him.

"It's okay. Lock all the windows & doors properly." Igor said.

"Yes."

"Well, where will guards stay?"

"Tell me, drawing room is right place for them or not?"

"Yes."

They locked all the doors and windows. Before going to sleep again they checked them properly.

Igor was not habitual of sleeping in dim light and he could not adjust it. He wanted to get the bulb switched off but Olga would be afraid of darkness that was the reason she always slept in dim light. Condition was tough and adjustment did not follow by him.

At last, he got out from the bed and moved to tell her his problem. He said while awaking her, "I cannot sleep in light. Please switch off it."

She turned off the light but she was afraid lying on the bed. Although she did not tell anything to him because she knew that, he came only for her help and she did not want to impose her priority on him.

Igor had slept and after half an hour, Olga went to the guest room and lay close near him. She was feeling relaxed and after sometime she also slept. Her warm breaths were striking on his cheek and then he awoke. He felt burden also. It was Olga's *plushy hand* on his chest. He perspired and felt the heart beats quicken. He held the hand of *a qualitative figure* softly, put over her gently, and left the bed after covering her half by blanket. Taking a pillow and a heavy bed-sheet, he slept on the sofa in the hall.

Now at that time, his eyes were beaming and he was thinking something while quivering because he never slept with any other girl until before. He was not able to bear that situation. He could not believe that he had slept with a *great sylph like*. He numbed at that time but while thinking he lost in sound sleep.

Next morning, Olga awoke first and found her alone on the bed and then she got out from the bed and walked to see him where he was. She found him in the hall. He was sleeping on the sofa. Without disturbing him, she freshen herself and prepared tea for all and then she roused him.

She asked him when he awoke, "Why did you leave the bed?"

"I was scared when I saw you on the bed with me. Your corporal tangible and warm breaths made me fear because I never slept with any other girl."

She passed bright smile and said, "Get up. Only one hour is left to go. Be fast."

"Yes."

"Are you really afraid of girls?"

"No, it is not right but…actually, if it were true, I never talk to you." He asked a little moment later, "Why do you ask this question?"

"This situation can create problem when you will spend life with your partner."

"If I am right, you have grown up."

"Yes dear. I have grown up but I was joking."

In fact, he had a dream to marry Olga. He loved her very much but he wanted to know her correct answer and wanted to know what she wanted. He did not want to impose his love on her. He left the sofa and stepped out to the rest room. Outside, someone was ringing the bell. Olga went to open the door and took breakfast from the vendor. She found another one.

When they had worn their uniform, they took breakfast.

Now both of them were ready to go to school.

"Let's go." Olga said.

"Wait, my dear."

"Why? We are late."

"My mother will be coming here."

"Oh!"

Time was 7:35 a.m. and chagrin on his forehead was showing acute disappointment. Now he was in tension. The rules of his school were hard and he had deposited fine last day.

"What's probe with you?" Olga said after seeing chagrin on his forehead.

"You know very well about it."

"Don't worry. She will be about to come."

"But we are late."

Then hearing horn sound of the car, he came out and found his mother. She gave one lunch box to Olga and another to Igor. After receiving the lunch box, Olga respectfully thanked her for this hospitality. Igor's mother dropped them off just before the school gate.

In the hospital, the condition of Irina was so-so and she was feeling the twinge of pain and not feeling well without Olga. She had her tension. She did not want to leave her alone but what could she do extra besides it. She wanted to make her used to of the bad world and she forced her while putting stone on her heart. Memory with Olga was being remembered by her. She recollected past sweet happy moments of her daughter and tears were brimming through the eyes on her cheeks. Pearls from her eyes were showing the extreme love of one mother to her daughter.

She came from the dream world when doctor sat by her.

"Are you well?"

"Yes doctor."

"Dr. Irina, do you think were you right?" He imputed her.

"I cannot say anything doctor but I was right. First of all, she had raised the question and the second point is that nurse had told me right about my condition that I am not keeping a good health. I know, I am suffering from Anti Partum Haemorrhage and there is no guarantee of my life. After much thinking, I decided to tell her all the things about it because without me, none can teach her but everybody can play with her for sex. I must not say like this but I am a mother that's why I have her tension. I have decided to send her America for her further studies but the problem is my step mother was once a prostitute that's why I forced you to tell her such things for security purpose. The death of my father was not in my bereavement but when my father knew the truth of his wife, he could not bear it and died. We have royalty in our blood. To accept a prostitute is out of our royalty. You can understand my tension. She can humiliate my daughter because she hates me. Anyhow, I cannot tell her about this truth and cannot teach her negativity of the society because she is but a child but I can make her strong for bearing the obscene of the wicked world that's why it was compulsory to me to teach her and this thing will keep her alert. After making prologue, I decided to teach her about the sex education."

"Yes. You are right. Sorry. Now I appreciate your decision."

"Only I know how I could compel her for living alone but…but my heart has pounded. My heart is like a broken mirror and there is no well hit in my mind to do extra instead of it. Sometimes, man is too helpless to do anything against fate."

"But why you did it?"

"Doctor, you will get success in operation then no problem. On the other hand, if not, it means this is the time when I examine her activities that's why I let her off from my hold to live alone. Suddenly one great problem arises that she has not prudence which she can use because we can find school for knowledge but cannot find school for wisdom and you don't know she is reserve dignity also. She does not like to talk to everyone but now in this situation, she will have to talk to different types of people. Nobody can teach it but anyone can gain it along with the world. This thing will make her extra mature and this is the demand of time. In this period, she can come forward while getting deeper sagacity with sharp outlook ready to create good adjustment with the society and can discard the undesirable impulses and fear. I want to know will she get over successfully. Therefore, I am taking a big risk and I have no other alternative also. I believe she is able to handle any situation."

"Really you are for deserving being respected. You are doing well but it is risky."

"It is my pleasure doctor and I also know it is risky but I have no other option. By myself, I cannot describe…one more thing is that she has fallen in love and you know in love we should have to know about love and lust and this thing also create a compulsory situation to me to tell her."

"It is also right." He said while passing a light smile and then he moved back from there.

———◆———

In the classroom, Olga remembered the love of mother's lap. In fact, she did not know the correct definition of love but able to breathe the air of love and feel the sensation of love. She also loved her mother so much.

When the school had got off, Olga came to meet her with Igor. She found her mother reading a book.

She disturbed her and wished 'good afternoon'. Face of Irina had blossomed after seeing *the Circean face of her daughter*. She kissed her many times and her lips and cheeks were wet. Her sensation felt it as a beslobber.

Irina asked her about the activities of the last day and she told her clearly everything. She was not satisfied but happy after knowing the courage of her daughter.

Igor asked, "Why do you want to make Olga independent? May I help you finding a good servant?"

"No, my dear. Thanks for it. I have deposited money to the Manager of the Hotel. He will get her provided food at meal time. If it is Olga, you should not bother about her. I never want to hand over my daughter to housekeeper. I never trust servants."

"Aunty, Olga can live with us. I welcome her. If you permit her, she can live with me."

"Thanks but my wish is to see my daughter competency of living alone."

He did not ask any question further. Olga was also silent. Irina gave them apples and they ate sitting silently.

———————————————

After twenty minutes, she told them that they should go. She had known that Igor had slept one night for the security of Olga and perhaps he might be able to change the theory of her daughter's heart. She also like him because he was not only a sapient gullible boy but also diligent.

Reaching home with Olga, he spent much time in talking to mother through phone. He also helped her in some housekeeping work and then set in for doing home work with her.

After an hour, Igor got out from the bed. He washed his face and went to the shop to get the punctured cycle repaired and also purchased packets of biscuits for Olga. He returned home within half an hour. He went near her and said to take biscuits. They took biscuits together and again absorbed in studies. He was doing good effort in this final term because he wanted to take the place of Wolf in the class that's why he wanted to clear the concepts of all the subjects.

While studying, three hours had gone by. Olga took cessation but Igor was doing his work.

After sometime, Olga heard the voice of the door bell and she went to open the door. She collected the food packets from vendor. Olga turned to Igor and requested to take dinner with her.

They watched one movie after taking dinner. He left her company soon for studying and after an hour, he fell on the bed.

Ten minutes later after Igor, She switched the power of T.V off and slept after midnight feeling tired from studies.

It was the time of sparrow chirp and both had done their routine work. Zinaida Igorevna Levina, mother of Igor, had dropped them off but scarcely had they reached the school when the bell rang.

Olga saw Wolf taking entry from the main gate of the school. He was passing through the parking area. She shouted, "Wolf. Wolf."

He came near her to shake hands but Igor had gone to the class silently.

"How are you?" Wolf asked.

"Fine and I have one question to ask."

"Question!"

"Yes. Day before yesterday, why did you leave my home without meeting me?"

"I cannot waste my time for you. Isn't it?"

He walked towards the class room after passing the rough comment. Olga was disappointed because she had spent one day for him. The previous day he was absent. Therefore, she asked the reason today but he ignored her.

Apathetic Olga went into the classroom alone. She sat with Igor on the first bench of middle row.

All the lectures had completed. School time had over, they both moved to the hospital directly and Olga gave description of the previous day to mother. She was literally happy.

Igor dropped her off. He said to Olga, "Wait for me. I will return soon."

Olga said, "As long as you are with me, I need not worry about anything. You are not only my friend but also my escort."

He laughed gently, slid inside the car and said to driver, "Go."

Now she was feeling totally loneliness. After taking bath, she engaged in studies. The wall clock was showing six p.m. but she had been studying. Hearing her name by someone, she was extremely happy. Leaving her work aside she went near to meet him.

He was Wolf Kotzwinkle. She said to him, "Why do you come here while you do not want to spend time with me?"

"Okay. Bye. But your question is totally rueful."

"Please stop…" She could not say anything more.

"Why? Have you had any problem?"

"No but sorry. Don't go."

"Well. What are you doing?"

"Obviously, I am studying."

"Oh! Which subject do you read?"

"I clear the concepts of Mathematics."

"Mm. May I help you in solving out some problems?"

"No, I have solved. Well! Would you like to take coffee?" She asked.

"Sure."

"Okay." She moved to the kitchen but she turned back and said, "Will you take French leave from here?"

"No."

Then she took a way of the kitchen.

He was very happy because he also wanted the company of that *beautiful houri* showing to others that he had also a girlfriend but being a plumed serpent he never showed black emotions. He loved her beauty but hated her achievements. He felt her like a thorn in his aim. He was a topper but Olga also and she defeated him many times that's why he wanted to show his good ability and talent not only in front of teachers but also in front of every Student. He wanted to prove that he was a prodigy while Olga was a prodigy.

Teacher loved Olga because she was a hard worker and burnt the midnight oil to get very good marks in the exams and also versatile. She took an optional subject also with manual work while the manual work classes were only for the boys. Cooking, arts and crafts belonged to the girls but she chose manual work taking special permission from The Director. She would also attend special classes on Saturday while many students used to attend school for five days.

Great coincident with Wolf was that he understood Olga as a topper and Olga understood him a topper. In study, one was like a dog and other was like a cat.

Olga prepared coffee and on the other hand, Wolf was thinking how he could waste her precious time. He knew that she loved him eternally so he wanted to gain the full profit from that matter. It was true; his adopting power was better than Olga but his defeating problem was his own over confidence.

Olga came with two coffee mugs and drank together.

"Can you go outside with me for strolling?" He proposed Olga.

"Sorry. I am busy now but you can spend time with me here, if you want."

"Please Olga."

"I can give you company tomorrow."

"Why?"

"Igor is also about to come."

He began to envy and without saying anything, moved outside the room. "Thanks for coffee but I do not spend time with girls in their home."

Olga felt odd but even after she cried for making him back but he avoided her.

Again, she was unsuccessful to fulfil her wish to spend time with him. She was upset. She had missed her boat. Now she was thinking, "Why did she not go outside with him? She could have phoned Igor for coming late."

With upset mood, she went to study but her mind had immunized for him. "How a stupid girl I am! I have lost one more chance again." She said.

Now Wolf had known the critical situation of Olga. He was thinking during on the way that he would give her company next day.

Igor reached there. He found her unhappy. "Why are you upset, Olga?"

"No, I am not upset. I am hearty." Making herself normal, she said.

"After all…"

"I am fine." She said.

Then they started talking on the matter of figure skating practice. Suddenly, Olga changed the topic. She started conversation to know how to make strategy for qualifying the exam successfully. He saw her in excitement and found her confident for achieving the top rank in the coming exam.

That day was spent as usual, nothing more, nothing else.

———◆·◆·◆———

Night's candles burnt out and both were in the school campus.

Something was special; Wolf came near Olga with happy mood and said, "How are you?"

"I am fantastic." She said. Taking a deep breath, she asked, "Is something special today?"

"No but why are you asking this question?"

"Because I see you so happy today otherwise you live in self-conceit."

"Yes, today I am happy but it is obvious in itself, the boys live in self-conceit."

"I am going to class." Igor said to Olga making interruption in their talking and he had gone to the class lonely. Wolf entered the classroom with Olga to cause to pass time in talking. Just ere reaching, Wolf said, "Well nowadays are you living solitarily in a solitary confinement?"

"First of all it is not a solitary confinement but my auspicious paradise and I am living with Igor. I have his security."

"Cool down, Olga. Don't be red."

"Wolf, why do you ask?"

"Yesterday, I thought, you are living alone that's why I decided to assemble with you. Therefore, I feel to know your choice."

Olga jumped with happiness and she could not believe her ears that it was his words. "Oh! Sure."

"Really."

"You are Welcome. You can come with me after the school."

"Okay."

She was covering the great length of happiness. It was the first time in her life when Wolf asked her for company. In the last three four days, it was the only day in which she attended all the lectures conceptually. The school got off and Olga reached to meet Wolf. He was going to the vehicle stand. He was in the day dreams. Olga held his shoulder; suddenly he came on the earth and said, "Who is it?"

"Friend…It is I. Olga."

"Oh! Actually I am thinking something."

"About me."

"Shut up. Why should I think about you? For your kind information, you are not as important as studies. I am thinking about the schedule of my studies."

Olga disappointed but she said in polite manner, "Let's go."

"No."

"Why?"

"Not just now. I will come in the evening."

"I think you will not come."

"I think you know better than I. So much madness is not good. If I say, I will come so obviously I will come"

Olga was not sufficed. Suddenly she said, "Mr. You told me in the morning to give me company. I have no need of your company. Is it clear?"

"All clear."

"You can pass only slang."

"Oh! Don't be red. I Promise. I will come...I will certainly come after informing my father."

"It depends on you but I will expect you in the evening."

After this, she went home. She was feeling boredom and wanted to swot-up but she could not help her own. She was worrying about Wolf. Her squirming was indicating that she liked him so much but she was unknown from his wish. It was exparte love probably.

She was feeling every second is equal to minute, every minute is equal to century, and every hour is equal to epoch. Her time had stopped. Hours crawled like by millennium even if she was striving to study.

She saw time lying on the bed. Watch was striking four o' clock. Somebody was ringing the door bell. Hearing the sound of the doorbell, she was extremely happy. She felt that Wolf would be there. When she found Igor, suddenly, her body language changed. He had understood the whole matter.

Without saying anything, he turned back and then Olga held his hand and said, "Where are you going?"

"I am going home."

"Why?" She said melodiously.

"I have read your face expression. I think your company is Wolf today."

"Hey! Take it easy. I took you for Wolf."

"Sorry. You should catch only one frog at a time and then it is good for you otherwise no result will be there."

"Please come in. You both are my best friends." She said putting her hand on his shoulder.

"Leave it Olga. Let me free."

"Sorry."

"In friendship..."

"Neither sorry nor thanks." Olga completed. "Well! Come back."

"No. Sorry."

"Do you come or not?"

"........."

"I say, do you come or not?" She shouted.

"........." Now being a statue, he was looking at her face with cute expression.

"Okay. Now I break up this friendship…"

He put his finger on her lips and said, "Yes. I am with you. Yes. I am back for you and I am not going. This break up can break me into trillions of pieces. I can live far from the world but cannot live without you."

Then Olga kissed him while hugging.

They went inside the room and started playing chess.

Igor asked, "Will Wolf give you company?"

"Yes. You will also. We will enjoy."

"No."

"Why?"

"It is because he is not a good boy. If it is your notion that he is a good boy, you should take his company."

"Dear…How can you say?"

"Leave it. You cannot listen to."

"Why?"

"Please, leave it."

"Anyway Igor, my mood is for going to the hospital. Can you spend time here unless I will come?"

"Why?"

"Wolf will be coming here so you can stop him here."

"I cannot help you in this matter."

"Being a good friend…"

"I am not a good friend." He said in a squeaky tone.

"Please, do it for me."

"I say no and the words I say mean it."

"Please accept my request."

"You are very selfish. You made me back for this work. Stop at all Olga, you do not know, he is not a good boy." He burst this time.

Olga saw him strangely.

"I don't have pent up feeling but I don't like him. To be a topper is another thing but to be a man, having a positive and healthy mind is a perfect thing. He is selfish, mean, greedy, haughty and arrogant. One day you will feel the pangs of remorse. I don't want to provoke you against him but you are my friend therefore I alert you. I don't want to see you in harm."

"Don't blame him like this. As I know, he is a good boy. I do not know why you treat him a bad boy. He is a topper and any topper cannot be a scoundrel but I know he is arrogant." Olga said because she did not want to lose that opportunity one more time. She said after a moment, "Will you help me in this matter?"

"Don't give me pressure."

"I hope you will not violate my oath."

"Olga! It is not good." He said angrily.

"Being a good friend, do it for me."

"Okay." He surrendered.

Then she went to the bathroom. He said himself, "How can I tell you that he had given me an intimidation strictly for breaking friendship with you. He is a roadie type bastard."

On the other hand, Irina's condition began to deteriorate. Her chance of survival was negligible. Doctors had lost their hopes and had stricken their flags. He gave clear cut refusal to Irina. Her tears came out through her eyes after imagining the cute face of her daughter. She was not afraid of death but she was scared after feeling the future and life of her innocent daughter. Now she was badly sad.

Suddenly she dialled her landline number. Igor received the phone, "Hello! Igor is speaking at this end."

"Oh! Igor, how are you? I am your aunty."

"I am fine. What about you? Are you okay?"

"I am also fine. Where is Olga?"

"She is changing her dress in her room. Don't worry aunty she is coming to meet you."

"You should take care on the way."

"Aunty Olga wants to go alone."

"Why?"

"Actually, Wolf is about to come here to meet Olga that's why I am here. This is the matter I cannot come to meet you. I am here to convey him Olga's message. Another main reason is that I am to go back."

"Why?"

"I do not like Wolf. He is not a good boy and today he is her company."

"Okay. Tell her for bringing the photo of Wolf if she has. I want to see his face."

"Yes. I will tell her."

"Okay." Moreover, she ended telephonic conversation and took a carefree breath.

———◆◆◆———

Igor informed Olga that there had been a phone for her. He told her everything.

Olga shook her head in a manner of accepting.

She reached the hospital. Now she was in the mother's ward. Irina won her in arms and celebrated her close. "Are you well?"

"Yes. But what…When will we live together, mom?" She said immediately.

"We will live together soon."

"Mom, I have a tension of your unhealthy condition."

"It is same here, my darling. I want to tell you something that you will not come here to meet me and never be worried about me. You are to prepare for exams without taking any tension of my health. Your exam is not so far."

"No."

"It is my order to you. Strictly, you are to obey it. Is it clear?"

"Clear but it is not fair." She said having a downcast mood.

Irina said kissing her, "My baby. I love you and I will be with you soon."

"I love you too and I hope so."

"Well! Show me the photo of Wolf."

"I do not have."

"But you must have. Wolf should be in the group photo of your class."

"No. He is not in any of the group photos. I do not know why?"

"Okay. But I want to say that I do not like this boy. This boy is American and I hate Americans. I hope you will not meet him."

"But why? Americans are not bad. He is a topper and good boy also." She said while bewailing.

"I do not want to hear you. What I am saying just obey it."

"Once you will meet him, he can change your theory against Americans. I know he is arrogant but he is more intelligent than I. You will see your daughter in him."

"Don't say anything. I am your mother and I know what is good for you. Moreover, obey me like a good girl."

"Mom, I cannot survive without his company."

"Stupid, just shut up. This American is not good for you. I am saying it means having some meaning." She shouted.

Bearing the scold, she began to weep. Irina wiped her tears and made her normal. She said, "Olga, I am your mother and I don't think anything wrong for you. He is not able to you."

"Why? What is the reason behind? Without seeing him how can you say this? Have you ever met?"

"No but It is not explainable. I hate Americans so how my daughter can love them."

"Why? Americans are also human beings."

"Olga, you are doing continuously argument with me. It seems that you have forgotten all the morals."

"No mom. But he is my love. I love him heartily. I cannot live without him. He is the finest track of my life. I like his ability of accepting challenges."

At last, she had to accept her obstinacy but she was not happy. She knew that if she forced her, she would not be able to attend her exams properly. Therefore, she took her own words back. However, she did not forget to take promise from Olga that she would not come here to meet her until the end of the exams.

Olga asked, "Mom, last time you told me that you would back home after six-seven days and now you are saying that I will not come to meet you until the end of the exams. Is everything in your favour or not?"

"Everything is fine here but after the operation your brother and I will live under the care of doctors and nurses. That's why."

"Okay."

Irina wanted to tell one more thing but she could not tell her. She complained, "Oh! God, what type of a game you are playing with me and my daughter."

———— ✦ ————

Wolf had reached her home but he found Igor. He said, "Where is Olga?"

"She has gone to the hospital to visit her mother."

"Why?"

"Her mother is hospitalized."

"Oh! Yes, I know. She told me. Well, tell me one thing, how did you feel when you spent night with Olga?"

"Shut your dirty mouth."

"Why are you angry? Tell me."

"Stop at all."

"Okay. Okay. When will she come?"

"I think…She is about to come."

"Is it confirmed?"

"Yes."

"Well! Will you favour me?"

"Tell me!"

"Now I am going but you will not tell her that I was here."

"Why?"

"I want to see her eagerness that she loves me or not."

"She takes me after you. She loves you more and more."

"I want to see the depth of her love. I don't want any wall in our relation. If you find she loves me, I hope you will go off from her life."

Igor said, "You are right. Who am I to create obstacle in your relation. Well…do you love her respectfully?"

"Obviously, I love her."

"Okay, I will favour you."

"Thanks!"

Wolf had made hay while the sun shined. Igor could not see through his trick what politics he was going to play with him but he was entrapped by him easily.

Wolf had gone from there. Igor was thinking about the reaction of Olga. He was confirmed that Olga loves Wolf but he was not in a position to leave her permanently. She was his life. He could not have lived without her but he did not want to force Olga for getting her love.

───────◆───────

Igor saw Olga coming. She reached near him and asked, "Did Wolf come?"

"No."

"Oh! What type of a boy he is. He never makes on time."

"Will you answer my question?"

"Ask."

"Do you really love him?"

Olga was serious. She knew Igor would not bear the truth. She loved Wolf but she did not want to leave him also. Wolf was her soul and Igor was like a heart beat for her but she gave priority to Wolf because of his intelligence. His graph of studies remained same but Igor grading graph varied too much but she liked his talent. He was her partner in figure skating that's why how could she say straight forward.

She said, "Igor, if I want to choose, I will choose him."

His eyes filled up with tears.

"Congratulations, Olga." And then he left her home immediately but there was pathos in his voice.

Olga shouted, "Come back!"

But he cleared out from there.

———————

"Oh, no! I should not have told him directly but I hate telling a lie." She said, "He is lovely by heart."

She was upset now. After all, he was her good adherent. She moved to washbasin and washed her face. She poured water in glass for taking it. No sooner did she take water than she heard the sound of doorbell. She found Wolf there.

"How are you?" Olga asked.

"Hey! No formality. Well, what are you doing?"

"Nothing!"

"It means you are free. Shall we go?"

"No. I have tension."

"Why?"

"I inflicted sorrow to Igor."

"Why?"

"Leave it."

"Well! You should not do this."

"Yes. I think so but why are you coming so late?"

"Hey! Don't blame me. I made it on time but you were not here when I came. You had gone to meet your mother. Your friend did not tell you?"

"No. He told me that you did not come."

"Oh! He told a lie. He does not want me in your life. His worst demerit is his jealousy. He dislikes me strongly."

Olga was shocked. She could not believe that Igor told a lie.

"Don't take tension. Let's go." Wolf said.

"I will not forgive him."

"Oh! Leave it. I don't want to see you in a bad mood. Enjoy with me happily. Let's go."

"Wait. I am just coming."

"Okay!"

But she was disappointed. Olga trusted him because he knew that she was not there and how he could know that she was in the hospital without coming here. Her mood was bad but last time she did not accept his proposal that's why she was agreed to his proposal.

Olga locked all the doors and went to the park with him but sweet moments of Igor were striking in her mind. She was upset too. Olga felt his way of talking not appreciable.

She said nothing but she felt nothing good.

Wolf offered, "Would you care for a cup of coffee?"

"No."

"Please."

"Okay. Come!"

They took coffee and bill was paid by Olga.

Olga said, "I think we have spent much time."

"Yes."

They reached home. Wolf said, "Good bye."

"Why? Live here with me."

"It is not possible."

"Why? Could you not live with me? Think, how can I spend night alone? Please stay here to abate my fear."

"What does it mean? Do you flirt to me?"

"No stupid. I want your company because I have your need. You should understand my condition seriously."

"For what?"

"Oh! Wolf, it is not a time of joking. I want your security. I cannot spend night alone. I have need of your support."

"Okay!"

He phoned his father and updated his position. He took permission for staying in his friend's house. He permitted him after a very long discussion.

Olga asked, "Why did you tell a lie? Even you are going to stay here."

"If I told him that I would be with a girl, he will not allow."

"Oh! But you should not have told him a lie. It hurts me that you are a liar."

"Just leave it! One should change oneself according to condition. It is not a lie. For giving you security, I did so otherwise I never tell a lie. You also know I am straight forward."

She did not say anything further and immerged in her studies and Wolf was watching a movie. At nine o' clock they took dinner together.

Olga moved to study then he asked, "Would you like to watch one movie with me?"

"No. I am to complete the chapter of Literature."

"Please Olga. I am feeling bored."

She saw him helplessly.

"Please."

"Okay!"

They stepped inside the TV room and lost in watching movie. Wolf wrapped her arm around her waist. She felt scratchy sensation.

"What are you doing?" Olga said seeing him oddly.

"What I did?"

"Don't touch me like this."

"Why?"

"It stimulates my sensation."

"Well! You are so beautiful and I lost my patience."

"Why are you talking incoherently?"

"It is my inner voice. You are *bewilderingly beautiful*, my dear. *You are adorable too.* Your beauty is a *synonym for greatness.*"

She laughed magnanimously. Wolf saw her startlingly.

She said, "I suggest you to sleep to take sweet dreams."

Then she scurried back to her room.

Cock crowed. Olga did not find Wolf. She searched him in every room but she could not find him. When she saw opened gate, she understood everything.

She got fresh and prepared lunch. She heard a voice when she was busy in the kitchen.

"Where were you, Wolf?" Olga asked

"I was in my home."

"Why?"

"Use your mind."

"Okay I understand. You went there to wear your uniform and for taking the school bag."

"Yes."

"But you did wrong. You should not have gone like this."

"I did not want to wake you up because you slept after midnight. I suggest you to take proper rest."

"Thank you." After a second, she asked, "Would you like to take breakfast?"

"No. I have taken."

Olga took breakfast and made her ready in thirty minutes. Now she was ready for going to school.

He proposed to her friend that we should go for school.

"Yes."

She locked her house and went to the garage for taking her cycle.

They reached school and now they were in the class room. Olga sat with Wolf. Igor was not happy. He muttered, "Olga, you are not a good judge of character. He is playing with you."

Teacher was going to teach students after taking attendance then Igor said excuse me madam.

"Yes, Igor."

"Madam, my copy-book of mathematics and report-diary are not in my bag. I think someone stole my copy-book and report diary."

"Who can steal your note-books, Igor?"

"I don't know madam but I want to search in everyone's bags."

"Okay."

Igor found his notebook and report diary in the bag of Wolf. He said to teacher, "Madam, Wolf stole my note-books."

"No madam. I am not involved in this work." Wolf defended.

When teacher looked inside his bag, she also found one obscene book. "Wolf, what is this! You read such type of a cheap book; I never think so. It does not grace you. Shame on you! You also read such an adult books in this little age. Oh god! It is very bad. What punishment should I choose for you?"

"I am an impeccable boy. You can believe in me. It is a conspiracy. I think Igor plays a game with me."

"Game! What type of game?"

"You want to trap me."

"N…No. He…He tells a lie." He said while stammering.

"Madam, he is telling a lie. Ask him when did I steal?"

"How can I tell the answer of this question but as I remember, my report-diary and copy-book were in my bag before assembly."

"Why are you disparaging me?" He said to Igor. He turned round his face to madam and said, "Madam, I am not fool. I don't have any need of his Mathematics note-book. Everybody knows I am a topper. I can teach him Mathematics. I don't know what is going on and who did it." He said further, "Think it again. Would any thief take evidence with him? Why am I getting myself ensnare?"

"Yes, you are right. There is some truth in what you say." Seeing his confidence, class teacher said.

"Madam, it is his work and he want to calumniate me." Wolf stated.

"Is it your work?" Teacher asked to Igor.

"No."

Then Olga stood. "Excuse me, madam."

"Yes Olga."

"Madam, I don't know who did it but Wolf is not involved in this matter because he has been with me since morning."

Class teacher believed immediately because she knew Olga never tells a lie but heart of Igor has broken into millions of pieces when Olga supported Wolf.

Then class teacher asked all the children, "Who did it? I will not punish him. Tell me. Trust me. I will not punish."

Four-five students said simultaneously, "Madam, Igor can do this. He wants to defame Wolf. He feels jealous of Wolf that's why he did it."

No one supported him but some students who wanted to support him were confused how to save him.

"Why did you do that?" Teacher said.

Igor said nothing. His silence was the proof of his mistake. He could not make her clear off but he wanted to make everyone clear breast. He had no any witness, no any proof and unfortunately he was not supported by anyone. His stainless conscience had been wounded and he took punishment by teacher. He knew that Wolf had it done by someone but after that he accepted punishment silently because Olga loved Wolf too much and he did not want to break her heart after raising the level of that matter.

He cannot do this type of work. He is a very gullible boy. Olga thought. She was also in scrupulousness. She was unable to make her conscience clear that Igor did it. She knew his nature but without proof she could not do anything for him. Her voice of conscience was distracting her.

A cold livered boy had won that bad game and now he was thinking that he had had success to down his fame in front of Olga and others. Nevertheless, it was the great writ of provision- God helped the bad egg. One lenient boy suffered without right judgment.

Teacher said after taking class, "I want to meet your parents."

Igor silently bowed his head but he was feeling damnation.

After the school, Olga asked, "Why you did? You know you hurt me."

"Sorry."

"I know you did only for me but why? I ever treat you my ideal friend but you hurt me. I know you wanted to humiliate Wolf. Students were right that you feel jealous."

"No."

"You are not speaking the truth."

"No. It is true."

"One more time you tell a lie."

"No."

"Then tell me did Wolf come yesterday?"

Igor was shocked.

"Tell me." She shouted.

"Yes."

"Then why did you give me wrong information?"

He was quiet. Every situation was against him.

"You are a liar and I hate you. You do not want to see me with Wolf that's why you wanted to humiliate him in front of the class teacher so that you can get me easily. No, never. But you have lost me."

He said nothing and went off from there silently. His heart was in his boots. All the students were passing jibs but he said nothing.

Olga said behind him, "I hate you Igor. I hate you."

Igor reached home and stepped silently towards his room but he could not hide himself from his mother's eyes.

At that time, his mother spoke nothing. For a long while when he did not come out from the room, his mother went to meet him in his room. She found him on the bed while weeping.

She went near him and put his head on her lap. Removing his tears, she moved her fingers on his forehead smoothly. Igor was weeping bitterly as if someone had died. His tenet of simplicity, tenet of fame and tenet of fidelity had died but now he became normal when he felt him in the lap of mother. His mother had read what the matter had passed through him. His eyes were showing everything with clear words.

"Why are you weeping, Igor?" She said kissing him.

"Mom."

"Yes. Tell me."

Igor told her everything from beginning to end. He was afraid what would be the reaction of his mother after knowing this matter but his mother treated him gently. She believed in his character. She said politely, "Don't worry. Forget it as a nightmare. In future, ever live far from the bad boys. Bad character boy is like a rotten apple which makes all the fresh apples rotten."

"Yes mom. Mom… Do you make out me erroneous?"

"No."

"Thanks mom. I am not varlet."

"I trust blindly, my dear. Well, forget it."

"I will try."

"Don't worry. I will meet your teacher."

"I am not worried what will teacher say. However, I cannot live without Olga. Now, she will not talk to me."

"She will. Don't take tension. She will be yours. It is my words."

"No mom. She hates me. She will not."

"You can believe in me. It is neither my intuition nor my prediction but I am confirmed she will come in your life."

"Is it true?"

"Yes. It is true. Wolf did not dignify you but dug his pitfall." She said further while kissing him, "Come on. Take lunch."

He took lunch with his mother.

Olga phoned Wolf, "Wolf, were you engaged in that matter?"

"No. I vow."

"Wolf, I know Igor very inch. He cannot play such type of tactics."

"Olga, I can assure you that I did not do that. I have just taken swear of loyalty to the truth of my own. Teacher chided him was right. He is befitting to say berate words. Do not worry about him. He is for to be upbraided." He said modestly, "Why are you taking tension of Igor. I know he is your fast friend that is the reason you are not accepting his indecency."

"I cannot say anything about it yet but my voice of conscience is giving me a violent shaking. He can be duped by others. He is credulous. If I find you defaulter, I will never talk to you."

"But I was duped by him. I am an eye sore to him. Igor is not a good boy. He is not your friend but he keeps up appearance of friendship." He said for washing her mind.

"I cannot agree. He loves me more than I love him, he loves me more than I love you and he loves me more than you love me but I also know you were not in that incident because you were with me." She said while feeling unconcerned before putting the receiver on the phone.

His presence with Olga could save him and made her sure that he was not an objected boy.

Clock's hands were taking the rotation but she was sitting like a statue in deep down position, and her eyes were pale and misted by tears. She was not in her own control and wanted to forget that matter of Igor but she was not absent minded. At that time, she was grimmest jawed and very puzzled.

She was feeling repeatedly that Igor could not do such type of a work and totally helpless to know what the truth was. She wanted to come out from the marsh of pale reminiscence of the day but that incident was not getting out from her mind and heart.

She did not want to rely upon Wolf because Igor would always told her that he had not been a good boy and in the hospital, mother was also against him. She was confused to understand the matter. Now she had tired while thinking of and she wanted to drift for a sleep. She got into the room and turned off all the switches of tube lights, locked all the doors and lay down on the bed in severe deep dark. Now she was not afraid of dark and felt comfortable in darkness and uncomfortable from tension. She was thinking continuously about the mind-boggling incident sprawling on the bed.

It was the time of midnight, she got out from the bed and dialled the number of Igor but suddenly she put the receiver back on the cradle.

She felt desperately hard. She went to the kitchen, drew out one bottle from the rack and drank water. She mumbled, "Was he wrong?"

She lay down on the bed but suddenly got out and started moving restlessly around the bed. While thinking, her mind had gone in cipher. She fell on the bed and lost in sound sleep.

Next day, Zinaida went to meet his class teacher.

"Good Morning, Madam. I am Zinaida Levina. You had asked my son to ask me to see you."

"Yes. I had asked him to do so."

"I am here with you."

"Thanks. I want to tell you that he has got into the bad habits."

"He has told me that incident yesterday."

"You know! Good! Well! What do you say? He should not."

"I respect teachers so I am not going against you but there was no fault of Igor. I am not saying this thing because he is my son so please don't take it otherwise. You also know him very well because he is also your student. It is done by any other student and what do you think?"

"I feel so but majority of students were against him."

"It may also be that those supported Wolf can be his friends."

"Yes. It can be. Again, I will investigate this matter and also bring it to his notice. I will make him make out being a teacher. I promise to do so."

"Thanks."

And then she requested teacher that she might be allowed to go home.

"Okay." Teacher said shaking hand with Zinaida.

CHAPTER 3

Dr. Anton Aleyksevich Turbin had written the letters to other specialists of this profession for the operation of Irina. A team of Doctors had come from Saint Petersburg. With the help of her Lawyer, Dr. Irina did all the formalities on her own responsibility. She did not want to create any difficulty for Olga that's why she inherited her all the properties and bank balance to her daughter. She made out lawyer everything and then all the formalities which belonged to him had been completing by his side.

Doctor asked her if she was ready for operation. She nodded then doctor declared next day for doing her operation. She wanted to meet her daughter but she crushed her every wishes because she did not want to give her tension during the exam time.

She called in Anton and asked about Roman. Doctor said, "He is in my cabin."

"I want to meet him."

"Why?"

"There is negligible hope of success in this operation that's why I want to send six thousand roubles to Olga."

"Okay but how can you count on him?"

"He is a very gentle person. I have talked with him and he did his responsibility honestly so I can count on him."

Doctor passed smile in the manner of acceptance.

Then she requested, "I have need of one envelope."

He gave her.

She drew out roubles six thousand inside from her reticule and put it into the envelope after mentioned the name of Olga.

Doctor ordered nurse, "I want to see Roman immediately."

"Yes, sir."

He took ten minutes to reach there. "Had you asked for me?"

"Yes. Could you help her?"

"Sure. It will be my pleasure."

Irina said, "Sorry to give you one more trouble but I have need of your help?"

"Yes, please. No trouble at all."

"It would be very kind of you if you give this envelope to Olga?"

"Yes. I can give her."

"Thanks." She said in a moment, "Also make her clear not to come here. You will tell her that it is my strict order."

"Okay."

Then he left the hospital immediately.

He rang the doorbell. Olga found Roman. "Yes uncle."

"Take it." He said while giving her envelope.

She peeped inside after tearing the top edge of the envelope and found money. "Oh!"

However, she did not know that Roman also added one thousand roubles for her help. In fact, he wanted to help her by heart. His heart had melted for her.

"Thank you, uncle." She said to him.

"Welcome."

"Come in and have a seat."

"Thanks."

She served him water and asked, "How is my mother? I have not heard about her for many days."

"She is fine. She will be operated tomorrow."

"What?" Startlingly she asked.

"Yes."

"Just wait a minute. I am also going with you."

"No. You cannot go there."

"Why?"

"It is her order to you."

"But why?"

"I don't know but it is her strict order."

"Okay." She said hopelessly.

"Okay, allow me to go." Moving out from the house he said, "If you feel any problem anytime, you can call me without any hesitation. Take me yours."

"Thank you, uncle."

"Take care."

———————

Olga was perturbed and she was equally disturbed. Olga's eyes were not weeping but her heart, her mind, and her conscience were weeping bitterly. She was upset and her heart was heavy. She prayed to God for good health of her mother. She was trembling with fear thinking about the operation of mother. She thought. *Will doctor get success in operation?* Continuously she was praying to God and she did not take dinner.

It was the time of eve and she was unknown about her mother's condition. Again and again, she was praying to God that her mother would come in well condition but God knew that what the result would be. Her mother swears bound her that's why she could not go to the hospital for asking her condition and she did not know the phone number of the hospital also.

The Moon came among the stars but she was sitting quietly on the stairs of lobby. It was her love for her mother that she could not take sound sleep. It was after midnight she stepped inside the room and fell on the bed but she could not take rest properly because of eccentric fidgetiness. Her soul was quietude. She jumped out and took many rounds in tension beside the bed.

———————

Irina was also thinking about the future of Olga in mum position. She was sat all by herself soberly and staidly; upset too. Tears fell down on her cheeks. She was helpless and hopeless.

She got startled instantly. It was Doctor, who called out her by name. "What are you thinking, Irina?"

Without saying anything she wept bitterly. Anton wiped her tears using tissue paper. "Don't weep, Irina. Believe in god. Everything will be fine. Don't worry."

"Death is not the reason of my fear but I have a tension of my sweet daughter. How will she live alone without me? What will be her life it is a matter of thinking. She cannot live without me because of innocence. I love my daughter very much. I love her very much, doctor. Her life and career will spoil and nothing is in my hand to save anything. If god gifts me one chance, I will solve out this big problem. I have little time that's why I cannot do anything good for my daughter. What will be her future…Oh! No. After thinking about her future, my mind becomes puzzle."

"By the grace of God your operation will be successful. Don't be hopeless. Hope sustains life."

"But chances are negligible. I am helpless."

"I am not God but I will try my level best using my full experience. If not, I will adopt your daughter. Don't worry; Olga is also my daughter-like. She is also like my Oksana."

"You are very kind and I am much obliged to you."

"No question of kindness, it would rather please me. It is duty of every human being."

"Yeah but you are like an angel. You deserve deification doctor."

"Leave it and take proper rest. Don't make your condition worst. It will not good for your baby."

"Yes but I want to make myself satisfy."

"What can I do in this matter? Tell me. I will do it by heart."

She said a minute later after thinking, "Could I use your laptop?"

"Sure."

She opened her Email Id and sent one mail to someone. To whom she sent for what purpose only god knew after her.

She said thanks to doctor after using his Laptop.

"Mention not."

Olga's eyes were weary. She could not sleep whole night. She had been gazing the stars to find out the falling star for taking the wish for her mother but again she was disappointed.

Hardly, she could prepare her mood for going to school. She went to school without taking breakfast.

———◆◆◆———

Igor had been living upset after that incident. Her mother was trying to make him normal but could not. His mind has hooked for Olga and it seemed that he had afflicted by grief. He didn't go to school.

His mother said while ruffling her fingers in his hair, "My dear, why are you not taking food? Two days have spent but you are not leaving your stubborn nature. Why have you not been taking food for two days? Why? My dear, take breakfast and be ready for going to school."

"Mom, I am not feeling well. I miss Olga."

"Why are you fretting yourself? This thing shows you are coward. Olga wants topper in her life, so, make your academic strong. I know you love her but it does not mean that you will spoil your life for Olga. It is either silliness or lunacy. Face her and try to win her heart. If you find out the way to solve the unfortunate problem, you will have to show them your potential in education. If your academic will strong, everybody can listen to you what you will want to say or show otherwise you will always be avoided by everyone. Remember that day when no one supported you. It was because all greet the rising sun."

He bowed his face.

"Be strong, my dear."

He said, "Mom, can I get her again?"

"Obviously, truth has legs. If you believe in God, you will get her. Your libation for love can govern her heart for provocation the hidden love which is at present literally hushed."

He fell on her lap and Zinaida gave him a kiss on his cheek. "Get ready for school."

"Yes."

Now, he was ready for going to school. Her mother feed him breakfast and then after he said Good bye to mom taking the school bag. When he slid inside the car, her mother said in a very polite manner, "Bye-bye and take care."

"You too."

She slammed the door of the car when driver ignited the car for dropping him at the school.

———————

Last time of operation had come. Doctor asked, "Are you afraid?"

"No but I have a tension of her life."

"Don't worry. Everything will be in your favour. I am also with you. Don't worry and rest assured."

"God forbid!" Irina said.

Then he said to ward-boys, "Take her in the operation theatre."

He immerged in operation with three other experts. He saved her life but could not save her child. Again it was not a good sign to her.

When she became conscious doctor informed her. That news made her daze and hashed her conscience. Anton found her teary eyes. He tried to divert her mind but she straight forward said to leave her alone.

Understanding the mother in her, he got out from her room.

"It is fifth autumn in my life. Oh! God, your bounty of pannier of sorrows to me is really appreciable. You are only stone hearted. Only stone hearted." She thought.

Her eyes were swimming in tears. She followed complete silence.

She had been sitting like a statue for an hour. Doctor entered to meet her again. He started consoling her. He could calm down her uneasily.

Doctor said after seeing her sombre condition, "Why this pondering over. See! You are not fully recovered. Your condition is worst and I suggest you not to take much tension. Why are you losing your heart? It is not for the sake of you but for sake of Olga. Is it looking good to weep like a child?"

"No, but…"

"What is bothering you? God listen to your wish. He gives you a new life for purveying Olga and you behave like a silly child. I know you have throbbing heartache but if you suffer, you cannot nurture your daughter. Everything depends on your health and now your condition is too critical. Though you will be in my care yet I cannot do anything if you do not want to recover yourself. I know you get a severe shock but it does not mean there is sagging in your life."

"Yes but I could not give birth to my child. How will I face the questions of my daughter? She wants to live and play with her brother."

"Who can fight against fate? It is a rule of nature and nobody can either change it or understand it. Sportive display of god is infinite. That's the way things are. Now, it is not a time to mourn but think freshly to secure your future with Olga because you cannot get chances again and again. It is a golden chance to you to purvey her. I hope you understand me. It is not good to live with feeble hopes. Saturate yourself. Isn't it? You have to redeem from this lamentation."

"Yes doctor. You are right."

"Good! Your condition is worst that's why I cannot discharge you today. Give me three more days."

"You know better than I but could I meet my daughter?"

"Yes and presence of Olga will help you to recover."

"I think so."

"Okay. I send Roman for Olga."

"Thanks!"

Olga said sadly, "Roman uncle told me that doctor could not save my brother. Is it right?"

"Yes."

She was on the verge of tears and her face became deep down. She said, "I am very sorry to hear this."

Irina said wiping her tears, "I think it is a wish of God."

"Why does God write such type of irrelevant deeds for us? Why? What type of animosity he has with us?" Olga said angrily.

"Don't say like this. Why are you taking tension? I am with you."

"First I saw the death of my father and now you tell me the bad news of my brother's death. Mom, God is stone hearted. He is not with us."

"He is with us otherwise you could also hear the news of my death."

"Don't say like this. Speak good omen. I cannot live without you. I miss you every time. I love you, mom. I love you so much. Loneliness stings me. I don't want to lose you. Only I know how I spent these seven days in tension without you. I could not live easily and now I will not like to follow your any orders."

"I can understand my dear. Don't take tension. It is not a matter of more than three days and after that I will be with you." She said.

"Three days?" She asked startlingly. A moment later she said, "Why does it not today?"

"Her condition is improving but we cannot take risk after discharging your mother. She has need of nursing." Doctor made her make out.

"Why?"

"If medicines do not suit her, I will prescribe injection after seeing test reports. She needs more care because she can face the problem of bleeding."

"Will she recover easily by doing so?"

"It may be because treatment is going on."

"Doctor, I want to see my mother in well condition anyhow."

"I am doing my best job. Don't worry; you can play with her after a week."

"Is it true?"

"Yes and be happy."

Olga passed cute contagious smile and seeing her smile Irina passed a bright smile in response. Then doctor said, "Okay, allow me to go."

"I will call you soon." Irina said.

"No problem. You can divert your mind talking to Olga."

She nodded.

Olga started giving details how she spent her life without mother and also gave the status of her studies. Irina ruffled Olga's hair passing smile. Hours were crawling but they could not judge what the right time was. Doctor said entering the room, "Have you finished your conversations?"

"No." Olga said.

"Dear, three hours had gone by."

"What?" Startlingly she asked.

"Yes. Probably, you lost deeply in talking to your mom."

"After all she has come here after many days." Irina said this time.

"I can understand the emotions of this child."

"Well! Could you permit me to do my job?" He asked her.

"Sure!" She said moving aside.

Doctor checked her up. "Good symptoms."

"Is she all right now?"

"Yes. Carry on talking."

Then he stepped out.

Irina said a minute later, "Olga, go back home. It is not good for you to go home during night."

"No mom. I want to live here with you."

"You are to attend school tomorrow."

"I can take a leave."

"No. It is not good. Give me only three days and then after I will be with you."

Hopelessly she said, "Okay."

Olga spent three days as usual. However, she was not happy but trying to forget the death of her brother. It was beyond her mind what was going on but every time she had been making her busy doing some work. Although she was giving full time to her studies yet could not concentrate properly.

Her mother also wanted to be discharged soon. At the time of discharging, Doctor made him alert not to take too much tension and suggested her to take proper rest. Her condition was not good and doctor said before a minute of discharging, "You are not in well condition. You have need of regular check up and I suggest you to take medicine from time to time. I hope you will give rest to your mind. Is okay?"

"Yes doctor."

"Where is your Mercedes?"

"Here in the hospital parking."

"Okay. I send you with my driver."

"Thanks doctor."

CHAPTER 4

Olga was surprised when she saw her mother after coming from school. She wrapped her arms around her waist and said happily, "I am happy mom. I am very happy seeing you here."

"I too. Well! What do you want to take?"

"Mom, you will do nothing. You have a need of proper bed rest. I phone Petera."

"Good girl but I am able to do work."

"No. your work is to take complete bed rest."

"Okay, my dear. Could you give me a chance today?"

"No."

"You give me a chance. I prepare chicken soup for you."

"How sweet! Will you prepare for me?"

"Yes. I will and I can."

"Okay."

Olga prepared tasty chicken soup for her. They took it together and Olga moved to study after giving her medicines.

In the evening, she called up Petera. She gave time of meeting.

———◆———

Next day Petera met her.

She said, "I have your need again."

"Madam, I don't have time. It is very difficult to me to find next job. I suffer when anyone dismiss me without any previous information. It hurts."

"You can pacify your anger but try to understand my problem. I was in fix. I was totally helpless to take a decision."

"I have given time to someone."

"I can pay you roubles 150 per day."

"…"

"Roubles 200 per day."

She saw her strangely.

"I can give you roubles 250 per day but I want you."

"I want to ask one thing. May I?" Petera asked.

"Yes."

"Why do you want me again?"

"You are reliable and my daughter also knows you."

"What does it mean?"

"As you know, she is totally reserved dignity and does not like to talk with everyone. She is reticent and has coordination with you that's why I want you again and you are a good Abigail for her."

"Okay. You can give me Roubles 130 per day. It deserves."

"Thanks but I will give you roubles hundred and fifty."

"It is my pleasure."

Care taking charge of Olga was now in the hands of Petera. She also took care of Irina with full dedication. Her nature was gentle and did her duty perfectly without any arguments.

Olga was busy in her studies because her exam was at hand but the graph of her mother's condition was falling day by day. She again came in tension because she did not find the response of her mail and doctor was helpless to recover her health. She wanted to meet him immediately anyhow. He was his last hope. Anton was also trying to maintain her health giving the best treatment but again he found negligible hope of her surviving.

Irina started trying to live normal in front of Olga and also tried to give her proper time. When she got time, she tried to make her happy making comical atmosphere. Petera did not tell her Irina's condition while she knew the serious problem of Irina.

One day, Olga was in her school. Irina turned on her PC and sent same mail many times to that person. She had a hope of his reply. After that, with the help of Petera she collected every record and certificates of Olga and punched them in one file. She ordered Petera to help her for applying for the visa of Olga.

She got visa and also happy after getting the mail of that person. She gave him response with schedule. He also replied her.

She also phoned her lawyer and fixed appointment with him. She wanted some changes in the papers of property. She chose three co-sharer of her property this time. Lawyer nodded and began his work.

It was June being the month of exam. She was studying through and through. Only two days had left and she was studying the Russian Language. She had tension of getting first position in the class. She wanted to perform outstanding.

It was the day before the exam. She got up early in the morning and started revising all the chapters that she learnt.

It was quarter past ten; she moved to church entreating for the good health of mother and appeared in studies without wasting time after reaching home. Right 01:45 p.m., she took lunch. Soon she moved to bed and fell into nap setting the alarm.

After an hour she got up and washed her face and again merged in studies. Clock was striking seven and now probably the last two chapters of the Russian language had left to learn.

She took abeyance from studies and moved to TV room to watch cartoon channel. She watched television hardly twenty minutes. She took dinner with mom and immediately moved to study for learning the rest of the chapters. When she had learnt her whole syllabus, suddenly, she moved towards the lobby and started revising the syllabus for getting the confidence.

In a short time, she had revised all the chapters. She got back in the room and put all the essential stationary like sharpener, pencils, erasers, and other things in the pencil box. She sat the alarm before sleeping.

<hr>

Igor was also preparing conceptually. He was really doing good effort. Wolf was also on the same page but it was difficult to say that who would save the prestige.

<hr>

She woke up when alarm rang and again reduplicated all the chapters. After getting confidence, she knocked off revising and went to the bathroom. She was ready within an hour and after taking breakfast she went to school for taking an exam.

She appeared in the examination room and attempted all the questions. She went near Wolf and asked about his performance. He said, "I did two mistakes but what about your exam?"

"I attended out of out. I alert you that I will get success of getting the top position."

"Oh! What a confidence! It is strange to me that you are proving yourself just after giving first exam. Still, many are rest. You will not succeed because you are not an incarnation of success."

"Okay. We will see. I agree I am not an incarnation of success but synonym of success. Well! I do not want to be in arguments so, allow me to go. I do not want to waste my time."

"Okay and best of luck for the next exam."

"Same to you."

Without wasting time, she left his company and came home.

<hr>

She was giving her excellent performance in the exam time. She gave exam very fantastically and it was appearing that every exam was a small task to do but her mother condition was comparatively bad. Regular treatment was unable to recover her condition. Olga had been living sadly. When she got free time, she took care of her mother. Petera also paid attention for her help.

Irina sent one urgent mail to that person again. She was afraid that he would come or not but she got his reply soon. Now she was tension free but being a mother, she had tension of her daughter's future.

———◆———

The exam of Mathematics was left to pass out. She had two holidays for preparation and had tension of her mother also because she had known her actual condition but did not leave her hope.

She completed her seventy five percent of syllabus that day and then she was brain-taxing with the rest part of the syllabus of Mathematics. Her mind had immunized for her mother but she was striving to learn all the formulae of that subject.

———◆———

Other side, Igor, at his home, was very upset. He thought that Olga had been surging from some problems in Mathematics because last many periods she could not attend classes very well. He knew that Olga had many problems in Mathematics that's why he reached near his mom and said, "Could you do my one work?"

"Sure."

"Please, go to meet Olga and give her this mathematics copy-book."

"And you?"

"Don't worry mom. I will pass out this exam without any difficulty with good grades and I have Xerox of my note-book."

"Okay."

He had very good command on this subject so he was not afraid of the exam. His mother also knew that he loved Olga very much that's why he would not like her downfall in studies. Therefore, he wanted to solve her problem.

Without wasting a single moment, she went there and gave her copy-book of mathematics.

"Aunty, it is his note-book and he?"

"He told me to give you."

"Why?"

"Perhaps he thinks that you have some problem in this subject."

"Even then…"

"Take it. He has completed his syllabus."

"It is not a class test but a final exam."

"I know but I could not stand in front of his sticky nature."

"Thank you, aunty. Please convey my thanks to him also."

"Okay."

"Sorry. Please, come in."

"Thank you."

Olga went to the kitchen, came back with one glass of water, and gave him respectfully.

"Thanks." Zinaida said.

"It's my pleasure."

She stood after a moment and said, "Shall I go?"

"Please, sit down. I have been feeling boredom since morning."

"Why?"

"Mom has gone to the hospital with Petera."

"Is she all right?"

"She is not getting good health that is the reason she goes there for regular check up."

"Oh! Don't worry. I am here with you." She said pampering her.

"Well! Would you like to take coffee?"

"Thank you my dear but keep on studying."

"Please aunty. I can prepare."

"Not right now but I promise to take treat when you will get good marks. Is right?"

"Okay. Done."

She sat by her and Olga remained involve in studies deeply. After half an hour, Zinaida got out from the chair and stepped outside from the room. She said to driver for bringing juice. He moved to shop accepting her order.

Zinaida came back and sat on the chair next to her.

After sometime, driver gave her packet of juice. Zinaida poured the juice into the disposal glass and said while giving her, "Your refreshment. Take it."

"Thanks but why have you done this? You are my guest and…"

"Oh! Am I just only your guest? Hey! Take me your mother like."

"Sorry. My intension was not to hurt you but it is my greatest pleasure."

She ruffled her hair. Olga engrossed in studies after taking juice.

Zinaida said after half an hour, "Well, I want to go now. Can I?"

"Please…"

"Olga, I have some pending works so please, allow me to go."

"Okay."

Then she returned home. Olga was very happy from her nature.

She told Igor that Olga had conveyed him thanks. He passed pretty smile softly.

Soon he said to mom, "Mom, I want to go Yekaterinburg."

"Why?"

"Without Olga I am dead. She is my life, my love, my future and my aim also. She is everything for me."

"Shut up. It is too much. Olga! Olga! Olga! You stop it. You love Olga I have no problem because it is not a big issue and I know she is a good girl but if you spoil your life for her, I cannot tolerate it. You are my only son and you will be the heir of Levin Empire." She said angrily.

"That's why I want to go Yekaterinburg."

"Tell me the strong reason."

"She treats me a sinner and I cannot show my face and cannot stand in front of her. My image has diminished badly. I am not living with self respect. Try to understand my situation. Sorry. I cannot face."

"I am sorry. Okay. I will talk to your father." She said hopelessly.

"Thanks."

Olga completed her whole syllabus of Mathematics taking help from his note-book. She was thinking that he still did her care so much.

In the evening, she was free after revising the syllabus one more time. Washing her face, she watched one television show and after taking dinner, she slept.

Next day she was revising the subject sitting near her mother. Irina was teaching her short tricks then she heard the voice of doorbell. She ordered Petera for opening the door.

Olga found one person coming near her. She saw him strangely but her mother called him up by name. Olga astonished who he was. Irina said to Olga, "Go to your room."

She obeyed being a good daughter.

———————◆◆◆———————

"Good! Here you are! Have a seat." Irina said.

Andrei Ivanovich Rodionov asked while sitting in the chair. "What about your health?"

"I am on the last stage of my life. My end is near. Well! Would you take tea or coffee?"

"Thanks but don't say like this. You will be fine."

"Be formal here. What do you like to take?"

"Okay, tea will do."

"Anything to eat besides."

"No, nothing."

Then she ordered Petera for preparing two cups of tea. Petera nodded.

Andrei said, "It does not feel good but by God's grace you will be fine."

"I hope so but nobody can change the law of nature and It is true. Before happening wrong with me, I want to hand over you my daughter. I have got her visa that I will hand over you. Tomorrow will be her last exam and after taking her all the certificates and final result, I hope, you will bring her to America. I believe that you will purvey her like a father. Now, you are everything to her after me. I hand over you my daughter because you are my reliable sweet brother."

"Don't worry. I will bring her up with responsibility. She is not only your daughter but also mine."

"I knew that you would not throw cold water on my hopes. Well! You are rightful claimant of $ 7 million of my property and my step mother has right on my property of $ 30 million and my daughter is the heir of my 5 million roubles with all my assets. You will help her to get them."

"Why you do it? I have no need of money. Don't take tension. Olga will be safe in my shed."

"Thanks Andrei but you know about the nature of my step mother. I know she will admonish her that's why I am giving her $ 30 million to live far from my daughter."

"I am well known to her nature. She is not good for us but don't worry. She will be happy with us."

"Thanks brother but she is good for you. After all, she is your mother. Well! Why did you not give response of my first mail? You know, I came in tension."

"Actually, I did not open my Email Id. When I saw your mail, I wrote you back immediately. I tell you something that she is my mother but she is greedy of money and lives in St. Louis with her paramour. She does not have interest in me."

"Okay. I have tension of my daughter. Please, keep her away from her black shadow."

"Don't take tension. She does not live with us. Olga will be safe."

"I believe in you and now I am free from one big burden and can die easily because she has your support now after me."

"Think positive."

"Here is no light of hope."

Andrei maintained silence then Irina called out Olga. She reached immediately in her room. Irina said, "Olga, he is my brother who lives in the USA."

She wished him meekly but thought where this new chapter has begun.

Irina further stated, "Olga, I have decided that you will study in America."

"No mom. What are you saying? It cannot be possible. I cannot live without you. I am not going to leave you. Not at all."

"Olga, I do not want to keep you in dark. I have limited breaths and for your future sake I decide to hand over your responsibility to Andrei, your maternal uncle."

Her face became insipid. She said with wet eyes, "Mom, don't say like this. It is sophism. You will be all right. I know you will get good health soon. Please don't say like this. I cannot live without you. You are my life and I don't want to go far from your lap. I need of your lap, mom. Please, don't say like this. God will help you. You will be in good condition soon."

"Be strong my dear and be practical also. Give promise to me that you will bright our names."

"Yes." She said with dry throat.

Irina ordered Petera for bringing the certificates, passport, and visa.

She gave her immediately after taking out them from the cupboard. Irina handed over him and said, "I will give you those papers in the evening. Actually, I could not get time to transfer money in your account but my lawyer will complete all the formalities. You will not have to take much trouble for this work."

"Okay. And thanks"

"No need of it. After all, you are my brother."

———

Olga left her company and started weeping falling on the bed. She forgot about her last exam. She could not utilize rest of her time. Her condition was much worse than that of her mother but what she could do. Nothing was in her hand. Whole night, she had been praying to god for her good health.

———

However, her mother was discussing something with Andrei after giving him the papers of property. She was in tension but he was giving her full assurance. After all, she was mother of one daughter and could not get relief without doing satisfactory work for making her future safe. After much discussion with Andrei, she was literally carefree but her heart was pounding.

She said to Petera for showing him guest room. She showed him guest room and Andrei fell on the bed for taking rest.

Petera was preparing food for everyone and Irina was thinking something. Soon she came out from the world of thoughts and started writing a letter to someone and put it inside one book. After that, she took a tension free breath.

———

Olga went to school and attended the question paper of mathematics firmly, came out from the class room happily because she had done great job and she was free from one big burden. She cleared exam beyond her expectations. She was feeling before appearing in the examination that she would not be able to acquire more than eighty percent while she solved all the questions. She was really happy and now she was searching for Igor to give him thanks.

Her face was bright with luminosity in her eyes and her influencing smile was looking like a magical smile of sorceress. She was very happy and this happiness was *increasing the lustre of her face.* When Ashley saw her in full of jovial mood, she asked, "What happened? Why are you so happy?"

"I did hundred percent. This time Wolf cannot achieve the first rank."

"I know you are a topper and pride of our school."

"My pleasure. Do you know where Igor is?"

"Yes. I saw him going towards the exit gate of the school."

"Oh! Let's come."

They were going to the main gate of the school while talking then they heard the conversation of Wolf with his friends. He was saying to his friends, "Now I see that how will Igor get good marks? He wants to take my place but now, he cannot. Olga was also giving him importance seeing his versatile nature but how could I see her with him? She is my friend. Only mine. *This beauty is one who born once in an era. She is beauty of the age! Russian Sapphire! She is a precious diamond of this school.* How can I see her with him? For this, I disparaged him. Everybody knows it was done by him but someone, especially you people know it was got it done by me. Sultan did it when I phoned him to do that. It is veracity of that matter. When teacher punished him, my soul felt happiness. As I told you last time, I provoked Igor to tell a lie that I had not come to meet at her home. Do you remember?"

"We know. It was an evening incident when Olga went to meet her mother in the hospital." His friends said simultaneously.

"Yes. You are absolutely right. It was the evening before that incident occurred and that naive boy could not understand my politics. I did it to create a gulf between Olga and Igor. I got success too. Olga hates liar because she ever speaks the truth that's why I played that cheap trick. He told a lie to know her view to whom she loves but he could not know I would reveal this secret. Olga started relying upon me when I got success in washing her brain. She started hating him. That stupid boy accepted my fault because he loves Olga and did not want to hurt her heart. He knows that Olga loves me lot, that's why he took my sin on his head. In this situation, he would not be able to study properly and would have been mentally disturbed in the memory of Olga. Chance of Olga is also negligible because her mother is in trouble and at least due to this reason she might be able to find time for studies. I have also given her a strong shock because I played a psychological game. After all, she treated him an ideal friend. How can she forget him easily? Now it is confirmed that I will get the top position."

His statements pissed her off. Tears were coming through her eyes and her rage has erupted like a volcano. Now she was thinking that she did great felony with that innocuous boy. She grumbled, "I am a defaulter. Oh! Igor, I am really very sorry." She was feeling repentance of her deeds."

Immediately she came next to Wolf and pacified her rage on him giving three-four tight slaps on his cheeks in front of everyone. He was feeling insult. She said, "Cheater! You played a bad game to get me in your life. You took perjury. It will not good for you. What did you think…You would hide this matter? Wolf, remember it, truth never dies. I hate you liar. You are below pariah. You want me in your life but not now. I respect him and here in my heart, I have a special place for him."

Without wasting time, Olga went to the staff room with Ashley and told teacher everything truly. Now vendetta had woke up in Wolf's mind. He promised himself that he would also take retaliation. His fame had fallen down in the eyes of every student. He pledged himself, "I will spoil your life Olga. If I cannot get you, nobody can get you. I will destroy you."

———◆◆◆———

Olga said to Ashley to find out Igor. She wanted to confess in front of him. She enshrined Igor. Both were trying to find out him but he had gone from there.

They met again but neither of them got success.

Now Olga was weeping by heart and then she went to his home after seeing Ashley off. When she reached there, she called out him. His mother came out; found her in long face, she asked, "What happened?"

"Aunty, where is Igor?" Naively she said.

"He has gone to Yekaterinburg."

"How much time has passed?"

"I think he would have reached the airport with father because he took the route of airport directly from the school and possibly his flight would have taken off to Yekaterinburg. You are late but what is going on? Why are you in tension?"

She told her misdeed of Wolf.

Zinaida made her make out not to take tension. She said to Olga, "Don't weep, let bygone be bygone but he loves you deeply. He is going to Yekaterinburg with your reminiscence. He did not want to become a wall between you and Wolf. For the sake of your happiness, he has left Moscow permanently. Last time he told me- Sacrifice, thy name is love."

"Aunty, please sorry. I am a sinner. You can give me any type of punishment. I am ready to kiss the rod. He did not do anything wrong. My support to Wolf was wrong. I did great felony."

"I know what the reason was. He had told me everything."

She was weeping badly and did not want to excuse her anyhow. Zinaida fondled her politely, wiped her tears, and said, "My judgment is that you will live happy forever. Now stop weeping."

"Can he not come back?"

"I have said aeroplane has taken off."

"Aunty, could you forgive me?"

"You are not a defaulter. In fact, to err is human."

Now her face was dull and again she began to weep. She was very serious taking this matter to heart. It was not her weeping, but raining of tears because her fast friend has gone very far from her.

She said after sometime, "I want to go home. May I?"

"No. First you should take lunch."

"Thanks. I am not hungry."

"Shut up. You can go when you will take lunch and you ought to obey it."

"But…"

"Oh! Olga. Be seated."

She obeyed. Zinaida said to servant to set lunch on the dining table. She came after washing hands and feed her every morsel. Olga felt that her mother was feeding her and Zinaida was thinking that she was feeding her son.

When Olga had taken food, Zinaida again called her driver and said to drop her at her house.

CHAPTER 5

Driver parked the car and they set out for moving inside the house. When they went into the Irina's room, Olga found her mother in sleeping and Doctor, Petera, Roman, and Andrei were standing silently. Perhaps they were waiting for her but she could not understand why they were standing like this. Quickly she went near her and fondled her politely. "Mom, I did hundred percent. And I am free to look after you."

When she did not answer her, she asked, "Are you sleeping mom?" Suddenly without wasting a moment, she asked the doctor, "Is she sleeping? Is she all right?"

No one could get courage to speak the truth. Again, she said, "Mom! Get up. Why are you not giving the answer of my question?"

However, how could a dead body answer?

Then she shook up her mother's body but she did not get up. Zinaida came next to her and said, "I am sorry but your mother is no more. She is no more."

Now it was the dreadful time. "What are you saying? Say, you tell a lie. My mom cannot die. She cannot leave me alone. She cannot make me orphan. How can she go far from me while she loves me more than anyone else in this world? I know she is playing possum."

"Try to believe." Zinaida said.

Again she shook the dead body badly and found it stir-less. This thing was penetrating the inner feeling of the heart.

"Olga, you must accept it. It is true. Your mother's soul has gone to heaven." This time, doctor said.

"Doctor, you are a liar. You tell a lie. Say, this is not true. It cannot be possible." Shockingly she said to doctor but Anton was also in very deep sorrow. A woman, he loved more, had died. His eyes were numbed and he had a pity on. He was also shocked after her death. After all, the chapter of his love had finished.

"Why on earth should I lie to you?" Doctor said.

She could not believe but the truth was truth and she was not ready to accept her. Not only she shook her head in a manner of rejection but also every movement of her body denied that truth. Her mental condition had pounded and she was shedding tears of agony.

Again she shook her up violently and found no action by the dead body. At last, she accepted her mother had died. She knelt while out-crying. She said, "No! No. Oh! No God." All had over-owed after hearing painful voice of that cute doll. Doctor put his arms around her when she burst into tears.

In the house of Igor, she was weeping but now, there was a flood of tears through her eyes. Tears were dancing on her cheeks. No. It was the Tsunami coming out from her eyes and her heart was drowning in the dun sea of darkness. Her two lovely beings, mother and father, had died and now she was lorn, no hand on her head. Halo of glory on her face had dwindled.

Many hearts melted with pity on hearing her panic shrill. It was the voice full of pain. Now her condition was like a half dead.

First, her father and brother left her and now her mother, Igor also left her permanently and her love also played fraud. Now she was stark alone. It was her doomsday.

"Please, tell me all of you, what is my fault? First, my father died four month ago and now my brother and mother. Tell me; tell me, what type of punishment God gives me! What is my fault? Tell me, why do misfortunes come together? I have understood that God is only a statue of mud. It has no heart and law. Our cross is not a god but 'cross of sorrow' is a god. Statue of stone has no mercy. God is a body of arduous heart, nothing else." Her pitiful cry broke the peace.

"Olga, keep quiet. Don't weep. You don't know your mom was one of the best moms of the world because when she was admitted in the hospital, she knew that she would die and she wanted to meet you but she did not want to disturb you in the exams time that's why she wrapped herself in the loneliness of sorrow. She followed acute loneliness. She told me that I would put her corpse in mortuary till the last date of your exam but at that time, I could save her for you but I am sorry this time. Her last expectation from you was that she wanted to see you on the top of the world. It is not a time of weeping but a time of struggling to achieve the goal. I think you will not forget the sacrifices of your mom. What your mother did for you will always make you proud."

"Yes doctor. I will remember it. I promise I will fulfil the desires of my parents." There was glimpse of sorrow in her every word.

"That's my bold girl."

Zinaida was praying for the peace of her soul but her heart was trembling because one woman understands the heartache of another woman.

Her condition was very rough and she had lost faith in god. She was uttering in wailing tone.

Zinaida surcharged with emotions and encompassed her gently. Effacing her tears she said, "I can understand your situation but don't worry, I am not your real mom but I can give you love of one mother." Listening to her, she placed her head on her shoulder and said wiping her tears, "God gives me punishment because I did wrong with Igor."

"My dear, it is not true. You had no fault anywhere."

Andrei went near Olga and said, "Don't worry. I will purvey you. You are in my shed now. I know you are a reserved girl and also know that you don't know me properly but I understand I will make coordination with you seeing your nature and hope you will cooperate me. By the way, your mother has told you about me."

"Yes. Last time she made me clear but my heart denies…"

"I understand your feelings but here is no other way and it was the wish of your mom also."

She kept standing a few moments peacefully and said, "I will have to obey her but my wish is to abide in Russia until I get my report card."

"May we not back for your mark sheet?"

"No. Please."

"Well! Leave it. We will discuss later. Now we should think for the next step."

"Yes." She said wiping her tears but her beautiful face was looking like a withered flower.

The dead body had been carried outside by the help of everyone. Andrei made at church to meet Archbishop for preparing of funeral. Olga was weeping continuously putting her head on the Zinaida's shoulder. She was making her normal while pampering her. Doctor had stricken with grief seeing that bereaved girl. Andrei came back and the dead body stored away in the coffin and then all move towards cemetery. This was the time when neighbours could know that matter of death seeing the grief procession. Many attended for the condolence. Everybody was thinking about Olga's life and she was weeping badly and her situation was typical. Zinaida tried to calm down her through persuasion.

On the land of cemetery, Olga second time saw up heaved grave after father, she was bearing the bereavement, and Zinaida was pampering her. At that time, her flighty eyes were pale. Her face was dull and she had been standing like a half dead among 'in beings'. She did not want to see the sarcophagus but how could she go far from her mother's corpse.

Weather was also dark. It was not a tawny sunset but the sky was covered with black, dry, and dense clouds. Either it might be the indication of hiding well deeds by the devil clouds or it might be the indication of expressing the God's displeasure. Her emotions were ensanguined by the arrows of misfortune. She had a thunderclap. Legislation of providence made her life harried.

Standing beside Olga, Zinaida was thinking about her future. As a woman, she understood her sensitive feeling. After all, she was also a mother of one child and her maternal heart swelled up.

Obsequies were held. Many people had gone from there. Olga had been standing with her uncle for a long time. Zinaida wanted to say something but she could not.

Olga Silently moved to put bunch of flowers on the grave. Season of sorrow was in full swing these days for Olga.

Doctor went near her and said, "Could we back?"

Standing silently, she said nothing. She was weeping putting her hands on her mouth. Andrei thought, "God, do you have any mercy?" He was in feeble state in front of The Supreme Being. This time, he said to her, "Olga, you have to stand on the tip toe of expectations."

It seemed that all the beauty goddesses were pleased from her but law goddess, Themis was angry.

Now they had returned from there. Reaching home, he went to ISD booth and phoned his wife.

"Hello! Is Samantha speaking?"

"Yes."

"Samantha, I am Andrei."

"Yes sweetie. Are your sister well?"

"She is no more now."

"Sorry…I pray to god to give peace to the departed soul but it is very bad news. Rest is peace." She added, "When will you come?"

"I cannot say anything right now but I will be soon there."

"Why?"

"I think I will come after taking her result card and certificates."

"Okay and take care."

"You don't care a fig for that and take care too." Then he slammed the receiver on the phone and reached home.

Zinaida was talking to Andrei and Olga was weeping in a separate room lying on the bed.

After an hour, Zinaida left the company of Andrei and went trying to feed her but she did not take food. She was not feeling hungry.

She said politely hugging her, "Take me yours. I know I am not your mother but you can treat me as a mother-like. Do you have any doubt on my maternity?"

"No aunty. I don't want to put up with lot of discomfiture after hearing this."

"Good! Good news is that you and your uncle will live with us."

She fixed her humble eyes on her face without saying anything.

"Will you feel happy with me?"

"Yes aunty. It is my greatest pleasure that I am with you who cares me lot."

Zinaida hugged her while passing beautiful smile.

Olga seemed to be normal by dint of her love and felt her generous lady. Her maternal was very cooperative.

It was an eve of the second day; sitting in the chair Andrei thought that Zinaida was royal housewife and lived with husband in a dream house of nine rooms, four restrooms, three drawing rooms, two studies, two kitchens, two guest rooms, one cloak room, one swimming pool, and one den. That he had become crazy after seeing her princely grandeur because he was also a business man but in front of her husband he felt himself a teething child in business.

He went to meet Zinaida and said, "Could you allow me to talk to you?"

"Yes. Sure!"

"Could you send me the report card of Olga on my address? It is my request to you. Please."

"Have you made a plan to leave Russia?"

"Yes. Tomorrow I will go to meet her Director for requesting him to hand over you her mark sheet. I hope you will send me soon as possible with character and conduct certificates. It will help at the time of admission in America."

"I want to suggest you one thing."

"Yes please."

"America is new to her, so, it will not easy for Olga to adjust there. In my views, she should spend some days here with me. It will help to recover her. Her heart has broken after seeing the death of her mother. She has need of proper love and care. As I think, she needs these surroundings for becoming normal."

"You are right. I can come here for her. I think we should take her views on this matter."

"Yes."

They discussed with her on this matter. Olga was ready to live with her aunty and literally happy. By heart, she did not want to leave her country but it was her mother's wish to study in America that's why she committed to live with her for some days while she knew that she would have to leave Russia.

Before going to America, he visited Kremlin, Red Square, and the Tsar Bell with Zinaida. He felt Moscow a little Heaven. He owed after seeing her hospitality.

Andrei was making his luggage with Olga then Zinaida said coming into the room, "Sorry to disturb you."

"What are you saying? You do not disturb us."

"Let me also help you."

"Thanks. But I have done."

"Okay."

It was his flight next day so for this reason he was busy in packing. After getting free time from that work, he immersed in talking to her.

Andrei moved to market for buying one gift for Zinaida with Olga in the evening.

Olga was dealing with one shopkeeper because he did not know how to speak the Russian language.

Shopkeeper said, "Yes, May I help you?"

Olga translated to Uncle.

"I want one gent's and one lady's watch."

She made shopkeeper make out the meaning of his statement.

"See all kinds of watches here in this rack."

Looking at the case, Olga said, "Will you please show me that seventh one?"

"Sure, here it is."

"Nice! Is it good, uncle?" She said him in English.

"Yes."

"What is the price, sir?" Olga asked.

"Price is roubles seven thousand."

"Okay. Wait we will pay after choosing the gent's watch." She said.

Andrei chose one watch for her husband and said to pack them and gave roubles seventeen thousand after taking watches.

Next day, on right time, Anatolye Vladimirovich Levin, husband of Zinaida, dropped him at airport.

Andrei said before departure, "It is my pleasure that I spent some days here with you. How should... Well! Here is one gift for you. Please, accept it."

Zinaida and her husband saw him amazingly.

"Please, it is my request."

They said thanks after taking upon it.

It announced that plane had been going to take off. Andrei said to Olga, "Okay, bye. I will back to receive you."

"Yes."

Andrei shook hands with Anatolye and said, "Pleased to meet you."

"Same here. I hope to see you again." He said.

Now he had sat inside the aeroplane. It took off for New York and they returned home.

CHAPTER 6

Olga was quite happy with Zinaida but there was pain of losing mother inside any corner of her heart. She had been living alone. Every time she tried to make her happy and to abate her grief.

Zinaida also liked her by heart. By the way, she liked her reserve dignified nature and also wanted to see her daughter-in-law of Levin dynasty because she was a girl of prudence and understanding. Her relationship with Dr. Irina was good. She was a very intelligent lady having Ph. D in Chemistry and she would also teach English to Igor.

Igor had not been topper since childhood. He was average while he was a good figure skating athlete but when he came in contact with Irina, he could clear all the concepts of his subjects and began to get good marks. Olga also learnt how to play chess from him. He made Olga a good player of chess. That was the reason Olga started liking him seeing his diligence.

The cycle of events was as usual. Now result day was not so far, there were only two days to wait for. Olga was afraid lest Wolf should oust her in grades. She wanted him after her for bellowing out the fire of avenge. Perhaps she hated him.

She had no tension of losing marks but she was afraid after thinking what if when Wolf would get first position. She wanted to take the retaliation from the side of Igor and it was her confession.

Decreasing of hours was increasing her tension.

Now that special day had come. Her result was going to be declared and she was curious. Olga was happy but worried also. She went to the school with Zinaida aunty. They were together because they both had same work.

When Olga reached the School, at that time she numbed. Due to hot haste, she went inside the class room and asked the class teacher about the final result.

"You got first position."

She took long breath closing her eyes.

"What about Igor?" She asked.

"As I think, he gets sixth rank."

"No. How can it possible?"

"It is true and you should accept it." She said after a moment, "Where is your mother Olga?"

This statement pinched her deeply. There was lugubriousness on her luminous face. She put up and said politely, "I came here with my aunty to take result."

"Why?"

"My mother is no more."

"What!" She exclaimed.

"Yes madam."

"Sorry but how did…"

"Please leave it, madam." She said with teary eyes.

"Sorry, Olga. Don't weep. I am sorry. Rest in peace."

She said nothing and sat down on the bench taking permission from teacher bowing her head in silent gesture.

Class teacher had a pity on her. She knew that her father had also died and now she had no one.

"Are you living with Mrs. Zinaida?"

"Yes but I will be in America within two-three days."

"Are you going to America for further studies?"

"Yes. My maternal uncle lives there. He will come tomorrow."

"Okay. I hope you will study firmly. It may also possible that you face many impediments in your life but you will have to show your potential and eminence anyhow. I want to see you a big wheel. You have capability of doing everything. You will work out for this. Obviously you are the pride of this school. You are a potent girl."

"Thank you, madam. I will work hard for my best future."

"Good."

Olga signed on the register and took her report card from teacher. She was happy seeing her grades of every subject.

Zinaida was also happy because her son being competent to maintain his rank in the bad circumstances when his fast friend was not with him, and his dignity had cumbersome. It was the typical time when there could be a down fall of his year.

Ashley got the third rank so Olga left the class room to congratulate her who was talking to her friends in the park. When Olga was busy in talking with Ashley, Wolf entered the class room with father. At that time, he was in good mood but when teacher complained to his father, he disappointed. Words of his class teacher were pecking on his mind. Now he wanted to take revenge from Olga.

He was bearing the scold of his father. Revenge had blazed in his heart. Zinaida was also making him make out. Teacher also made him understand but at that time, he could not want to do argument because his father was with him and he was disappointed after seeing the report card.

Wolf was a stiff-necked student. He said while coming near her, "From where the whole world stops thinking, there I start thinking."

"Oh, cheater! It is my dialogue. Don't put my cap on my head and do you remember what I said to you? I am synonym of success." Olga threatened him.

He mumbled, "I shall cook your goose."

Ashley said, "She is a girl and Wolf, you should not say like this. You should respect her because you were wrong."

"Just shut up." And then after he moved towards his father.

Ashley said, "Stupid!"

"Obviously, he is an apache." Olga said and left her company after shaking hands because she saw her aunty going to The Director's office.

Zinaida met the Director with Olga for the purpose of 'Transfer Certificate' and 'Character Certificate'.

He said, "You can take tomorrow."

"Thanks Sir." Olga said.

"Welcome!"

Zinaida set forth to car. Olga requested Zinaida, "Aunty I want to go to cemetery to share my happiness with my mom."

"Yes. Sure!"

She said to driver, "Moved to Kalitnikovskoe Cemetery."

"Yes madam." Driver answered.

When driver applied the brake of the car right opposite of it, Olga got out from the car, slammed the door, ran toward the grave, and sat beside it.

She said, "Mom, I complete my promise getting first rank in my class but what about your promise? You are a liar. Tell me, why did you put me in dark? Only for that, I would fail. You could not think that what people would say to me. Do you listen to me or not? They will treat me an orphan. Now I am an orphan. Your daughter is an orphan."

She was weeping. Who could understand her sadness? Who could alleviate her agony and her heart-rent pain? Who could save her stake life?"

"Who will love me, mom? Who will give me the lap love of a mother? What will be my future without you? Mom, do you hear me or not? What type of a sin I did. What was my fault? Why did you leave me alone in this world…Mom?"

Now it was raining. Raining! However, it was clear weather when she left her school. No doubt, it was raining. Perhaps, it was not raining but a cascade of tears of Themis. Her woman's heart had melted. Possibly, no, it could also happen that it was her tears of happiness that she had won over all Juno, Venus, Hebe and Psyche. It was very difficult to judge which was correct. However, future of Olga would make her feeling clear either it was the tears of mercy or happiness.

Olga further stated, "I will not dissolve your penance. I will not breach your struggle. It is my promise I would die rather than defeat."

Zinaida said behind from her, "Olga, be quick. It starts raining."

"Yes." She said with dry throat.

They reached home. Olga was thinking about her future but her face was deep down. Her heart became tremble when she thought about her life in America. She spent rest of her day in thinking. She could not sleep at night also.

Next day, she got her 'Character and Transfer Certificate'. Andrei was also in Russia. Now, the time of her departure was near.

When Olga came back home, she found him. Her face became dull. She did not want to go there but no other way for her. Her luggage was ready. Once again, she checked her all the essential things of her requirement. She had everything of her needs.

———————◆◆◆———————

All three were standing outside the airport at right time. Zinaida found that Olga was weeping. She said, "Dear, why are you weeping?"

"I don't want to leave my country. I want to live here. Here with you. My heart is heavy. Something strange in my mind makes me restless."

She asked to Andrei, "I can take her responsibility. What do you think, Mr. Andrei?"

"Sorry but Irina wrote me in a letter to purvey her. I cannot go against her will. I don't want to give you a load of her responsibility but don't worry; Olga is now under my secured responsibility. This is my visiting card. Whenever you want to talk to her, you can dial my number."

"Thanks. Please, take it also." She said giving him hers.

"Yes." He took it from her.

It announced that plane had been taking departure. Andrei said to Olga, "Be Quick."

"Yes."

Suddenly, Zinaida went near Olga and hugged her. "Take care."

"Yes. You too."

Andrei shook hands with Zinaida and said, "Pleased to meet you."

"Same here and I hope to see you again." Zinaida said to Andrei. She said further while hugging Olga, "God bless you, my child." Throat of Zinaida choked with emotions.

Now they had sat inside the aeroplane. Here at airport tears were shining on the eyelashes of Zinaida.

The aeroplane flew to America. When she found aircraft far away from her sight, she left for the house. Her heart was pounding. Fearful tragedy of Irina's death shocked her. She was upset in her room thinking about the life without her child.

CHAPTER 7

They reached America and now they were going home. It was the first time when Olga was in another country while she could not visit Moscow completely and finally she was in America.

She found hustle-bustle, noise and crowd in New York more than those of Moscow- heaven of Russia. *"Moscow is heaven in the world and New York? Oh! It is looking like hell."* She thought. Suddenly she asked, "Uncle, which country is more beautiful?"

"Obviously, Russia is a beautiful country…it has a heavenly city. Everybody knows Moscow is the most wonderful city of Palaces."

"Then why do you not live in Russia?"

"My mother land is St. Louis but my business is in New York that's why I live here and another reason is that I do not know how to speak the Russian Language but I have spent my childhood in Russia."

"Uncle, it will not be easy to adjust here easily. It is a warren city. My Moscow is better than your New York."

"I can understand your situation but it depends on you how you can settle yourself here easily in the atmosphere of this city. As I think, you will adjust here completely."

They reached home and Andrei rang the door bell. The house was not so big but its exterior looking was good. Samantha opened the door and said, "Hello, Olga! How are you?"

"I am fine. What about you?"

"I am fine and happy that you are with us." She said moving her thumb on her rosy cheeks. She added, "Okay, I prepare something for you."

"Thanks aunty but I am not…"

"Take us yours."

"Yes."

"Wait! I fix something special for you."

She said nothing.

"Well! Your English is good." Samantha said.

"Thank you."

"I felt that you are pure Russian."

"Yes. I am a pure Russian. My language, my blood, my soul, my culture, and my patriotism are Russian and no one can abstract them from my blood as long as I will be alive but I know how to speak English. I think it is not my disqualification."

"Sorry, it was not my meaning. I did not want to hurt you."

"Leave it. Well, fresh up." Andrei said.

"Yes. Where is bathroom?" Olga asked.

"Oh! Yes." Samantha showed her everything. After sometime, Olga was fresh. She went to meet Samantha after changing the dress. Samantha was astonished because she did not see such type of an *utmost, winsome, and beautiful doll. She had enamoured on her inflaming cuteness. In addition, her immense beauty had captivated Andrei in Russia also.*

All had gone to sleep after taking dinner. It was 6 a.m. Samantha and Andrei were sleeping. Alarm clock started ringing. Olga got up. Within an hour, she freshened up but Samantha and Andrei were sleeping like a duck.

Olga went to the kitchen and searched milk, pan, sugar, tea, cardamom, and other essential materials for preparing tea. After sometime, she got success in her work. She prepared morning tea and stood at the door of the room where Uncle and aunty were sleeping inside.

She knocked the door.

No reaction was there.

She again knocked the door.

There was no answer.

She tried again.

"Who is there?"

"It is I."

"Oh! Come in, my dear." Samantha said opening the door.

She wished Samantha and went into the room for giving her bed tea.

"Good morning." Samantha wished. She said further, "Oh! You prepared tea for us. Thanks. So nice of you."

"Welcome."

"What is the right time?"

"It is eight to ten."

"Oh! We are late, Andrei." She said while arousing him.

"Mm. Let me sleep."

"We are late, Sweetie."

"What right time is going on?"

"Eight to ten."

"Oh! No." Quickly he left the bed.

"Uncle, Here is bed tea for you."

"I will take it latish."

"What would you like to have in breakfast?" Samantha asked.

"I take tea only."

"Oh! Feel at home. No need to be formal."

"I am perfectly at home that's why I prepared tea without taking your permission. I know it is out of moral and I should have taken permission but I did not want to disturb your sleep."

"It is false, my dear. You did well." She said while passing smile.

"It is my pleasure."

"Good girl. Well, I arrange for brunch."

They took brunch together and then Olga started reading one book. Andrei left for the office.

It was the time of one p.m. but Olga had been reading the book since morning.

"Olga, lunch has prepared. Come on." Samantha said coming into the room.

Both took lunch together and then Olga fell on the bed and started missing Igor. She had forgotten the chapter of Wolf and wanted to start new chapter with him. But how will she? She did not know and spent many hours tossing in bed.

She got out from the bed and went to Samantha and said, "If you have some pending work, I can help you."

"No work is left to do. Do you know how to play chess?"

"Yes. I know very well."

Samantha was a very good player of chess but that day she was puzzled. It was the first time when someone could stand more than an hour. She was feeling herself as a dilettante in chess. Three hours had passed away and there was the situation of adjournment but Olga employed active defence while building a strong bridge. Finally, Olga won. Samantha was very happy and impressed by her game. In the last ten years, she lost her first game while she was the University level champion in chess.

"Congratulations!"

"Thank you."

Olga looked at the watch; time was right twenty to six. She moved to complete the book.

Samantha thought, "She is a very intelligent girl. Really, she is a beauty with *brain*."

By heart, she adopted her daughter. She own had no child so she wanted to take care of Olga. She was eager to cascade over her full maternal love. In fact, Andrei was benedick and his age was near to twenty four. They had no child that's why they accepted her member of their family. He made many nights romantic with Samantha but not for the baby but for naughty desires.

Next day, Andrei was about to go to office. Olga addressed him, "Uncle."

"Yes."

"When will I attend the school?"

"After one and a half month."

"Why?" Startlingly she said.

"Yes. Here, session starts in September but here in America you will see different school style. Here in schools, you will face different teachers of different subjects so you will have to adjust with the atmosphere of the American School carefully. It is not based on Russian pattern."

"I can adjust with the American pattern because this pattern is similar to our secondary school in Russia."

"Good! I think you are going to be fourteen."

"Yes."

"It means you are able to take admission in class eighth."

"Class eighth!" Startlingly she said.

"Here school is not divided into three sub schools as in Russia. Here classes start from nursery to twelfth. According to your age, you can take admission in class eighth."

"Oh! Could you buy me the books of class eighth?"

"Why?"

"In this period, I can complete my syllabus."

"But here, system is different. Teachers give assignments."

"It is very good. If I am pre-prepared so I can complete my assignments properly."

"Okay. I will provide you the syllabus."

"Uncle."

"Yes."

"I want to take admission in Class ninth. Could it possible?"

"Yes. You can but you will have to pass out the entrance test."

"No problem. I can pass. I want to jump so I want syllabus of class eighth with some books of class ninth. Could you provide me, please?"

"Okay. I shall provide you."

"Thanks!"

Then Andrei moved to office.

<hr>

Olga made her busy in many works because she did not like wasting of time.

Samantha took lunch with Olga and she was astonished seeing her maturity. When Olga completed her lunch, she moved inside her room.

Samantha found she was arranging her certificates. "What are you doing, my dear?"

"I am arranging my all the report cards and certificates in the file."

"Oh!"

She sat near her and started helping her. She could not understand the Russian language that was written on the certificates.

She said pointing her finger on the certificate, "I think it is your result card."

"Yes."

"What is your position?"

"I got first position."

"Okay. It means you are a topper."

"Yes."

"Well! What is your date of birth?"

"Twentieth of July."

"Hey! It is not so far. I will give you grand party."

"It is my pleasure, aunty but, I think, no need of it. I am not a child. I have grown up."

"You are just a child for me." She said passing her smile.

She responded smilingly.

———◆———

It was Twentieth of July, Samantha arranged the party on her birthday, and now Olga was going to celebrate it first time in America; out of country. She was remembering those moments when her mother and father used to celebrate her birthday but now she missed her parents. She was showing herself happy by face but by heart, she could not tell anything about the heart panic sorrow to others.

Her eyes were full of tears before joining the party. She was looking at her parents' photos intently with wet eyes and her heart was pounding. Then she heard the voice of aunty, "Olga."

"Yes, I am just coming."

She wiped her tears and went into the hall where party was on the full swing.

She was in a white frock and looking very beautiful. Carnation lips, Rosy cheeks, two braids of platinum hair, and beautiful blue eyes were stunning the persons.

Her beauty fascinated all. That extremely beautiful doll was blotting in a beauty of moon. Everyone was praising her beauty. She stood out in all because of her supreme class beauty.

One person said giving her present, "Happy birthday, the cutest girl of this world. May you live long! Here is your birthday present."

"Thank you."

All were discussing on her beauty and cuteness. Obviously, she was looking like a very cute doll. There was a boy in that party. He went to meet her. "Hello! How are you?"

"I am fine."

"Could I join you?"

She said nothing for a second but suddenly what she thought, she said, "Okay."

"If you don't mind, could I ask your name?"

"Olga Sergiyevna Rodionova."

"Oh! My name is Mark Sagan."

But Olga did not pay attention.

"Are you not in a mood of talking?"

"No. It is not so."

"Then tell me something about your choice, hobby, and anything special which belongs to you."

"My choice, hobby, and specialty are to give importance to studies."

"Study! I feel ennui from studies."

"It is your look out. I think you are suffering from Alexia."

"Well! Leave it. If you don't mind *you have unconscious beauty. There are no words in the English dictionary that I can describe your beauty. No words, no lexicon, no language, and no languages over the world have beautiful words to make a beautiful poem on your beauty. Now I am adding new idiomatic comparison in standard English- as beautiful as Olga. By the way, the more said about your beauty, the better!*"

"Leave it. It is too much and I think you should enjoy yourself this party."

"Please, let me say." He started, "*Till the last date of the earth, no girl can acquire your place. You are an extremely enamoured doll. You are well endowed by nature. You have Empyrean beauty and empyreal look.*"

"What a stupid chatter box he is." She was imprecating him in her mind.

"Would you like to ally with me?"

Then Samantha called her, "Olga, come on. Cut the cake and share the pieces among all present here."

"Yes. I am coming." She made up to aunty without giving him answer. While feeling relax, she said, "Thanks God."

"Olga, first blow the candle off." Andrei said.

She did it and then cut the cake.

All started singing a birthday song. Olga distributed the pieces of cake among all.

When she gave cake to Mark Sagan he said Thanks.

"Welcome."

Guests immersed in celebrating the party. A few were looking her again and again and their eyes had settled on her cute face.

On the other hand, in Yekaterinburg, Igor was also celebrating her birthday with friends but he hid the matter that that party belonged to her girl friend. It was the grand party by him.

Condition of Igor's heart was like that of Olga. She was remembering the care of parents and he was remembering her. In Russia and in America, birthday celebration had made magnificently.

Olga was happy after seeing the dedication of uncle and aunty.

CHAPTER 8

Next day, Andrei had gone to office and Olga helped her aunty in the housekeeping work. She played chess again with her and again she won.

In the evening! Taking entry he called out her, "Olga."

She came near him and said, "Yes."

"Your books."

"Really." She said happily while jumping. She added, "Thanks. Uncle, thank you."

Taking books in her hands, her eyes brightened widely.

Samantha felt, "She is very fond of studies."

Days were rolling and Olga remained in completing her syllabus.

———————◆———————

One day, Olga came out first time from the house with Samantha. The boys who were playing in the garden were astonished after seeing her beauty. Those who were talking with their girlfriends started looking at her while forgetting their partners.

"How pretty angel she is! She is a very beautiful vision in the world. Amazingly, she is an encyclopaedia of beauty." One boy described.

———————◆———————

Vacation had over. Olga had completed her sixty percent of syllabus. One day, Andrei went to the neighbourhood school with Olga for admission which was one kilometre far away.

The first sight of the school after two months filled her with jubilation. She was feeling herself one of the luckiest girls in the world.

At the door, Olga asked, "May I come in, Father?"

"Yes."

She moved into the room with Uncle. Andrei introduced her to Father.

The Head of the School asked many questions and she answered him confidently, properly and politely. Then Father called to teacher and said to give her entrance exam.

After an hour, she came out from the examination room. Andrei asked, "How was your exam?"

"I attended completely."

Again she met Father then he said, "Your result will declare after three days. Have you had your result card?"

"Yes." She said while giving him.

The Head teacher could not understand then Olga made him make out.

Father came in dilemma, he asked, "You are fourteen years old and going to take admission in class ninth."

"Our Russian pattern is different. We go to school at the age between six and seven and our school is divided into three sub schools; Primary, Secondary and High but here children take admission at the age of three so here pattern is different. I have completed three years of secondary. I want to jump class eighth that's why I am taking admission in class ninth directly."

"Oh!" Taking breath he asked, "Why did you come here from Russia? Will you be able to adjust with our surroundings?"

"It is because my parents had died and I can adjust." She said while bowing her head.

"Sorry but your uncle did not tell me about this incident?"

"I told him."

"Why?"

"I do not like to gain profit while showing weakness."

"It is a good spirit. Can I know the reason?"

"My father would always say that those who show their weakness can never be great."

Listening to that statement, Father was impressed. He said, "You are a good girl of your parents. I never saw a student like you in my whole life." Further, he said, "Whatsoever will be the result, leave it, and now, I give you admission in my school. You are a renascent girl in my viewpoint."

"It is my immense pleasure but sorry, please. I am not a special pupil. Rule is equal for every student. Being a good student, I will come here on behalf of my result."

Again, he was very impressed. Now, he was much worried about her result more than Olga. He wanted somehow to see her in his School.

Again he said, "Have you had some other certificates of co-curricular activities?"

"Yes but all are in my uncle's home. Fairly, I am twice winner of 'Fancy dress competition' at school level, three certificates of 'debates', two gold medals in swimming at school level, first prize in science Olympiad, silver medallist in figure skating at state level and also winner of chess championship at state level."

"Excellent. I want to see you in my school only."

"Yes. You can keep trust on my work."

"God bless you!"

"Thank you." She said to him respectfully.

She returned with uncle. She was feeling that she would pass the exam and become the student of that school. She was excited and touching the sky because after the death of her mother, she had lost her hope that she would set up her studies.

She went near aunty and fondled her.

"Aunty, you do not know, Father was impressed and he was giving me admission without seeing the result of the entrance exam."

"Oh! Yes."

"Yes."

When Olga hugged her, she felt oneness with her and kissed her many times.

Further Olga said, "Well, I am going to study. If you want my help, please, you can call me anytime."

"Olga, games also play an important role in our life. Games keep the body healthy. Do you never play any outdoor games?"

"Yes. Sometimes I swim when my heart says but in Russia, there is my friend; name Igor Levin, who ever strolled with me generally in parks, malls and other places. He is my fast friend and did my care too. He worked out my every problem easily and I used to practise of swimming in his swimming pool."

"You do not know Andrei; she is a very good player of Chess. She defeated me twice in a row." Samantha said to husband.

"I know. One more thing is that you are a University level champion but she is a state level champion."

"Oh! Yes."

"Yes."

"But she did not tell me."

"Maybe, she could not get chance of telling you. However, you do not know Samantha; her friend's father is a very successful business man. He lives in a dream house, may be in dream heaven. His house is as big as that of my sister."

"Obviously, your sister had full hold in her father's business and he was also one of the big businessmen of Russia."

"Yes. Our one hotel was in Switzerland, two were in Russia and three bars and one hotel are here, in America."

"I know but what about the hotels of Switzerland and Russia?"

"My sister sold all of them."

"Why?"

"Her husband was an ordinary person means he was The General Manager in the Oil Company and my sister decided to live an ordinary and happy life with him. After the death of her mother, she felt shortage of love in her life. She wanted someone who could love her and she loved him madly and he too. It will not be wrong to say that she preferred love to money." He said with deep down face.

"Hey! I am sorry. Leave it. I prepare something for you."

September 7, time was half past ten morning. She was in the school campus and saw her result on the notice board. She was top listed and was very happy now. She went to meet Father.

"May I come in, sir?"

"Olga...Yes. Come in."

"Good morning." She wished him.

"Good morning. I know your result. I am proud of you."

"It's my pleasure. Father, these are my certificates and medals."

He blessed her after seeing the certificates of a bonafide girl. He said, "You can join our school tomorrow."

"Yes father but…"

"Yes. Go on."

"Father, New York is new for me so I want to deposit you all my original certificates and result cards with passport for safety point of view. Please, accept my request."

"Don't worry; all your certificates, medals, and results are now safe here in our records room."

"Thank you."

"God bless you."

She reached home with Uncle.

———————◆———————

One day, Anatolye said to her wife, "See! Olga has gone to America and I think our son should be with us now. He is our only child and I cannot live without him. I love and miss him so much."

"I too. Think about the mother in me but I am afraid."

"Why?"

"When we will tell him that Olga has gone to America, it can hurt him. He will not be able to live without Olga."

"Only you can make him understand easily because you are a mother and I hope he will understand you because he is deeply attached with your heart."

"Okay. I will try."

"And I get your next flight booked."

"Thanks."

Zinaida took the next flight of Yekaterinburg and went to meet Igor. Seeing him in solitude, she said putting his head on her breast, "How are you, my son?"

"First, you tell me how is Olga?"

Her heart pumped fast. She made herself normal in a second and said while smiling, "You are much eager of Olga. You did not ask about your parents' condition. We also love you dear."

"I love you too but it is not my answer. My question was how Olga is!"

"I think she should be fine."

"What does it mean?"

"Actually, I do not know about her."

"Why?"

She was afraid and said while dropping a kiss on his forehead, "She has gone to America."

He was shocked and his eyes widened. He asked restlessly, "Why? And why did you not tell me?"

"Her mother is no more and now she is living with her maternal uncle in America."

"Oh! No. You must have to tell me this incident. Why did you hide?"

"I did not want to see you in tension. I could know about her death at the very last moment but do not worry I was with her to reduce the heaviness of her heart."

"My tension is nothing in front of her critical condition. What she had been thinking relating to me but you should have to tell me?"

"I am sorry."

"That big incident happened and I was not with her. What she had been thinking about me? Really I am not her good friend while I should have near her in her very hard time. How ridiculous I am! Why I decided to leave Moscow? Oh, God!" He said while weeping.

"Don't weep Igor."

"I will not forgive me."

"You did not do anything wrong. If you knew about it, obviously you would not come to Yekaterinburg."

He did not say anything then Zinaida said, "Well! We should take a return now. We will live together happily."

"No. I want to go America."

"What?" Startlingly she asked.

"I want to go there and I cannot part from her."

"But why?"

"She cannot live in America due to her uncommunicativeness and will not be able to make coordination with American people. After all, who else can know her very well except me? She likes to hold aloof. She has need of my company. She will die there and I will die here."

"Hey! Don't say like this Igor. Your parents cannot live without you. We love you Igor. Try to understand our..."

He cut in and said, "You try to understand my situation which is more critical than that of Olga. I cannot live without her. I have decided to go there to meet her."

"Igor, why don't you understand?"

"Why do you not understand me? Please, talk to father for my life sake. Please, just try to understand me otherwise, I will die."

"Igor it is too much and don't say like this. It hurts. Sometimes you want to go to Yekaterinburg and sometimes you want to go to America for studies. What's up with you?"

He put his head in her lap and said while flooding tears, "Mom, I cannot live without her. Please, try to understand my situation which is going very critical day by day. Her separateness can take my life."

"It is not an easy task. How will I make your father understand for this?"

"You should anyhow. You will have to do this for your son and once you have told me that Olga would be mine. You should stand on your words."

She surrendered and said, "Okay. I will talk to your father."

"Promise."

"Yes. I Promise."

"I hope you will make him agree." Igor said.

"I will see."

"Mom, you are to do this for my life sake. Olga is my life, love and everything. I cannot live without her. She is a soul of my body."

"Okay. Don't worry. Let me talk on this matter."

"Thank you."

"Well! Shall we go?"

"Sure!"

Now Igor returned home with her mother. When he met his father, he kissed him. Anatolye was happy. He said, "How are you?"

"I am fine and you?"

"I am also fine dear. Here is good news. We are going to France for a family trip."

Zinaida interrupted, "Listen to me. I want to talk to you on a serious matter."

"What? Serious matter? Is everything all right?"

"Yes. Please, come with me. I know, you are tired and I should not raise this matter right now but I am restless to tell you something. Please."

"Okay."

Zinaida put the proposal of Igor in front of him and discussed that matter intently. After a very long discussion, she could convince her husband. When Igor knew that his father had given concurrence, he was very happy.

———————

School session had started in Russia. Wolf asked Ashley, "What is Olga doing nowadays?"

"She had left Russia for further studies. After the death of aunty, she moved to New York with her maternal uncle."

"Oh! And what does about Igor?"

"I don't know. If I am right, he is in Yekaterinburg."

"Okay. You can go."

He burst into a peel of laughter. Ashley was sad seeing him in laughing. He went on loudly, "She is only for this. An orphan bitch. I feel so happy."

———————

Olga felt her future good when she went to attend classes first day. All the teachers were impressed but the most important thing was that she was popular in the school, especially in boys. *Her beauty was the subject of discussion and she was the beauty magnet to boys in every way.*

All the boys of class ninth at the time of recess period encircled her and asked about her choice, hobbies and also about the culture of Russia. *It appeared that swarm of black bees was haunting over a beautiful rose bud.* Olga felt irritation.

Some students raised their hands for friendship but she gave clear cut refusal politely, "No. Sorry, I want time."

Someone treated her arrogant and someone respected her nature but she liked mature than fickle.

One week had passed but she did not make any friend. She did not want to make new friends because in the period of last five years she had been living only with two friends.

Zinaida phoned Andrei from Russia. He said, "Hello!"

"Hi! I am Zinaida from Russia. How are you?"

"I am fine. And what about you?"

"I too. Where is Olga?"

"Sorry. She is in her School."

"Okay. In which school does she read?"

"K^{12} International School."

"How is she? Actually, my son wants to talk to her."

"She is fine."

"Okay. I will call you later."

"Okay. When she comes, I will tell her about your call."

"Thanks."

Then she put the receiver on the phone. Now she had known where Olga was studying.

Now she was ready to go to America but she did not tell Igor that she had got the address of her school. His father was not happy. He said while kissing his wife, "It is not easy to live a long period without you darling."

"I know body cannot live apart from his soul but for his life sake it is necessary for us to accept his stipulation. His condition is worse without her but don't worry I will keep in your contact."

"I will wait for your call."

Then she said good bye to her husband and took her seat with Igor. Aeroplane took off from there to America.

Igor had reached there. His father had bought an apartment for them where they were going to live. Some bodyguards were there for protecting them. He took late admission but he was happy because he was going to live again with her friend to whom he loved by heart.

Amrit Saxena was the topper of class eighth. Now the competition had started between them because in the class assignments Olga scored the highest marks and now he was upset seeing the efforts of Olga but miracle was that he fell in her love. He wanted to give her proposal but main problem with him was that she lived totally alone every time and did not show her interest in the class fellows. More than ten days had passed away but she did not make any friend.

Olga was in the love of Igor that was the reason she was not interested in making friends. The real matter was that she was in New York, a city that never sleeps and she did not take long to get into the swing of the things and persons of New York and she wanted to know the nature of the people.

One day in the recess period, Olga was taking her lunch sitting on the bench. Amrit sat by her and said taking deep breath, "Hello Olga."

She turned her face and said, "Fine. And you?"

"I am also fine."

"Is any work...?"

"Yes. No. Could I take your some minutes?"

"Sure. Yes, carry on."

"Why do you not make friends? Why do you live alone?"

"I do not have any need of any friend. I am happy with me."

"Even...If I propose you for friendship..."

"Well! Why do you want to do friendship with me?"

"I do not have any answer of this question but I want to do friendship with you. I hope you will not deny."

"No. Without getting the answer of my question, I will not accept your proposal. Everything has a reason that's why first of all you will have to tell me the reason."

"First promise me. If I give you the reason, you will accept me as a friend."

"You are clever but reason should be logical."

"Okay. You steal my sleep. You are my sweet dream. *You are my dream doll and I never saw such type of a beautiful girl as you are in America. You are as fresh as rose bud. Two sapphires of your eyes enchant me. Your contagious smile is as sharp as the sharp edge of a sword."*

Olga was deep down. She remembered Igor and there were tears in her eyes. He used to describe her beauty in a very good manner. Seeing tears in her eyes, Amrit took her handkerchief and wiped her tears gently. He said, "I am sorry that without taking your permission I touch you."

"It's okay. Thanks."

"I do not understand why are you weeping?"

"You are just like my Igor. He is a very gentle boy. Well! Leave it."

"Who is Igor?"

"Igor is my love. I love her and I am just like a fish out of water without his presence."

"Sorry. I knock the wrong door."

"No. We can be friends. You are a good boy of pure heart. I like loyal persons."

"Thanks."

Then they shook their hands.

Other side, it was the daily routine of Igor to remember every lovely moments of Olga. Perhaps he could not find Olga but he was living with love symbol of Olga__ a gifted white rose. He was a dote doer.

He was trying to do his level best to maintain his performance. He started studying with double effort only for getting her love.

He did not make any friend but he would give importance to everyone. His nature was different than Olga's.

One day, while sitting in the school garden under a tree, he was engrossed in the memory of Olga with her photo. He was looking her photo intently then one girl came near him and said, "Hello, Igor."

He gave no answer.

"Hello! Where are you Igor?" She said while giving him spasmodic jerk.

"Who? Oh! You are."

"What are you thinking?"

"I am thinking about my friend."

"What is your friend's name?"

"Leave it. Is any work?"

"Why should I leave it? Tell me, please."

"Olga Rodionova."

Suddenly she said teasingly, "Girl friend!"

"She is my first and last friend. I did not make any friend except her."

"That's why you do not make any friend here?"

"Yes."

"If I am right, this photo is of Olga in your hand."

"Yes."

"Can I look at her photo?"

"Yes."

He gave her photo. She wonderingly said, "She is more beautiful than I. She is superior to me in beauty. If she fights the beauty contest it means she will oust me."

"Are you preparing for the beauty contest?"

"Yes."

"Best of luck."

"Thanks but what are you doing here? If you like her so you must be with her."

"I don't know where she is in America. Her father and mother had died and now she is living with her Uncle and Aunty. I come here to find out her but could not. I do not know where she studies."

"Oh! Sorry, I am deeply grieved at her parents' death and I also don't want to hurt you."

"No. I am all right but that matter also hurts me."

"Do you love her very much or she is only a friend?"

"Yes, I love her very much. She is an integral part of my life. I have left Russia for her."

"Well! I fall in your love. I am very fond of your cuteness, your solitude, and your purity. You are not like the other boys."

"But I cannot love you."

"Why?"

"I cannot cheat her. She is everything. She is blood in my vein, thought of my mind and soul of my body. She is throbbing of my heart."

"She is lucky. One in trillions gets such type of a loyal lover. Well! Come with me. Your Olga is studying here in this school. It is also a coincidence you took admission in that school where she already studies."

"Is Olga here?"

"Yes. She studies in class ninth. I have seen her many times. Come with me." She said while holding his hand.

Igor followed her. He found Olga talking to someone. He was none other than Amrit. He said while coming in front of her, "How are you Olga?"

She was surprised. She said, "Am I dreaming?"

"No. I am Igor, your friend. And how are you?"

Tears rolled down on her cheeks. She said, "I was upset when I could know about the truth of that matter. I went to meet you in your house but you have gone to Yekaterinburg. I want to say sorry while I know it is not much enough to wash my wrong doings. I am your defaulter and I am sorry Igor. I am really sorry that I could not judge your pure heart. I hurt you. I had taken my consequences. I have no one. After my father, mother also left me alone in this world."

"No need of sorry and don't say like this. You are not alone. I am with you. Who says you have no one. I am yours. I will take care of you and my mother is also with you." He said wiping her tears.

She smiled and said, "Thanks. What have you come here for?"

"I come here for you. How can I leave you alone in this new place? I took admission in class eighth but why did you take admission in ninth class?"

"I want to go back Russia as soon as possible that's why I save one year taking admission in class ninth."

"Okay."

Oksana gave him a chocolate and said, "Share the bite of chocolate for the new start of life."

"Thanks." Igor said.

They shared bites of chocolate and then Olga said, "Is she your friend?"

"No. My class mate. She helped me while telling me about you."

"Hey! You are rude. You should not say like this. Now she is our friend. She helped you to make me meet."

"Okay. As you wish."

Then Olga said to her, "I am Olga Rodionova. I live in Moscow but I am here to complete my education."

Oksana passed affable smile. She said, "My name is Oksana Turbina. My father lives in Moscow and he is the specialist in gynaecology and works in Yuri Memorial Hospital. I was adopted by him because my parents died when I completed my eleven months. My father is unmarried. My father first worked in St. Petersburg but again he left that city after sometime."

"Oh! Sorry Oksana but our past life is same. Well! What is your father's name?"

"Dr. Anton Aleyksevich Turbin."

"I know him. He knows my mother. He did treatment of my mother. What a co-incident, Oksana? What a great co-incident?" Olga said.

"I also know him." This time Igor said.

"It means my father was unsuccessful in the operation."

"He got success but…leave it Oksana. I don't want to go in my past life but I am happy that I have a new friend belongs to my country."

"I am happy too."

Olga introduced them to Amrit. Now they four were friends. Olga said, "We are fantastic four of this School." They shared lunch and after recess period, they returned their classes.

After School, She met Igor. They were happy. Igor said, "Olga, you will not tell your uncle-aunty about our presence in America."

"Why?"

"I do not know but you will not."

"Okay. I will not tell them."

Then after seeing Olga off, Igor moved to his apartment.

———◆———

One day she was sitting inside the class-room alone. All the students were playing outside in the ground. One senior boy came near her and said, "Hello! How are you, attractive butterfly?"

She saw him while beating her brow.

"Don't look at me sharply." Peter McPherson said.

She said nothing and moved out from the class room. He ran and said holding her hand, "Please, Don't avoid me."

"Leave my hand. I say, leave my hand." She shouted.

"Okay. Do you want to go on beach with me for making a date?"

"Shut up stupid."

"Please."

"Do you want to receive the letter of expel?"

"Okay. Could you join my group? I am ready to welcome you in my group."

"Listen to me carefully. Please, don't force me. All your ways will not work. I am high and dry. Otherwise, something will happen wrong with you."

"It is a suggestion or a warning."

"It is an intimidation not a warning."

"Okay. I am giving you a chance. You can think. It is my promise to you we will not force you."

"Have you told? Now, you can go."

"Okay."

Then he stepped forward from there without wasting time.

"Stupid." She grumbled.

Time was moving at its own pace. Exam commenced. Olga was preparing her syllabus. Amrit was also preparing his syllabus but he was feeling that he would not be able to maintain his rank.

Olga gave all the exams properly and now she was waiting for her result while completing the next syllabus.

Result declared and Olga got third position and she was not happy but she had a distinct identity in her class.

All the boys wanted to do friendship with her. She was a '*dream girl*' for all but some vermin persuaded her for date but she was the dignified girl. After all, she was the popular girl.

After the exam, Father announced for Fancy dress competition. However, it was fancy dress competition cum beauty contest. Now Olga was preparing for fighting the contest.

Everybody knew that she would be the winner. Every student was fond of her beauty.

Time of the beauty contest was not so far and other girls had tension about the victory. They knew that she was all rounder. They were thinking that they had been doing formality. They knew that all the boys would give vote to Olga. All those girls were sure Olga would be winner.

Now it was the final day of contest. Olga qualified all the earlier stages. Now Jury were asking the questions. One asked, "What is the meaning of your name?"

"Olga has two meanings, divine woman and success."

"What is your aim?"

"Honourable sir, I want to join the Russian Army."

"Why?"

"It was my father's wish. Before collapsing, my father lived in Kazakhstan but he left Kazakhstan and started to live in Moscow. He wanted to see me in the Russian Army. That's why I want to give my services for my country honestly and now my aim is to fulfil the desire of my father."

"Will you not like to win the beauty contest at International level...if you get chance?"

"Sir, it is the side advantage. It may possible it will change my path because popularity is also a snare. If I can achieve this opportunity, I will add lustre in the name of my country and parents."

"As you know you are in different environment so will it not raise some problem in your aim?"

"First of all I want to say sorry but my answer is to give in is not in my nature and I never live according to condition, I ever effort to change my condition according to my desires. I never learn to rely on condition. I know very well my work is my God and my workmanship is my worship." Confidently she said.

All that school mates turned out to applaud her. Entire auditorium began to resound with cheers. There was glimpsing of confidence in her every words, at last she won Fancy dress competition cum beauty contest.

She was very happy and gave thanks to parents. Igor was also happy. Oksana was on the second place. Olga gave treat to her friends after the end of the contest.

<hr />

Now she was spending her days happily. One day Samantha went to St. Louis where her mother and mother-in-law lived. She lived one week in St. Louis with her mother.

Olga was living with her Uncle. She saw many monuments, museums and other places and watched movies and also enjoyed herself many trips with him.

Every day Olga missed Igor and Samantha aunty. Samantha also wanted to meet her as soon as possible but she could not get time because of busy schedule with her mother. Her mother was ill. On the other side, Igor also missed her.

When Samantha returned home, she was in tension. She was confused to share something with husband. One day Andrei asked while taking her in arms, "What happened, Samantha? I find you alone nowadays and you are living upset. What is the problem? Tell me, did my mother say you anything wrong?"

"No, I am fine darling."

"Sweetheart, tell me your problem. Don't hide, dear."

"When I met your mother in St. Louis, I told her about Olga. She was against her. She was imprecating her."

"Yes, I know why she did it."

"Why?"

"I am telling you one secret but I trust that you will not say it to Olga."

"Yes."

"My mother was once a prostitute. She wanted to do the marriage of my sister with one person whose name was Joy. He was the son of my mother's friend but my sister loved Sergei. Anyhow, she got success but my sister gave him divorce after six months."

"Why she did it?"

"Joy was fraud. My mother's eyes were on my father's property. She had tension lest my father should handover everything to my sister so she wanted to grab my father's property after my sister's marriage with Joy. He was a black sheep. My sister held hand of Sergei for life time and left America permanently after giving him divorce. My father loved my sister that's why he inherited her seventy percent of his property and could not bear her segregation. In her bereavement, my father died. Truth is he got a heart attack after knowing about the truth of my mother's past life. After this my mother treated her responsible for the death of my father that's why she told you Olga ominous."

"Oh! When you know your mother's nature very well, why do you not leave her?"

"I want but she is not ready for this."

"Why?"

"The reason is that we both have same right on this property. She never agrees with me in this opinion while she spends much money for luxuries more than we do. Well! Leave it and I hope you are not credulous. Olga is not ominous for us. And in fact, I am not going to die. I am your defaulter also because I ever crush your sweet emotions. I never did for a baby because my mother is a prostitute and I do not want her black shadow on my child."

"Speak good omen, darling but I want my own baby."

"Okay, forget it. Now, Olga is our daughter so we should focus on her."

"Yes but I want mine. I am keenly desirous for a baby. Please, feel my extreme eagerness. Our world is incomplete."

"Okay, so you want a baby."

"Yes."

His gorgeous mouth sensually invited her for taking kisses lying on the bed to calm down her fever.

"Okay, change your mood." He said while fondling her.

Samantha said, "Leave me. What are you doing?"

"What am I doing? I love you."

"No, but Olga can see…"

"Don't worry."

He moved to lock the door and windows of the room and then he switched off the light. He fell on the bed with her. She was delighted in his arms.

"Are you ready for crossing the limits?"

"Leave it."

"Hey! I am going to complete your wish so cooperate gently."

In addition, she took off the sleepwear and unbuttoned the shirt of Andrei and kissed him passionately from neck to chest for making connubial. His hands rested on her waist and he could feel the smoothness of her body. He drew her towards him and her heart started pummelling.

They both were out of clothes and worked to make a passionate climax. He was sucking her breast and titillating her pap.

Andrei scorched her in the heat of natural phenomenon and she felt that everything has burnt all around.

She put her hand on his hips and rolled over the bed with him. He was kissing her and Samantha was adding pleasure. That night was naughty yet romantic and blissful to each other.

When Andrei took face to face position, Samantha bit his lips slightly. He said while kissing her neck, "Is it a bloody kiss?"

"Hot. Red hot. As hot as red blood."

That night they had been talking about her coming baby. Next day they both were naked on the bed. Samantha roused Andrei while putting on the clothes.

"Let me sleep, darling." He said.

When he did not get up, she sat on him and said, "Put on your clothes otherwise Olga…"

"Oh! Yes." He said with bright eyes.

Soon, Samantha leaned on his head and kissed him. Andrei put one hand on her naked and firmed breast and second on her hip and again fell with her on bed. He put his lips on her couple of lips, kissed her whole body many times. He asked, "How did night spend fast?" Again, he closed her tightly.

She was shy and gave him jerk slightly and said, "Don't be romantic."

She put on her gown and moved to the bathroom.

———◆———

After three days, Samantha again went to St. Louis. The condition of her mother was not well. Again, Olga was living with her Uncle. She was happy with him. One day, Andrei's mother came to live with him. He welcomed her but Olga's life came in trouble. Two weeks had spent and her life was continuously going to hell. After his leaving for the office, Tory started doing wrong with Olga. She was savagely treating her slave.

Andrei was not happy seeing her mother's behaviour. One day he phoned Samantha to come back but no one picked up the cell phone while bell was on the route. Again and again, he tried to make the contact with her but she did not pick up the phone.

He was going to dial the number again and suddenly he heard the sound of the door bell. He opened the door and found Samantha.

"Why are you not picking up the phone?" He said while kissing her.

"Surprise." She said while passing a contagious smile.

Samantha was very happy. Obviously, she was meeting her husband after a month.

"Come."

"Ya."

Olga came near her uncle and when she saw her aunty hugged her politely. Samantha kissed her.

"Andrei." She addressed him.

"Yes."

"Is she okay?"

He said nothing.

"Olga, are you all right?"

"Yes. I am all right."

"No. You tell me a lie. Your face is telling me everything." She asked further to Andrei, "Is this work of Mother-in-law?"

He nodded. Samantha hugged her politely and said, "Don't worry. Now I am with you. No one can say anything."

Tory Rodionova, mother of Andrei, came from the bathroom after taking bath. Seeing Samantha with Olga, she frowned and said ruminatively, "Okay, Okay. Stop loving and take a hot shower. I think you are exhausted from journey."

She neglected her and moved into her room with Olga. She gave her place on the bed and then she stepped out to the bathroom.

That linear behaviour of Samantha increased the rage of Tory. She went near her and said, "What did I make you comprehend? Should we forget it?"

"Leave it and your criticism is not based on fact. She is a child and every child is divine and my duty is to obey the every instruction of my husband. He is my world maker. I cannot be tyrant with her. I am telling you don't force me. I cannot follow you. Sorry, I cannot do anything wrong with her. It is against humanity."

"Her mother was also a child and she painted me black and white. Every child should obey the instructions of guardian. Nevertheless, Irina did not obey us. I am telling you she is demonic."

"Irina did it; not Olga."

"Stupid..."

"Mind your language and remember it, I have adopted her and now you cannot think anything bad for her otherwise...you can think."

"Shut up. Don't be emotional. She is a bitch."

"Second time I say mind your language. She is not a bitch but a beautiful witch." Then she moved into the bathroom.

The nature of Tory was not good for Olga. She tried to disturb her every time and in this hard circumstances Olga was not able to study properly. Now again her life was upset because her exams were not so far.

However, she had full support of her aunty. Having the support of Samantha, she could study properly. In the school time, she tried to utilize her free periods and recess periods. Every single second was precious to her but Igor took care of her very well and supported her with full dedication.

Tory ever tried to excruciate her but support of Samantha gave her happiness and courage. Olga did not say anything to anyone while the nature of granny was like an executioner.

She did great effort because her exam had started and her efforts gave him good result. Again, she gained good marks. She won over the callousness of a woman and her admonition.

Her stars were not working properly. Sometime bad luck overtook the good luck and sometime good luck overtook the bad luck but time of sadness was very long than that of happiness.

She had forgotten the callousness of granny and now she had merged into studies again. She was steady on the track of her studies.

One month had passed away but Olga was bearing the sarcasm, humiliation, and oppression by granny. She was preparing her foundation for the future but present condition made her helpless. Now she had lost her hopes but love of Samantha was making her energetic. She had her full support.

One day, Tory met a lawyer. He was her lover also.

"Darling, the heir of this property is living with us."

"I don't understand."

"You know my husband had died in the bereavement of her daughter and before dying he named almost all his property to Irina."

"Yes. I know it."

"Now Irina is also no more…"

"I don't understand. If Irina has died it means you and her brother are the nearest owner of property and you can claim on it."

"First of all listen to me, now, her daughter, Olga has come to live with us. Now she is the heir of her mother's property."

"Andrei can also take her property."

"He cannot do this. Money is not an important part in his life. If so, he could divide the rest of the property with me but he did not."

"Oh! You have only one safe way if somehow you can take her signature on the papers, you can be the heir."

"Oh! Yes. Why did it not strike me? Difficulty is that I have given her much admonition."

"Then start loving her. You will have to win her heart anyhow. She has authority to choose or give property to anyone."

"You are right. I should have to love her."

"Obviously but you can win her heart giving her too much love."

"Darling, how fantastic it is! I will have millions of dollars."

"Yes sweetheart."

Then he moved to cupboard and took out one bottle of whiskey. He made two pegs, one for Tory, and another he drank it immediately.

He locked her in arms and said, "Have a couch."

"Leave it."

"Why?"

"Shut up…"

"Am I wrong? In early days, you were a high class prostitute. Many people had slid inside you. After the death of wife, Ivan married you in feeble condition. He was unaware of your cheap job otherwise he did not marry to you. He gave you shelter and good standard and now you are planning to snatch his property. This thing shows your filthy standard while he gave you better standard and I know, he died not in the bereavement of her daughter but your exposure of hidden secret was the cause of his death."

"Hey! Shut up. How you can say me like this? I have also right to take some part from his property. It doesn't matter what was I but I was her wife and legally I have full right."

"It is an act of meanness while you have some part of his assets, isn't it?"

"Okay. Don't down my dignity in front of me. You will also enjoy these dollars."

"Now what are you thinking about present?"

"I have to accept your proposal of couch otherwise you will be criticising me."

"Smart lady."

"But you are a black mailer."

"Because I am a Lawyer and I know every defence."

Then he held her in arms. "Really, you have spark in this age." He said.

She didn't speak anything but lawyer had devilish gleam in his eyes.

He lifted her dress and his touch made her breast tingle. He leaned down on her for cupping her hard rounded breast. She moaned lustily when he kissed her passionately. She was lamenting. David Weinberg scorched her romantically capturing her buttocks. He started twisting her nipples which were looking like pink berries that stick straight out. She hushed, "Good. You are doing well."

They were panting. After sometime, David Weinberg maintained the clothes and said her to put on the clothes. She did it and moved home.

After a week, she returned New York and now her nature was changed. She did not excruciate her and started loving her. Olga also pleasurably accepted it. She felt that it had been also the gift from God. Samantha was happy after seeing her nature but she was also aware because she knew that she had been a high class prostitute and can play fast and loose.

One day, she said to her husband, "Your mother's nature has changed but I think something is fishy."

"I want less contact of Olga with my mother. She must live far from her. As I understand, she wants to take Olga in her confidence and want to know about my sister's property. As I am right she comes here to induce her. Sorry but Olga will sleep with us in our room."

"No problem and no need of sorry. I understand what you want to say. I will take care of her."

One day, Andrei handed over her some papers.

"What it is."

"Irina, your step daughter, before dying, chose you for $ 30 million."

"What?"

"Yes. You are heir of her $ 30 million. Take this visiting card of her lawyer. He will help you in transferring money."

She could not believe but her eyes were bright. She read that papers without wasting time. She said happily, "Oh! Yes. She did." Taking a long breath, she asked, "What did she give you before dying?"

"She transferred $ 7 million in my account."

"Oh!"

"And for Olga?"

"Five million roubles."

"Why she selected me for this"

"How can I say?"

"But I understand why she gave me $ 30 million. It is a price for living far from Olga. No problem, it is good for me. Why should I take tension?"

Andrei also knew the answer of her question but he did not want to give her to raise the matter. He thought, "How much hunger of money she is!"

Tory was very happy. Now she was the heir of $ 30 million.

She took next flight of St. Louis and went to David Weinberg. She knocked the door. He opened it. He saw her in happy mood. "Today you are looking very happy. What is the reason behind of it?"

"Now I have $ 30 million."

"O, yes."

"Yes, my darling. See these papers."

After reading the papers, he said, "Congratulations."

"I decide to open a Bar here. I have also $ 10 million in my account."

"Obviously. I think we should expand this business."

"Yes. You are right and we will make a plan on it as soon as possible."

"Okay."

Tory with David was enjoying their luxurious life while Tory and Andrei were the owners of night clubs, bars and a hotel and shared fifty percent of the profit.

Days were rolling. Olga passed out class ninth and got third position. She was not happy. When Igor asked, she said, "Third rank."

"What? Again you get third rank." He said shockingly.

"Yes. I am sorry." Olga said and her eyes filled with tears.

"No. You are joking. I cannot believe. My Olga cannot get third rank."

"But it is true."

"Then who got first?"

"Amrit."

He said to Amrit who was near Olga, "You should not have got the first Position. This position is only and only for my Olga. Those who become the reason of giving her tears, I can take his life. I will not leave you, Amrit."

Olga said, "Hey, Igor. You are rude. Don't say like this."

Now Amrit said, "No doubt Olga is a hard worker and everybody knows she did her best. You can understand. It was not easy to her to learn typical and hard terminologies of each subject in English. In Russia, Olga used to give exams in the Russian language and here she gave exams in the English Language so it would have been tough to her but difference in grades is not so big. My GPA is 4 and her GPA is 3.33. I believe next time she will be a topper."

Igor said, "You are a topper so we want party. This is your punishment."

"Oh, sorry! I have no bucks."

"He is a bankrupt but no problem. Igor will give us party." Oksana said.

"Why should I give the party? I got only B minus."

Olga said, "Don't worry. I give you party."

This time, Igor said, "No. I can give. I was just kidding."

"Don't worry. Come with me. I can give you party."

Olga gave them party but Igor was not happy.

Olga asked, "Why are you so sad?"

"I am going to Russia but I don't want to go far from you. I cannot live without you. Your absence in my life will offend me."

"You must go. Your father is waiting for you. You should have a consideration of your father."

"That's why I am going but…"

"Oh! I am fine here with Oksana and Amrit. Don't take tension. I will talk to you through phone. You must go."

"Okay. Tomorrow I will take flight."

"We will be with you to see you off." Olga said.

"Yes. We will be with you." Amrit and Oksana said simultaneously. "Thanks."

<hr />

Olga was not happy. Her chest was tightened and soul was restless. She did not want his going to Russia but she could not compel him to stay there with her. She was in tension and feeling something would fall out ill omen with her. That night she could not sleep properly. She had been turning whole night. She missed Igor every second.

<hr />

Next Day, Olga was in his apartment with Oksana and Amrit. She met her aunty. They were packing their luggage. Zinaida was happy seeing Olga in her apartment. She kissed her cheek.

Seeing Oksana behind Olga she said, "Who is she? Your classmate?"

"No. She is a classmate of Igor and he is Amrit. My classmate."

"Oh!"

Oksnana said, "Zdravstvyuite!"

"Zdravstvyuite! Vi zinayte po-russki?"

"I am Russian. I am Oksana, adopted daughter of Dr. Anton Aleyksevich Turbin."

"Oh!" Zinaida thought, "It cannot be a coincidence. Why is Oksana here? Why Dr. Anton sent her here for studies where Olga is already studying? If I am right, it is just only for the security sake of Olga and it means someone can harm Olga."

She did not say anything but politely she asked, "Well! What will you like to take?"

"Nothing. Thanks." They said.

She asked Olga again, "What happens? Why are you so sad?"

"It is a very short time meeting while I could have met you but I could not get time."

"Don't worry. I will be back here by September."

"I will wait for you eagerly."

They helped her in packing. Amrit placed their luggage in the trunk of the taxi. Now they were ready to go to the airport. Igor slid inside the cab with mom. Olga wiped his tears while her eyes were also teary.

Olga said, "Bye."

"Good bye and be careful in my absence." Igor said.

Zinaida also said, "Olga, take care in my absence and take my visiting card. Call me when you feel something out of situation. We will take immediate action through embassy."

"Yes, aunty. Don't worry." Olga said.

"We are with her. Don't worry aunty." Amrit and Oksana said.

"Okay and you all of them take care too."

"Don't take tension and have a happy journey."

She smiled and said to driver for dropping them at airport.

They returned from there. Oksana moved to the hostel but Amrit was with Olga. They had been talking till evening.

Amrit said, "I think, I must go. I am late."

"Yes. You are late. You should go."

"Okay bye and take care."

"You too."

One day, one relative of Andrei came. He invited them in the party. They assured.

Next night, Samantha and Andrei were ready to join the party. They asked Olga but she denied. She knew that if she went there, everybody would start to give explanation of her beauty and this thing would irritate her.

They were in a hurry so without making fuss they left for the party.

It was the time of midnight then phone rang and picked up by Olga. Her face was white and impoverish after hearing that news. Her Uncle and aunty had died in a car accident.

She was sapless, restless and wept badly. Her eyes were swimming with tears. Now her whole life had become sapless. She transferred that news to granny through phone. Tory was shocked.

She imprecated her, "You are the root of this accident. Your black ominous shadow gulped down the life of my son and daughter-in-law. My husband had also been died by the evil omen of your mother." She burst in anger.

"No. You are wrong. Death is a natural phenomenon." She said while weeping.

Heart of Olga had broken off. Her world had demolished.

Next day, they completed funeral. Olga was weeping badly. She was invoking herself a curse. It was the third time when she was seeing the dead bodies while burying. She was looking like a season of autumn. The dead bodies had buried.

Tory lived normally some days. When that matter became cool, Olga was seized by her.

She locked her in a dark room sticking the tape on her mouth. Now no one was there to save her. Truly, after the death of uncle and aunty, she was scared badly.

Granny could have changed her colour like chameleon again, she could not think. Her life became humpty-dumpty. Tory beat her every time and gave her stale food to eat. It was she who did not take that food and lived seven days without taking it.

She phoned David.

"Hello"

"Tory is speaking."

"Yes."

"Andrei and his wife are no more."

"What?"

"Yes. His reckless drunk driving caused accident."

"Is it right?"

"Yes."

He laughed badly as he could. He said, "It is a good advent of luck for us. Is not?"

"Yes. Sometime fortune finds favour in others. Now luck is pleased with us. Now I am only one of my husband's properties."

"Yes. I know. You are really a very lucky woman on the earth. Every wish is in your lap. Everything is going good with you."

"Yes. What should we do with Olga?"

"Stop worrying baby. When we will have had all property, we think about her. At present you have no need to do anything wrong."

She spent ten days continuously in weeping without food and water. She was feeble and feeling herself an odious. Her condition was not explainable. There was a great shock on her heart after the death of uncle and aunty.

Tory was in her room. Mobile started tuning; it was the phone of David. She picked the mobile and said, "Yes David."

"Do one work."

"Yes. Go on."

"Drop her at orphanage."

"What if I sell her to pimps?"

"Can you deal with pimps for Olga? It will be risky."

"Don't worry. Still I know many pimps. I can do it easily. Well! I am coming to St. Louis after chaffering with pimps."

"Okay."

She disconnected the call and started searching the papers of Olga's property but she could not find. "Where are these papers? Why should I leave rouble five million? I must ask her for these papers." She muttered.

She stepped into the room where she kept Olga in. Tory roused her while kicking her and asked, "Where are your roubles 5 million?"

"I don't know anything about roubles five million." She said while bearing the brunt of granny.

She gave her tight slap on her cheek, "Tell me bitch. Where are papers?"

"I don't tell you a lie. I do not know about any papers."

"You cannot save yourself. Your aunty, your godmother has died. Actually, I do not want any heir of this property that's why I am going to deal with pimps for you. Now, your next place will be a brothel." She laughed and said after a moment, "My husband named almost all his property to your mom and I did not want that. Your mother failed my plan after giving divorce to Joy. He was also with me in this plan but after sometime he fell in love of your mother while he had his first wife and he wanted to give her divorce for Irina but fate took tossing and turning. Irina gave him divorce first. Your mother married with Sergei and started living in Russia. After one month, Joy also moved to Russia and after this, I could not know anything else. And now you are heir of roubles five million that I want to take it from you."

"I do not want money. You can take it whole. Leave me for making my future. I did not come here to get money. I don't know about any papers but I have my own ATM card in which have $ thirty thousand. You can take it."

"Where is an ATM card?"

"In my room."

"And Password."

She said after telling her password, "Please leave me alone. Don't spoil my future."

"Future!" She said while beating her, "Look! It is your result card and now I am going to burn it."

"No. No granny. It is my future."

She laughed loudly as she could. She went on, "You cannot make your future. There is no importance of future for a prostitute."

Olga was afraid and Tory lit the lighter and burnt the report card and then she also burnt the certificate of 'beauty contest'.

Olga's heart had broken. She lost her whole energy.

Tory said, "I know you can get them again but I will not make you free to go to the school for this. I will ruin you."

Olga could not do anything but her life was going to leap in the dark. Her innocent feelings have been injured. The tears were streaming down on her face.

"Why are you spoiling my life for money? I don't have any need of money. I came here for completing my education and I have also given you my ATM card so please leave me alone."

"Shut your mouth." She abused, "Bitch."

"You are a woman and woman has a big heart…"

"Don't make me emotional. I am not fool and not soft-hearted. I am not like an ice cream. Your warm emotions cannot melt me. Americans are not emotional."

"Even then I am your daughter's daughter."

"She was my step daughter."

Then she came outside from the room after entrancing her.

She tried making contact with whore-mongers. After sometime, she got success and wrote the address.

After this, she took unconscious Olga there. She met the Master of the racket of demi-reps. Tory entrusted him Olga and got money by him. They did not tell their names and hid the faces from each other.

Tory said, "Listen to me carefully, Olga is inside the car, you can take her and my responsibility has over. It is just among us and after deal we will unknown to each other and her responsibility is in your hand. How can you use her it is your problem?"

"Don't worry. I feel that you are new in this business."

"Why?"

"It is because your vibrations in the voice are revealing many things."

"Oh! There is irritation in my throat."

"Oh! Now you can go."

"Okay but I suggest you to sell her at De Wallen in Amsterdam, the capital of red light area. You can get a good price."

"It is my job and I can think what is good for my business."

"Okay. It's your look out."

Then she gave key to another man who was also the member of that gang. He went to the car and lifted her on his hands. He astonished after seeing her *miraculously reigning cuteness*. His arms were quivering while he had sexual intercourse with many minxes. Seeing to Olga his heart started pounding. "Oh! God, she is but a child and not proper for this work."

Perhaps he had also conscience. His face was white and he was helpless to do anything for that cute doll because he had to obey the order of the Master. Thinking something, he locked her in a room.

"I don't know you and you don't know me. We are strangers now."

"Don't worry. In this business, we keep our word."

Then without wasting time, she was out of there.

CHAPTER 9

When her mind started working, for a minute she could not understand where she was. She said, "Where am I? Is someone here? Does anyone hear me?"

No answer.

She went near to door and found it was locked from outside and accordingly she knocked it. One corpulent man came inside the room and switched on the lights after closing the door.

Fearfully she said, "Who are you?"

"Don't shout. Your effort is useless because it is a sound absorber room. Got it?"

When she came near her, Olga yanked that Yankee in opposite direction. "Don't touch me. Leave me alone. Don't touch me."

"Don't worry. But understand the..."

"What are you?" She cut in.

"I am a social devil."

"Don't talk in riddles. Please, tell me where I am and what you are."

"How should I tell you? Rather, I am a procurer and you are at the perch of brokers. We will hand over you to brothel keeper."

"What is the meaning of procurer and brothel keeper? I did not read these words."

"Oh, God! How can I make you understand?"

"Tell me."

"What will you do after getting the meaning of these words?"

"Please. You don't know I have lost everything. My father, mother, brother, uncle and aunty have died. Now I want to know what my future will be. What you are going to do with me?"

"It is baseless to think about career while indulging in this field. Well! Procurers are those who provide prostitutes to others for gratification. Brothel keeper means a holder or Instructor of the prostitutes."

She was afraid after hearing the word 'prostitute'. Words of Doctor had started hammering in her mind__ light minded, quean, AIDS, Tears, rape, venereal diseases, and vaginismus.

Fearfully while weeping she implored in deplorable condition, "Please leave me alone. I beg you for my life. I do not want to go in this bad work. I am afraid of AIDS, rape, and Tears. I can earn my bread and butter somehow but please. Let me free. Please."

"Nothing is in my hand. I cannot do anything. My other friends wanted to inject drugs in your veins but I forced them not to do this with you. They had made their mood of gang rape because you are vinaigrette of beauty but I know very well how I could save you from them. First time we bought a juvenile, otherwise those girls who belong to above eighteen want to do this shameful work for money meet us for clients and then we take commission from them. We are the suppliers of the girls. My Master bought you for $ fifty thousand. You are useless for us. Therefore, we are going to hand over you to brothel keeper. Further you will be sold to any prince of Arab because Russian girls have good prices in the market."

"Listen to me."

"Yes."

"My beauty is now calumny to me. I don't like my cursed beauty. I hate my face. I hate my beauty. Please, I request you to throw acid on my face. Please throw acid on my face but I don't want to do this work. Please." Olga said while weeping.

Hearing her lines his heart started pumping fast. He had a pity on her. He went near her and wiped her tears. Now his conscience awoke and his body started quivering. He said politely, "Don't weep. You are a brave girl."

"It is your words. This does not behove you. One who earns money after spoiling life of others says to me not for weeping." She said, "What type of a business is this? Don't you know I have a respected age and you are treating me a business object? Shame on you."

"Olga you don't know about this wicked world, as I see, it has two aspects first is to quench the thirst of passion and second is to earn more and more money after doing ill legal work. It is a short cut of earning lots of money. For your knowledge sake, more than one million Americans are living with HIV in the main cause. For social evils, cultural reasons and biological reasons, women infected directly through sexual contact. 41 million HIV positive people are living all over the world because ninety percent are hispid. Since the beginning of the epidemic, almost 78 million people have been infected and about 39 million people have died of HIV. Olga no one can save you now. You will have to immerge in this work. I know very well that it is an ill-legal work but I do it for my family and it is also the demand of the society and fairly speaking, I am trapped too. If I try to leave this work, I cannot go back. We do not want to do this work but we cannot free ourselves from this work of prostitution because we are embroiled in this work deeply. I can only feel for you but cannot do anything for you, sorry. If I set you free, they will kill me. And their network is big. You cannot hide you from them."

Nothing had left to say after hearing him. Now her heart had sunk in darkness.

Two days had spent and Olga did not take single morsel of food. After seeing her stubborn attribute five men went inside the room. They beat her badly. One lifted her shirt. Now her back was totally bare. Four men held her tightly while Olga was protesting them. She was flouncing in their hands. One man lit the cigarette for torturing her. After puffing, he was about to burn her bare back while touching the burning cigarette then John bullock shouted, "Stupid, What are you doing with this child? Rascals, go back." He went there after hearing her painful voice. Seeing Olga in wriggling condition his heart stopped beating.

They followed her order then John Bullock went near her. He was feeling very guilty and helpless.

He sat by her and said while moving his finger on her chin, "Olga, please take it. I cannot see you hungry. If you have little place for me in your heart, you will take it."

She recalcitrated then he hopelessly turned out from the room. When he was closing the door, Olga said politely, "Please, come here."

He looked at her decently.

"Yes. Please come."

He sat beside her. Olga started taking food but she could eat half out of full.

"Please, complete it full. You have not been taking food for two days."

"Thanks but I am not feeling hungry."

"Olga, don't be hopeless. I will talk to my Master again perhaps he will set you free."

"Thank you."

She knew that he was telling a lie and his effort would be baseless.

He left the room and stepped towards Master. "Can we not set her free?"

"Is your mind working properly? I think you are working with senile mind. I gave $ fifty thousand for this girl."

"I know but…"

"Shut up. Don't be emotional. In business, mind plays an important role than heart so work consistently. Focus on your work leaving her aside."

"It is true that life is full of enjoyment without girls but not full of enjoyment without bucks but listen to me. It is not our work of selling the girls. Our work is to take the commission from girls and to transfer that amount to Godfather of the prostitution. All the women belong to eighteen to thirty but she is in girlhood and also like my daughter Britney."

"Don't lick my mind. I can understand your feelings because you are father of one daughter but sorry, I cannot help you."

"You know voluntary prostitution is a legal profession. Forced prostitution is ill-legal and how we will get immigration papers and she is fourteen years old and age of consent for non commercial sex is sixteen and prostitute must be eighteen years old."

"Saudi Arab is striking in my mind and for this I selected Marten. She has a very big racket and she knows some pimps of Arab. She can do something and we can earn big amount. She is a golden fish."

Hopelessly, he met Olga again and said, "Sorry, I could not do anything."

"Now I hand over myself to god."

"But Olga...A shiver is running through me after estimating your future in this work. You don't know Arabians are lusty."

"Ha ha. Don't worry."

"What is the reason of your sudden change?"

"One door ever remains open when rest all the doors become close and I am waiting for a sudden flare. It can show me a way in this darkness."

"I am astonished."

"Yes, it is a matter of astonishment. Please, tell me when will they hand over me?"

"They will hand over you tomorrow."

"Please, you can go now. Let me think something for the solution."

"How will you save your life?"

"If I get chance to phone Zinaida aunty somehow, she will definitely come here to save my life."

"Tell me her mobile number. I can do it easily."

She told him but at that time, it was engaged. He moved to ISD booth but he disappointed. He was back and said sorry to Olga. Now she had left her last hope. She told him that he should try again. He tried but again he could not get line.

Hopelessly she said, "It seems god forgot to write my fortune."

John remained standing quietly. He stepped out from the room after a minute.

Next day, Olga had been reached up to the car in unconsciousness. They took a way towards the red light area of New York City.

When car stopped in front of the brothel, they got out from the car with Olga, went inside and handed over her to Marten. She was the brothel keeper and seven courtesans worked with her.

She said after seeing her, "Is she?"

"Yes."

"Are you mad? I cannot purvey this girl for making her prostitute. She is not in a proper age for this work."

"I do not come here to listen to your summons. I am doing my job. Now decision is in your hand. You know some panders of Arab."

"I did mistake. Why did I transfer money in your account?"

"Don't waste my time. If you want to cancel the deal, I can find another one."

She spoke nothing.

"Take your money."

He placed the bundle of dollars on the table and then with Olga, he moved from there.

Marten said, "Stop. Don't cancel the deal."

"Okay. Take her in your responsibility and what you will do with her, it belongs to you."

"Yes, it belongs to me."

He handed her over to Marten again & then he set forth to the car.

In fact, the heart of Marten had melted seeing the cute face of Olga. She did not want her in this social evil and she could not have believed in others that's why she was ready to deal with him.

When they left the brothel, Marten thought, "Generally prostitution is my work but I have also conscience. After death, I will have to answer God. It is our helplessness and nobody realizes it and cashes our feebleness. I think she is in early thirteen or fourteen and this is not a perfect age for prostitution. Man is stone hearted but I am not. Her age is for enjoying the life not for engaging into the prostitution. If I set her free, where will she go? Now it confirms that she is orphan."

Heart of one prostitute had melted.

"Feebly I want men libidinous then I earn but I can take more than infinite sorrows of one helpless girl." Marten mumbled herself.

She stopped thinking and moved out from the room while shutting the door.

Fifteen minutes later, Olga came in consciousness; she came outside from the room and cried, "Where am I?" Is someone hearing me?"

Two women came near her and said, "You are in one of the brothels of red light area in the New York City."

"What is the meaning of red light area?"

They were astonished. She felt that Olga was virgin. One prostitute said, "She does not know what red light area is!"

Then Marten came near her from another room and said, "Hello!"

"Good joke. What are you?" Ruminatively she said.

"I am a brothel keeper and seven high class prostitutes work here under my instructions. You can take us as a page three minxes."

"It means I am eighth one."

"No."

She astonished. "Are you going to hand over me further to anyone?"

"No."

"Then you will make me free."

"I can do this but I cannot trust others. You are safe here. Don't worry."

"Can you not leave me alone? I do not want to live here in this jerry hell and do not want to do this bad evil."

"I am not also interested to serve you."

Then one prostitute, Diana Hood said, "Marten, she does not know the meaning of 'red light area'. She is pure. We should not do sin with here. She is not a whore and not able to do whoredom."

"If I will set her free, other mafias can capture her for natural fulfilment and also cash her for the prostitution and we cannot believe in others. I know about the werewolves of New York. What can I do for this one whore of raw-age, I also don't know?"

"Yes Marten. You are absolutely right. She is a whore of raw-age in our racket."

"I accept it. She is the first juvenile whore because those girls come to attend brothel are above eighteen."

"No. it is wrong. I am not a prostitute. Mind your language."

"My words are not for you. Do not worry. You are safe here and we do not force you for this social evil."

"You also know it is not a good work then why do you accept this profession? Why does your government not ban this? Do you not feel guilty?"

"We are feeble and come in this work for the requirements of the society. By the way, it is not true. Everything has two aspects thus it has also two sides. First is that government also earns money in the form of tax so government cannot ban it. Second is some prostitutes are forced and some prostitutes are here to earn money because they are very poor. Man is not totally wrong but woman is also faulty. Nowadays, woman does not respect her own sex. The biggest satire is Women are making Womanisers. You are a child and you do not know about the wickedness of the world. Now prostitution has made daily need for people. Possibly, you do not know at the time of Second World War, the Japanese government provided prostitutes and brothels to soldiers. When American soldiers were fighting in Vietnam, brothels filled with teenage girls. They raped and beat brutally. At present, everybody wants to quench the thirst of passion that's why they want women only to fulfil the desire of sex. Woman is a sexual object and resource of exploitation only."

"But I cannot live here and this place is not suitable for me."

She smiled at her innocence. She said, "I can bear the charge of your studies but remember one thing; you will never come out from the room because I do not want to bring you in the contact of the people's eyes. I will send you to the hostel as soon as possible."

"I do not want your ill-legal wealth. Please, leave me alone."

She said rudely, "Why do you not understand your condition? It is a bad world and you cannot live tension free alone. It will not be an easy task for you to live alone in New York. New York is one of the costliest cities in the world. I am telling you if I set you free obviously, other lupines can make your life spoil. They can force you for sex because you are *regnant princess. Your very attractive face can increase the temptation of people.* You are comparing the world with your own behaviour. It is a good thing but sometime it is necessary for everyone to understand the colour of people who are living in the world. Don't you know? The character of every person is different like the face of every person and we cannot trust everyone. I alert you don't be stubborn. In America, there are two types of pimps. Some pimps are direct dealer and others are those who deal through internet. If you, by mistake, come in the contact of them, they will upload your nude photos on the website for auction and you will lose your life with dignity." A moment later, she said, "Sorry to become angry at your behaviour. You know, I can earn more than $ two million after selling you. You are antique piece in the world of prostitution. Your rate will go high but I will not do."

She arched an eyebrow and had been standing silently.

"Don't be hopeless. Let me give some time for preparation because it is not so easy to me but we can save you. We are not independent because we are slaves of brokers of women. They are big Mafias. If they get this information, they will kill all of us. We have no value while we give them thousands of dollars." Marten said.

"Thanks."

"But remember this thing; anyhow you will not come out from the room because your presence in front of people and those mafias can maim your future."

"I will remember it."

When Olga was about to turn towards the room, one person went there. He was a yearly old client. He said, "Marten who is she? Is new one?"

He could not see her face. He was behind her back.

"Where do you spring from? However, do not show your interest in this girl. She is not for prostitution."

"Mind your language. Remember it; I do not fulfil my lusty desires with juvenile." He added, "You don't know when I was in Russia, I met one girl,

Olga Rodionova. At that time, she enchanted me but her *cute face* shook my conscience. I took her as my daughter-like after regretting. I felt myself raffish at that time. Really, her innocent face had changed my thoughts. Her parents are no more. She has no one. She left Russia for further studies and I left Russia for her because she is insecure here in New York. She is living with her uncle but I do not know her address."

Olga moved to see his face. She recalled her memory and remembered; it was he who got her from school and also dropped her at her house.

Sweetly she called him, "Roman uncle, I am here."

Her presence made him stupefied. His heart pounced. He was looking at her intently with astonishment without blinking. He was finding some words to ask but his condition was like a dumb.

"Y...You, you are here. How did you come here? Are you all right or not? Where are your uncle and aunty?" He asked many question linearly in a flow.

"Uncle, I do not know how to tell you about my terrible life but after the death of my mother, my life is wet in the rain of sorrow and continuously going to hell."

"Don't worry. Now I am with you. Now, you are safe."

Then he said to Marten, "I am going with her. Now she is my responsibility."

"How can I believe in you? You can disrespect her?"

"Marten." He shouted. "Don't measure my temper."

"Don't shout Roman."

"Marten, I cannot leave her here for this work."

Then Olga said, "Marten, I want to live with him by heart. I know him very well. He is a good person."

"Is he a good person? Those who involve in prostitutions are never being the good persons."

"But he is good for me. I know him." Olga said.

Hearing her statement, she raised brows.

"Yes. It is my wish." Olga said again.

Perhaps she wanted to leave the brothel somehow that was the reason she accepted his company.

"You can think Olga."

"Yes. I have thought. His protection is better than yours."

Then she nodded.

A twinkle of hope flashed into her eyes. Olga was about to start going with him then Diana came before Marten. She whispered in her ears, "We can show mercy with Olga because she is a child and every child is all-in-all incarnation of god but Roman is not a child. It is true he is our yearly old client but I want that you should take money from him in exchange of Olga."

"I want to earn one spiritual reward of my one good act…"

"Don't be silly. All can also earn virtue but not. Then why should we think of it? You know people very well, they make us prostitute. Their requirement and our critical condition force to join the brothel and bars. Tell me, can literate society offer us a warm reception? Can we live while holding our head high? Now it is our bread and butter and we cannot kick it."

"You are right but…"

"Don't be emotional."

"Leave it Diana."

"No Marten. You have to do it otherwise I can call…"

"Okay. I understand. Don't black mail me." Then she said to Roman, "Come back, Roman."

"Yes."

"You can get her when you will give me $ Fifty five thousand."

"$ fifty five thousand! It is too much. I cannot afford." He said startlingly.

"Sorry. Then I cannot help you."

"No. I will give you money within two days but you have to give me promise that you will not serve her to others and save her from Mafias. You can understand that her life will spoil."

"Yes. I will remember it and you can trust me blindly."

Roman went outside from the brothel. Olga ran after him. She shouted, "Roman Uncle."

However, he went off from there ignoring her. Sitting on driving seat of the car, he drove fast to his apartment.

Angrily Olga said, "You are really a mean. You are just a business woman not a woman of emotions."

Marten bowed her head. She could not say anything and went off from there silently.

Diana started saying, "Olga, if he comes here with money, we will understand that he really wants to adopt you otherwise he wants you for…you can understand. I know his financial condition. He cannot bring more than $ five thousand."

Roman was inside his room. He thought to take money from Doctor Anton but by heart, he wanted to do for her on his own. For this, he changed mood to take money from Dr. Anton. He went into the store room without wasting single second and merged in finding out one previous news paper.

He hopelessly said, "Where is that news paper?"

After sometime, He reached computer cafe and started surfing on net for searching the advertisement.

He wrote one address on paper of one person from the visual display and moved towards to the house of addressee, met him, name was Michel Lambert.

"Hello Michel."

"Fine. Who are you?"

"Sorry for disturbing you. My name is Roman…I read your advertisement in newspaper."

"Yes."

"Sir, with reference to your advertisement on newspaper I come here to talk on the matter for giving you kidney."

"Yes, please come."

"Thanks."

Michel said to him to sit in the chair. He sat then Michel stated, "Sorry, I have done deal with one person. Now he is ready to give me kidney of her mother because she has her blood group O."

"What did they demand?"

"He demanded nothing but I compelled him to take $ forty thousand."

"I want only $ thirty five thousand."

"But why?"

"You want a kidney to save the life of your son and I have need of money to save the life of my daughter. Please. Understand me. We are on the same boat and you can understand my condition. My blood group is as same as your son. Our Antigen in red blood cells is same. See! As a layman, the best transplantation of kidney depends on the genetic order. Only twins have same genes. If not so same genes can find in relations like father and mother. You cannot give your kidney because your son and your wife have same genes and she is not alive. My kidney is a foreign part for your son. His antibodies will not allow my kidney but our blood group is same so he can survive after taking my kidney. He will live on medicines."

He immersed in thinking.

"I know you have done deal but you can cancel." Roman said.

"I give you money when you will have given me kidney."

"I can give my kidney today. I have little time."

"As you wish."

They went to the hospital and then Roman gave one kidney for that boy while taking responsibility on his shoulders.

Doctor got success in operation.

Next day had spent and Roman did not go to the brothel then Olga was losing her hopes. She was sitting while putting head on her knees, squeezing her legs with arms. Roman was her last hope and she was repeatedly praying to God.

Day after that day, Doctor did not let him go. He was worried about her. Olga was also in tension where he was.

Third and fourth day, he also did not go to make her free from that place.

Fifth day, he took money from Michel after taking leave from the hospital. He was feeling pain in stitches but even then, he moved to red light area for giving money to Marten.

He said to Marten inside the brothel, "I could not get $ fifty five thousand but I think $ 40000 is much enough. Please, allow Olga to go with me."

"I know about you. You are flat broke. Where did you earn this big amount?"

"I think it is not compulsory to me to tell you this thing. You should be interested in money so take it."

"Okay. I hand over you Olga."

"Yes. But you will not raise her matter. It is my request."

"Don't worry. Purvey her as a father."

"Once again, I request you that you will not raise the matter of this girl in front of mafias. They can spoil her life."

"Don't take tension. She is safe now."

Then she moved to one room and called out her, "Olga."

"Yes."

"Roman has come."

"Is he really?"

"Yes my dear."

Then she ran near him.

He held her hand, covered her face and got out from there.

He opened the door of car for Olga. She slid inside the car and then Roman started driving the car after taking driving seat.

She was very happy after coming inside the open canopy from an evil quagmire.

Olga said during on the way to his apartment, "Don't you afraid of AIDS?"

"Yes. I do."

"Then why do you spend time with cheap girls?"

"I do not go there for amusement and I am not habitual of cheap girls. Actually, the truth is your granny was once a prostitute and you are not safe with her that's why your mother told Doctor Anton for getting his daughter admitted in K^{12} international School for your security purpose but she forgot to tell the address of your uncle before dying. Dr. Anton sent me here to protect both of you. I had a doubt that your granny could have sold you so for this I would go from brothel to brothel in search of you."

"Oh! Today I understand why my mom forced to doctor for telling me Gynaecology and sexology. She was a perspective lady. Thank you, mom."

"Yes. You are right and you also don't know when I gave you an envelope in which you found money, I added one thousand roubles in it. I also used to spend my nights before your house in the park for giving you security."

"Oh!"

"Yes."

"Thanks." Olga said warmly.

He turned his pre-owned car on the way of shopping mall.

He bought some clothes for Olga. She was very happy.

Now she was in his apartment. Roman gave her snacks and told her that he was going for some important work.

He said to Olga ere leaving the apartment, "You will not go here and there because I am going for some important work and I will either return in the evening or in the night. Is it?"

"Yes." Olga said.

Olga was very happy that she came out from one big hell and she had the hope again for making the future. She was afraid of Tears, Vaginismus, AIDS, and venereal diseases. These words were striking in her mind continuously when she was in the brothel because Dr. Anton Turbin had imparted her sex education but now she was feeling easy.

Roman reached to meet Michel. He said, "Thanks friend but I have no words to give you thanks."

"No Roman. You did my help. I gave you only money and nothing else from my side. One cannot give one drop of blood but you gave me your kidney. Courageous person takes risk."

"It is my pleasure."

"You don't know I can also give my kidney to my son but I am suffering from Bright's disease. Today I reveal you that my genes are same but I mentioned wrong in the newspaper."

"Oh!"

After a short while, Roman took permission from him to go.

He nodded while shaking hands.

"I want to give you thanks once again." Roman said.

"Welcome."

Then he moved to hospital. After completing his duty hours, he reached home and it was the time of half past eight.

He rang door bell. Olga opened the door then he found her dull pale eyes.

"Why are you weeping?"

"I am weeping on my inauspiciousness. You do not know, I have odium that my inauspiciousness had taken the life of my father, mother, brother, uncle and aunty. I have a fear that my odium can gulp your life."

"Oh! Leave it Olga. Everything belongs to God. Time, death, life, and changes belong to The Supreme Being. We are only puppets and nothing is in our hands. Now you have to wash out your blind faith and I hope that you will never raise this matter again. Is it clear? You are a girl of present era so be practical and now you have no need to worry. Try to forget it. Fresh up and change your dress. We are going to the restaurant for taking dinner. Don't weep. I am not your father but you can treat me as a father-like, if you want. You can usher in new life." He said while wiping her tears.

"Yes. I never forget your obligations."

"It is my duty. See your face. You are looking like a withered flower. Go and get yourself fresh…And yes. I hope that you will not feel yourself hapless."

"Yes."

When Olga came back before him after taking bath and changing the clothes, *she was looking like a seraphic beau ideal* but her face had faded literally but *in dark blue jeans and in a yellow shirt again she was blossoming as a rose bud. It looked like that new bud had come out from the calyx. At that time, her green eyes were pale but fickle. In Spite of this, the great sharpness of her beauty could give a deep wound to others.*

He smiled seeing her face and put the key in ignition and drove the car to the restaurant for taking dinner. Olga took food properly after thirteen days. Long after, she took food fitfully and felt well. After taking lunch, she thanked god.

Here Roman had also completed his confession after saving the life of Olga.

They visited many places and returned home after midnight.

He said to Olga for taking sleep and Olga slept in his room. He slept in drawing room. One rest room and one kitchen were also the part of his apartment.

CHAPTER 10

Next day, Olga awoke early in the morning but Roman was sleeping. She was fresh but she could not prepare tea because there were no essential things for its preparation. Roman always took his meals outside. Kitchen was looking like the house of spiders and their webs.

Olga began to clean the apartment and astonished when she found many used bottles of whiskey. She was not late to understand that Roman was addicted to wine. Within two hours, she cleaned the apartment. Now it was appearing that she was at fine place. The apartment was looking like an old warehouse before two hours.

He woke up and found his apartment clean. He was surprised. He was very happy from Olga. After calling her he asked, "Why did you do up the rooms?"

"It is looking like a store room that's why I cleaned it.'

"Mm." He mumbled.

He went near her after an hour and said, "Wait for me. I am coming after arranging the breakfast."

"Okay."

Now he had gone from there.

He returned and took breakfast with Olga. He rubbed his finger slightly on her cheek and said, "Now you can start your new life."

"Yes and Thanks to save me from the hell."

"Have you got your admission in school?"

"No. But…"

"Carry on. Take me as your father."

"Is it right that you will bear my charge of studies?"

"Yes. You can go school when session will start."

"Oh, thanks!" She said excitingly.

"Be thankful to god. I am not to be thanked."

"Yes but you too." Then she rigged to god.

"Your school is not so far. It is just about five kilometres far from here."

"Uncle, I have passed my ninth class and main problem with me is that I want syllabus of high school with uniform and stationary."

"Don't worry; I will buy your books, note-books, and uniform." He said to Olga after taking breakfast, "You will not go outside from here until I come back. Okay?"

"Yes uncle."

He turned to hospital. He met doctor first and said, "Doctor today I want to take leave."

"No. I cannot help you. Today I am busy and I have need of your help."

"Doctor, try to understand my problem, I have need of this leave. Please."

"Sorry. Can you not tell me before two three days? Then I could have thought about your leave. You were on a three-day leave. Yesterday, you worked only half-day. Sorry, today I am very busy and I cannot permit you for a leave."

"Well, Can I take half-leave?"

"Okay, after two p.m. you can go because I will have done my job."

"Thanks doctor."

He was very upset now. He thought, "If I do not go there on time so she will be hungry."

He was doing work with doctor. Moreover, at three p.m., he could free from the work. His mind was thinking only and only about Olga. When watch was striking two p.m., at that time his face was showing very acute tension. He wanted to go back as soon as possible but he could not get time. His mind was only thinking about her. When he was free to go back, he drove the car fast to the bank for withdrawing money and then after he was at his apartment. He knocked the door, Olga opened it, and then he said, "I am sorry. Really, I am very sorry. Hurry up, be ready."

"That's all right."

Immediately they reached the restaurant. "What would you like to take in lunch?"

"Sea food."

"Okay."

One waiter came near him and requested for using the 'Menu'. Without using the 'Menu card', he ordered sea food. Both took lunch and after taking the cash memo, they moved to the Shopping Mall. He bought books, copies, uniform, lunch box, pencil box, bag, and many more things.

Roman used to take food regularly in the restaurants but now he decided to keep one maid servant.

On the way, Roman asked, "Olga, can you say me…I mean; I want to hear daddy from you."

"Yes papa. Why not?" She said.

Now she was not feeling herself orphan.

"Why do you not marry?"

"I will give you mummy soon."

She laughed.

"Will you marry a Russian girl?"

"Why?"

"Russians love their partner by heart. Simple, the divorce rate of Russia is much less than other developed countries of Europe. You can also marry a Polish girl. People from Poland have a very good nature."

"I think you are right. I have also read that Russia comes after America, Switzerland, and Puerto Rico."

"My grand pa had American wife and her nature is very bad. I had to endure lot of trouble with her. She is sluttish. She burnt my certificate and result card and handed over me to whore mongers."

"What?"

"Yes."

"I handed over her my ATM card for saving my life but she showed no mercy. She excruciated me every time and gave me rancid food."

He let out her breath and said, "Don't worry. I am with you. Why are you not lodging report against her?"

"I don't want any obstacle in my studies. First of all I want to make my future. I don't have any purport taking her. Money is not an important factor in my life but to fulfil the desire of my parents is my first goal. It is important."

"Yes. You are right."

―――――◆◆◆――――――

That night they went to the restaurant for taking dinner and did shopping also. He took bread, butter, milk, eggs and jam for next day because he did not know how to cook. Olga also bought many other books of favourite writers and he let her bought.

———◆———

Olga was happy with Roman. He also understood her feelings and also cautious about her wishes. Olga also had a consideration. He, every time, made her happy and she too.

Other side, in St. Louis, Tory was happy with her partner. They were enjoying their luxurious life and had also forgotten the matter of Olga.

———◆———

Igor was not happy in Russia but her mother was happy, after all, she met her husband after a year. He dialled her Uncle's number many times but every time he found his phone switched off. He wanted to talk to her but what he could do while living in Russia but he celebrated her birthday splendidly with his parents. Amrit was also on the same page. He found her Uncle's home locked when he went there to wish her birthday. He was also eager to meet her but he did not know where she was.

———◆———

Igor was now in America because new session was about to start. Only one week was left in September. Olga had completed most of the syllabus but she also missed Igor every time.

CHAPTER 11

Roman took a break from his work and lived with Olga for a week. He supported her lot and helped in her studies. He took great care of her.

Session had started. Olga was to go to school. Roman woke up at five o' clock and fixed breakfast and lunch for Olga. He aroused her at six o' clock and then Olga moved into the bathroom. Here in the kitchen, he was boiling the eggs and set for her lunch box. When Olga came back in the room, He called from kitchen, "Come here Olga. Breakfast is ready."

"Uncle...I mean, daddy, I am just coming. Please wait."

She was actually wearing her uniform.

"Okay." During this interval, he put the lunch box inside her bag.

When Olga had worn her uniform, she stepped towards drawing room and took breakfast. Now she was ready to go to school. She placed some books and note-books inside the bag. Roman ignited the car, Olga slid inside it, and he dropped her at the school gate. Olga was very happy at that time.

Now Olga was in school and going to take classes of new session.

"Good bye daddy."

"Good bye, my dear."

Roman directly moved to hospital.

When Amrit saw Olga, he went near her. Pure and painful separation of Olga from his life could be seen in his eyes. His eyes filled with tears and he was floating in the river of emotions. He kissed her while embracing. He asked with dry throat, "Where were you Olga? You don't know I was half-dead without you."

Suddenly he made a distance and said shockingly, 'Oh...Oh! Sorry Olga. What I did? I am very sorry. I should not have done that. What I did? Oh! Please, sorry."

Olga passed a soft smile. She said, "Don't worry. I do not mind because prosperity gains friendship but adversity tries them. Anyway, in this adolescent period, youth flows in the high emotions of love because it is often perplexed stage conflicts between dreams and realities of life and sometime youth does something wrong while doing different experiments with people or on other things but remember in future I am not yours. Only Igor can do this."

"Yes. I will remember it."

They went inside the classroom and sat on the same bench.

In recess, Olga was taking lunch with Amrit, Igor and Oksana. Some knave boys started passing sharp comments. The volcano of her forbearance power had erupted.

Igor stood up to beat them but Olga stopped him. She knew that fight would overtake dangerously. She came face to face and warned, "Don't entangle with me otherwise I can tight loose screw of your brain."

"Good. I feel you are hot but your tongue is also very hot."

"I can give you a very hot slap." Olga threatened.

"But I can calm down your hotness."

His group started laughing because he passed her a filthy jib. Olga moved her hand giving him slap but he held her hand in air. "Oh filly, this splendour is not for you."

Then he cried. He felt the pain on his face of one fist.

"Now this thing increases my splendour, doesn't it?"

"Peter, it is not good."

"I am doing a good job but you did wrong. Now you have to say sorry…"

"If not…"

He gave another punch without saying anything.

"Yes. What do you think? Are you ready to say sorry?"

"No."

"I am giving you last chance otherwise I will really dislocate your many bones."

After thinking something, he accepted his proposal. He said, "I am ready."

"Good boy."

Then he told her he was sorry.

By the way, he did not want to fight with him because the gang of Peter was big. He ever lived with twenty boys of his class and by nature, he was bellicose.

That raffish group had gone from there then Peter McPherson took a direction of his class. Olga said, "Thanks."

"Welcome but no need of it. I do not want your thanks. I want friendship with you and I have given you proposal."

Olga saw him unusually.

"I know that you are angry at my behaviour. Last time when I met you, I think, at that time I behaved in wrong manner and now I am sorry. Olga it is right I am not a good boy but I have also some good characteristics which I cannot show. Now you have no need to take any tension about any stupid boys, I will flay them."

He moved but again stopped for a short while to say something to Olga, "Olga, It is my suggestion to you that you start living with everyone otherwise they will assume you arrogant. I know you are intelligent and want to live with toppers but it is not good. This behaviour shows that you understand others insignificant. You are creating a gap."

"No. It is not true. It is very tough to me to accept anyone but other side if I accept anyone, I cannot refuse."

He said nothing and moved away from there with his gang. Olga shout to make him back but he had gone avoiding her.

Olga had been seeing them. She moved to take classes with Amrit after recess. She said to Amrit while sitting on the seat, "Amrit, Can you tell me his last name?"

"Yes. McPherson. Peter McPherson."

"How can I meet him?"

"He is a popular boy of dangerous mind. Everybody can tell you about him. His nick name is 'gang master' because he has fifty boys in his gang and every time he lives with almost twenty boys. His only goodness is he ever uses his power for a right cause and no one can stigmatize him."

"By face he looks like a black sheep."

"It is your view but in earlier days he was a very simple and gentle boy. Every person used to tease him but…but he never gave them any response. Everybody put his name 'dumb and deaf'. One day some villain type boys beat him badly as they could. After that incident, he did not come to school for a month. When he came, he was in different colour. He also became a rusty boy but he never uses his power in wrong direction. Simply, he is the boss for every student of this school."

"Why did those boys beat him?"

"He talked to Patsy Nance. She was the girlfriend of Robin Fox."

"Robin Fox!" She said while beating her brows.

"Yes. He was the stupid boy who beat Peter with his friends."

"Oh! Is Robin fox here with us in this school?"

"No. Last year, he took admission in another school."

"Oh!"

"I feel he wants you in his group."

"Yes."

"What do you think about him?"

"You tell me."

"In my opinion, you should join his group."

"Why…What will be the advantage?"

"Olga, you are a very beautiful girl and every boy passes comments on you. Some propose you for making date so he can save you from all."

"It is selfishness but the truth is he also forced me for a date."

"No. Never."

"But he proposed me."

"Unbelievable. He can't."

"But he had proposed me for a date. Believe in me."

"Possibly he had melted by your beauty. The sharpness of your beauty gives him wound. It can be the reason that he proposed you. It means he is really taking interest in you."

"Well, what should I do?"

"You can accept his proposal."

"Are you mad? How can I make date with him? I think, your mind has slipped and flipped."

"Not for a date but for the friendship."

"Friendship." She thought deeply. "Okay, I will talk to him tomorrow."

"Okay."

She attended rest of the classes and went to meet Igor after school in his class. Amrit was not with her.

Igor asked, "Had you gone somewhere with your Uncle and aunty?"

"Why?"

"I phoned you so many times but every time I found your phone switched off."

"No. My Uncle and aunty died in the car accident. I am really a very ill-starred girl."

"Oh, sorry. May God rest their souls! Don't say like this. God examines you. He wants to see your potential and patience but here is one thing to ask. To whom are you living with?"

"I am living with Mr. Roman. He was the personal assistant of Dr. Anton Turbin."

"Oh!"

"How did you meet?"

"Leave it. It is a very long and painful story. I will share you anytime in future. This thing hurts me so please leave it."

"You can live with me. I welcome you in my apartment by heart. It will be my pleasure if you accept it."

"Sorry. I cannot cheat him. He is now my father-like and I say him papa but being a good friend can you do me a favour?"

"Yes."

"Oksana has no one except Dr. Anton and she lives alone in the hostel. Actually, Mr. Roman came here for the protection of Oksana. We also live Five Kilometres far away from Oksana's hostel. As I think, she is totally deceived from parents' love. You can give her shelter in your apartment. She will be happy in the care of aunty."

"Yes. You are right. I will talk to my mother on this matter."

"Thanks."

"Neither thanks, nor sorry in friendship."

"Okay." She said while laughing, "I forgot."

Roman was working in hospital. When he saw watch was striking 2 p.m. he drove the car to the school and picked up Olga.

Both stepped into the drawing room. He said to Olga, "Come on and take lunch."

Having washed hands she took lunch. When they had taken the lunch, Roman said, "Olga I will come at 7 p.m. so you don't go anywhere."

"Yes."

"You should take care."

"Yes. Don't worry."

He again moved to hospital for completing his duty hours.

Other side, Olga walked inside her room and changed her dress. She sat to do homework after changing the clothes.

Time was 7:30 p.m. Roman reached his apartment. He said, "What are you doing?"

"I am doing my home work."

"Now come on and take dinner."

"Daddy I have burden of work. Please, you take it."

"How much work is left to complete?"

"Three subjects are left."

"Okay, I will help you. Now leave it." He gave assurance.

She took dinner with Roman. After taking food, he helped in completing her pending work.

At 10 o' clock in the night, he said, "Olga, go to your bed and get up tomorrow early in the morning."

"I have no time to die. Please."

"Don't worry. I can do your home work."

"But…"

"Obey me. Go to your bed."

Then she lay on the bed after saying him good night.

Roman remained doing her home work and at 2 a.m., he was free to fall on the bed.

Next day, He prepared lunch for Olga and after dropping her at the school, he moved to hospital.

Olga waited for Amrit. When she saw, she went near him.

"Hello!"

"Fine. How is your life?"

"Not fine. So-so."

"Why?"

"Sorry but I have no answer of this question. Well, leave this topic."

"Okay but you can share your problem with me."

"Thanks."

"I think you don't understand me a friend."

"Hey, why are you giving a bit of my mind? You are my friend but I have not such a big problem. I am fine."

"Okay. Now this duke is ready to give his services to one of the most beautiful princesses."

"Great exaggeration!"

"It is not an exaggeration. *You are a Goddess of beauty.*"

Hearing his statement, suddenly she recalled the words of Igor. He used to tell her in Russia- Why do you not believe in me? *You have The Most High beauty. Cinderella, Snow white, Alice, and Barbie doll have no standard in front of you. They are dead less beauties. You are an extremely comely rose bud.*

She mumbled, "I love you…Igor, I love you by heart and excuse me for my wrong support to Wolf."

"Olga." Amrit called her.

She did not give him answer.

In fact, she was recalling her sweet moments with Igor.

"Hello, Olga. Where are you?"

"Oh! Y…Yes."

"What were you thinking?"

"I am thinking about Igor."

"Oh!"

"Well, Amrit. How can I meet Peter McPherson?"

"Do you want to meet him?"

"Yes."

"Let's come with me."

Olga followed him.

Peter said seeing her, "Hello!"

"Hello, Peter."

"I am fine. How are you?" He said politely.

"Peter, I want to say thanks again. I felt bad when you went from there while avoiding me."

"Sorry." He said more politely again.

"No need of it but I am ready to do friendship with you."

"Are you giving me a bribe?"

She saw him oddly without saying anything.

"It seems that you don't understand my intension."

"Yes."

"Olga I can read people through at a glance. You do not want my beneficence on your shoulder that is why you come here to accept my proposal."

"No, I will never make a date with you. I am giving you proposal of friendship."

He laughed.

While coming in normal manner he said, "It means you want to make me a body guard."

"What types of crackers are you setting off?"

"I feel you have known that any rascal student of this school cannot say anything when I will be your friend."

"You are absolutely wrong. Remember it; Olga Rodionova is a girl who has no need of other's help. I am self dependent."

Then she had stepped out from there without wasting time.

Peter could not get courage to make her stop but he mumbled, "Nothing daunted."

Now she was far from his sight.

Olga had forgotten him by and by. Peter also could not get courage to propose her again for friendship.

Roman received his salary. He withdrew money and went to the cycle shop and bought a lady cycle for Olga.

He said charmingly entering the room where Olga was studying, "Olga, close your eyes and come with me."

She followed her while closing the eyes.

Roman said, "Open your eyes."

When she opened her eyes, she found a cycle. She said happily, "Is it for me?"

"Obviously it is for you."

"Thank you."

"Being a good father it is my responsibility to procure you and provide you all the things that you need."

After some days, he kept one maid servant because there was an improvement in his financial condition. After all, he would not go to brothel and bars.

One day at night, Roman was watching the television and Olga was studying in her room. He felt pain. In fact, there was a formation of gleets in his wound where stitches were. That part of body converted into boil. He had been suffering from pain since many days. Now his situation was bad. He was totally unable to bear the pain. He took painkillers with antiseptics and moved to bed.

Somehow, he had lost in sound sleep taking sleeping pills.

Next day, he dropped Olga at her school and met Father for some discussion. First he told him about himself.

"Please, sit down but I am seeing you first time."

"First one was her maternal uncle."

"But she is very intelligent. Fairly speaking, she is an intellectual girl."

"Thank you." He added, "I want to admit Olga in the hostel for a week."

"Why?"

"I have some problem that's why I will have to get my operation. I live alone with Olga."

"Okay. Meet me after the school is over."

"Thanks but I have one request that you will not tell her anything about my problem."

"Okay."

"I can hope that you will not forget my words."

"Don't worry. You can trust me."

"Thanks. How much amount I can…"

"Leave this matter. There is no need for this."

"Even then…"

"Please, leave it. It is a small reward for our promising student."

"It is my pleasure but charge of mess."

"It will also be free."

"Thanks Father."

He came in his room and took nap after setting the alarm.

At 1:45 p.m., Roman got up from the bed, moved to the school, and received Olga. He went with her to Father's room. "May I come in?"

"Yes. Come in." He turned in the direction of Olga and said while leaning forward on his elbows, "How is your study?"

"Not bad."

"Not bad! What are you saying? It is your High School." He said getting startled.

"Yes, sir. I know and I will recover it soon."

"Are you all right?"

"Yes sir. I am all right."

"Okay. Yes, Mr. Roman." He said while looking at his face.

"Please give me a form."

"No need of it. I am giving you a letter and when you give it to warden; he will provide her one room."

"Papa, I am not going to live in the hostel. Please."

"Papa!" Father astonished.

"Yes. She treats me as a daddy." Roman said.

"Okay." Then he laughed. He made her understand, "Olga, your father is going to another city for a week. You will have to live without him only for seven days."

"Is it true? Are you really going out of New York?"

"Yes. I have some important work."

"Oh!"

Then he said to Father, "Thanks."

"Welcome."

He drove car to the hostel, met warden, handed over him a letter then he showed one room to Olga giving her key.

He said, "Room no. 35 is your room."

"Yes sir." Olga answered.

Roman returned to meet Father.

He said in his room, "Thank you Father for telling her a lie."

"No need of it. You told me that I would not tell anything to Olga about your condition that's why I did not speak the truth."

"Thank you."

"Welcome."

In his apartment; taking her clothes, again he took a way of the hostel. He gave her suitcase. Olga was not happy and he found her tears dancing on the cheeks.

"Why are you weeping?"

"I feel that something is going wrong with you."

"No. Everything is fine. Do you not believe in me?"

"I believe but my conscience is restless."

"Don't worry."

"I am worried about you. Are you okay?"

"Yes I am all right. Don't think negative. Okay?"

"Yes." However, she remembered her mother's word when she told her before the time of operation.

"Okay. Take care." Olga said.

"You too."

Then he reached hospital directly and told everything about the condition to doctor. Doctor started to diagnose his problem.

He asked, "What will be your charge?"

"Don't take any tension of payment. When you will want to deposit the money, you can deposit it."

"It is not my meaning..."

"Roman, you have been working here for a year and in this hospital all the workers live as the members of family. If I do not, who will help you?"

"Thanks doctor."

His treatment was successful but doctor suggested him for taking complete bed rest.

Here in school, Olga missed him so much and in the hospital, her absence upset him. He could attempt the impossible for Olga. He used to live a wild life before adopting her but her arrival in his life changed his life style. Now he started living like a civilized man. He could not fill his life with colours while drinking in nightclubs but now his world had filled with a rainbow of infinite colours.

CHAPTER 12

One day Olga was going to the hostel after school. One girl came near her and said, "Olga, Igor was calling you."

"But why? He could have come to meet me here. Well! Where is he?"

She did not say anything but indicated towards one car and said, "He is inside it."

Car was much far from the school. Olga said, "Why is he calling me there? He can come here to meet me."

"I don't know Olga but he is calling you there."

"Okay." After saying this she went near that car but did not find Igor. One man put handkerchief on her nose shrewdly and she could not protest. She was fainted and kidnapped.

That senior girl was studied in her school and she was also involved with the members of that gang which was involved in selling her to Marten. They had known that Olga was free from prostitution.

Amrit felt some suspiciousness. He thought, "As far as my knowledge concern, Igor do not know this girl and he comes with his BMW and this car belongs to Ford Company and he has no car of this model. And he cannot change his car within five minutes...Oh, Shit! Olga is trapped."

Now, he was late to do something for the help of Olga. He was shocked. Immediately he phoned Igor and he picked up. "Yes, Amrit."

"Igor, where are you?"

"I am in my apartment."

"Igor, Olga is kidnapped."

"What? What are you saying?"

"Yes."

"Where is she right now?"

"She is in the red car of Ford Model."

"Amrit, follow that car and remain in my contact. I am coming."

"Okay."

He disconnected the phone and ran towards his car. He ordered his driver to follow that car. His phone rang. He picked up.

Igor asked, "Where are you right now?"

He told his position.

"Okay. I am coming with my body guards."

"Come soon."

"Don't worry. Whenever I am with my Olga it means no one can harm her."

He disconnected the phone.

That red car stopped inside one garage and one man came to make the shutter down and locked it from the back.

Again, Amrit Phoned Igor and told him his right position and he fed that information in GPRS to know his actual position.

Olga was unconscious. She was locked by them in one room. When she came in consciousness, she was afraid. She understood everything. She tried to peep through the key hole to understand what the matter was going on. She saw the leader of the gang dealing with two girls and the girls were in pitiable condition. He was saying, "You earn only $ 500. Why?"

"I could not get clients."

He hit a tight slap on her face and she began to weep.

He said in rough voice, "I don't have any interest in your plea. If you do not give me a good business I will distribute the CD of your Porn movie. This can spoil your life and you will be responsible for that. Our business runs when your type of girls enchants the man for paid sex and we are not here to feed you. You are to fill up our pockets with money."

"Next time I will allure my clients. Please, don't beat me."

"I want $ 2000 tonight. Go and trap the clients."

"Yes."

She left that place with one man and Olga could not see his face. Then the leader interacted with the second girl. Olga saw dense cloud of fear on her face. He held her hair tightly and devolved her to another. He said, "Make her bare."

She protested lot but could not help her. Four men held her tightly and one man tore her all the clothes. He said, "No one can go far from us and you wanted to run away from here."

"No. Sorry."

But he kicked her breast. She cried. Again he hit her face ruthlessly and blood came out from her lips. He said, "How dare you to run away from us?"

She said while holding her leg, "Please sorry. It was all by my mistake. I will not. Please, sorry."

"No. It is not a proper punishment." Then he ordered his colleagues to fasten her with the chair and soon they did. He took an electric wire and touched it on her ear. She whined. Olga's heart pounced seeing inhuman treatment. She was frightened but what she could do besides seeing.

That girl said while weeping, "Please, leave me. I will not do it again. It is unbearable. I beg at your feet."

He did not listen to her and this time he touched the electric wire on her breast. She wriggled and her face was dull and white.

He opened the knot and laid her down on the floor. He put off her balconette BRA and crumpled her breast wildly and ordered two men to rape her. They started raping her and one man made a video. She was weeping and begging for her life but they ignored her. Olga said, "Her sorrows are more than mine. Oh, God! To be a girl is a curse. I want to be a boy next birth. Why do you make me helpless to help her?"

She was raped many times. When all had raped her, one man came with injection and injected drugs in her vein and now she was unconscious.

This time Olga numbed. He ordered them to get Olga in front of him. Olga trembled badly. Then he saw Igor coming inside the room. Igor's bodyguard killed the five men and now the Master of the gang was at the gun point. It was unexpected assault so they were not ready for the counter attack. Seeing him there, tears came down on her cheeks. "Thanks, Igor. But why do you come in trouble for my life?"

He asked from him, "Where is Olga?"

"In the room."

He ordered his bodyguard to leave that place with Olga immediately. Two bodyguards went inside the room and wrapped her completely and left that place within a minute. Now Igor asked, "What is your name?"

"Frank Baker."

"How dare you to kidnap her?"

"She is beautiful and can be a precious item in the world of prostitution. She can fascinate our clients easily and I can earn millions from her."

Igor could not control his rage. He slapped him then Frank said, "I will kill you bastard. You don't know me what am I."

He said, "I want to see what you are. Show me. I want to see the He-man in you. Show me."

"I will fuck your mother and also kill you."

"Okay." Then he took a hammer from one niche and hit it on her toe cruelly. He cried. Igor said, "Why are you helpless? Where is your gasconade? I will shatter your bravado."

He took a pistol from the guard and shot his leg. He cried and started abusing him. He ordered his bodyguards to beat him black and blue. They beat him like barbaric. Now he was half-dead.

Then Amrit said, "Igor, this is the girl who helped them for kidnapping Olga."

Igor slapped on her face and said, "Why did you try to harm my Olga?"

"I was helpless and had no other choice besides it. They are ferocious and wild. They used to beat me and forced me to indulge in this bad evil. I am the victim of their blackmailing."

"If you had no choice so you will destroy the life of my Olga. I can take your life but I will not. No one can touch her as long as I am alive."

"Sorry. I was helpless. You can slap me more. She is a lucky girl to have an audacious friend like you. I loved one of them and he forced me for prostitution. Actually, my life was hell. My father and mother is no more. I used to work in a mall to earn for my bread and butter and also for depositing my fees. This young dead man of twenty one, Paul came in my life and made a sexual relationship with me and made my porn movie but I was unaware that he would throw me in the work of prostitution. When I knew this truth, I forced him to delete it from camera but he did not and started blackmailing me. He made me a chippy. I was not by birth. Igor I know you provided shelter to Oksana and my wish is to live with you. I have no one. Please understand me. You can beat me. I am ready for this. I know I am a sinner and your defaulter also but please. I want to come out from this bad world. This world stings me. I was helpless and I did not have intension for destroying the life of Olga but they forced me." Then she began to weep.

"Okay. No problem. But I have a condition."

"I will follow."

"You will not tell about Olga to anyone. It is a secret between you and me. If you cancel this deal, I will kill you. I can go to jail for the life of my Olga."

"Done."

"Thanks." Igor said.

Now the police and Media had reached there and Igor was the Hero. Her mother informed the police when Oksana told her about that big incident. She hid the matter of Olga's kidnapping.

Inspector came near him and said, "Thanks Igor to help these two girls. How do you know about them and this place?"

"Actually, this girl belongs to my school and my friend, Amrit saw her kidnapping. He phoned me to help her, and then I came here with my guards to save her from them. It is also my duty. Five are dead in firing and now he is in your custody. He will tell you about the other rackets also and you can save other girls."

"Thanks."

Igor was about to go then one bullet injured his shoulder. That bullet could have taken his life if he did not change his position. His shot missed but guards of Igor took a rapid action and shot him. Bullet made a hole in his head and he died.

Now those girls were free and his guards moved with him to the Hospital for saving him. After an operation, he was fine. Olga, Zinaida, Okasana, Amrit were there and had been praying for him.

When he was out of danger, Olga came to meet him with his mother. Amrit and Oksana were also there. Zinaida said, "How are you, my brave son? I am proud of you."

"I am fine."

He asked Olga, "How are you?"

"I am fine but you should not have done that. They could have killed you."

"Your love makes me immortal and no one can take my life. My life is yours. I live for you and love to die for you."

"Oh, Igor. I love you. I love you so much. You should not be possessive for me."

But Igor could not say I love you. He found tears in her eyes then asked, "Why are you weeping?"

"I am not fit for you. Now I am rotten."

"Who says you are rotten. You are fit for me. I can accept you in any of the conditions."

"You are great Igor."

"No. I am not great and I did what one friend should do for his friend."

"Thanks. You saved my life and now this life is yours."

"I don't need of your life. I want you."

"Dear, I am yours."

"Thanks." And he smiled.

Olga said, "Now allow me to go from here. I am to go to the hostel."

"You can live with me."

"Try to understand. Warden can phone to my father and I don't want to see him in tension. Please. I will meet you tomorrow."

"Okay."

Next day, the news was 'Indo-Russian Unity Saves Two American Girls.' Now, Igor and Amrit were the Hero. Igor's father scolded him first and when he knew that he did so to save the life of Olga he congratulated him and gave him best wishes.

Police investigated with Helen Flanthrope, that intermediate girl. She told them everything except the matter of Olga. Police destroyed all the porn CDs and her movie which they got from that place. Now she was free and started living with Igor. Zinaida legally adopted her and she was happy now.

CHAPTER 13

Finally, one week passed away and Roman felt himself in a well condition. Now he had come to his apartment from the hospital. He was dying to meet her because he has her tension.

Immediately he arrived to ATM centre after taking debit card to withdraw money.

After withdrawing money, he went to the hospital to deposit the bill.

He came across the doctor when he was going to receive Olga.

"Hello Roman!"

"Doctor, I am fine and thanks."

"There is no need of thanks." He said smilingly.

"Could I go doctor?"

"Yes. I can understand you are eager to meet her."

He frowned for a moment. Suddenly he said, "What, after all, do you mean?"

"You are worried about your beautiful doll."

"How do you know?"

"I saw you with her in a Shopping Mall while buying books."

"Oh!"

"Go and meet her. Have a nice day."

He drove car to the Shopping Mall and returned home to drop off her new clothes. He would always try to give her happiness.

He went to the school at 2 p.m. to receive her. They moved to the hostel and took all the things from the room. Olga handed over the key to warden with thanks and came home with him.

It was her jumping jubilation after seeing new clothes in her room. Passing a very cute smile she thanked him.

"Welcome."

They took lunch together in the restaurant because his servant was on leave.

❖

By and by time was rolling and Roman was much too addicted of whiskey. One day he organized a small night party with four friends in his apartment. In his room, they were in mood to enjoy the lustre of the party. Roman was doing good hospitality.

At that time, Olga was studying in her room. Here in his room, one friend of Roman increased the volume while rotating the volume switch of the music system for appreciating it.

They were enjoying themselves but it was creating disturbance in her studies. She did not want to go there but at last, she could not stop herself. She came out from the room and stood silently at the door. She found all of them dead drunk. Roman was making the pegs for all.

The eyes of one man stopped on her figure. He felt more intoxication in her beauty than that of whisky. He said while having a cold sigh, *"Beautiful! She is either beauty bomb or beauty yard. No other girl can be as beautiful as she is. She is smashing."* He lost his consciousness and the level of grogginess in his mind was increasing his passion and he wanted to come in the contact of that intoxicant dew from the sea of whiskey.

He came near her and said abjectly while touching her bust, "Are you teen age adulteress?"

"Shut up. Shame on you. This thing does not behove you." She said angrily giving him spasmodic twitch.

"My god! *You are very hot.*" He said making her fun. *"Oh, what a chilly beauty she is!"*

He moved to Roman and said, "One hour has spent, and you did not tell me anything about this non-age punk. It seems after leaving the company of prostitutes, you have come in the contact of juvenile. Is she second Lolita? Tell me, how much money did you spend for this girl? I can give you triple for her. Hey! *She is nonpareil and I want her for one night…*"

He gave him punch on his nose and thick blood ran down on his lips. "Shut up bastard. She is my daughter. How dare you to say like this? I will

174

kill you mother's fuck. Get lost; Scoundrel, I say get lost from here otherwise I will kill you." He said blatantly and affronted him in front of all. He was continuously giving him box. It seemed that he would take his life for Olga. "Don't take the exam of my patience. Get lost."

He was shocked now. He said, "As I know you are unmarried then how you can have a daughter."

"I adopted her. And now she is my daughter."

"I am sorry. You must tell us. As you used to go brothel that's why..."

He cut in and said, "I do not want to listen to you and no arguments further. Get off from here."

His rascal friend left for his home. Roman said sorry to all and then all his friends also took the way of their homes.

When all were gone, he sat beside her and said primitively, "Why did you come here?"

She was quiet but her tears told him everything then after this, he could not say her anything. Silently she walked into her room.

After sometime, he went near her and hugged her politely.

He said, "Sorry. I am really very sorry. At that time I was wrong. I should have understood you."

"No. I must not have gone there to disturb you but they were appreciating numbers aloud and it was disturbing me. It was the reason I went there. I am sorry." She said while weeping.

He wiped her tears and came outside with her to watch one movie. She was happy after watching movie and came back after mid night.

Olga stepped in his room after wearing night dress. He was thinking lying on the bed. She said sitting beside him, "Do you love me?"

"Yes. I love you my dear. Is any doubt?"

"Well! Could you give me something?"

"I can give you everything. Order me." He said smilingly.

Olga also smiled in response. She said, "Please, leave the company of your friends. They are not authentic people. They are libidinous."

"Yes. I will leave them."

"Promise."

"Yes. It is my promise."

Her exam commenced. Olga was preparing for passing out the exam of high school. She studied properly but when she saw her result, her face became long. It was her bad luck otherwise her time passed happily. Again, she could not get desirable marks but this time she got success in the improvement of her marks. She got 89% according to GPA.

When Olga knew Amrit scored maximum grades, she was happy and gave him party with compliments on the success in the examination. He was astonished when he felt the sensuousness of Olga's lips on his cheek.

Unexpectedly he said, "Unbelievable. I do not believe that you gave me a kiss but the touch of your delicate lips can increase the highest passion of anyone."

Olga laughed and said putting her hand on his shoulder, "I did not give you kiss but it was your gift."

"I will take care of your gift till the end of my life."

"Oh! You are silly. One day, you will make me your slave." She said.

"Are you stooping towards me?"

"No. My stooping is only for Igor."

"I know very well but I am just kidding."

Amrit was very happy after taking treat from Olga.

One night, Roman was taking wine; suddenly he felt pain, it was extremely painful. He cried, "Olga, come here."

Feeling dart of shock she went there in his room

She was fearful after seeing his face red and sweated.

He said, "Olga, phone to doctor."

She dialled a number after searching in a phone diary. Doctor gave her assurance to come soon.

Olga asked in deplorable condition, "Are you all right? Is anything wrong?"

"N…No. I…I feel pain only." He said unsteadily.

"I am worried about…"

"Oh, don't worry. I say I am all right."

Olga was rubbing her soft fingers smoothly on his forehead while weeping. He literally forgot pain after feeling her sensuous touch.

Now doctor had come on time. He checked up him and said, "Your lungs have some problem and it seems that your kidney is not working properly."

He ordered Olga for leaving the room.

She followed his order but she stopped behind the door of his room.

Doctor said, "I think your kidneys do not work properly and there is some problem in your lungs also. Tell me right about your condition otherwise it is tough to me to understand your problem through external check up. I can help you in reducing your pain when you tell me the reason of your condition." Doctor said to him seriously.

"Doctor, I gave my kidney to one person for money because I had no other way to earn money for saving the life of my daughter and truth is that I am addicted to drinking."

Olga heard him; her face was white and peaked and Roman was unaware that she was listening to him standing behind the door of his room.

Doctor said, "I see. Now you can spend the night after taking these pills but your operation is compulsory otherwise your chance of survival will be negligible. Your treatment will be long."

"Total disbursement?"

"First, let me diagnose your problem."

"Doctor, you know everything even then you…"

Then he told him estimate of total expenditure.

"Doctor I cannot bear it. You can detect it from my salary."

"I can do it but arrangement is compulsory to you because team will be there for your operation. This is an issue of others specialists."

Olga was weeping badly in her room. She thought. *Obviously I am fully detestable and totally worthless and hapless. My bad omen first took the life of my father then after mother, brother, uncle and aunty and now my father-like is in trouble seriously. I am ominous. Yes, I am ominous.*

That lachrymose girl took her cycle and rode towards any place. She stopped the cycle in front of church and stepped inside. She fell in front of the cross and invoked to god for father, "Please, help me. Please! Please! Please! Jesus, you can take my life but do mercy on my father. He is a very good person. Please do your mercy on my father. I do not want to see my father dead. Please god. You ever take exam of devotee but today it is your exam. If you fail, no one will trust you. All will understand you a statue__ a statue of stone, a worthless dumb and deaf statue of mud, nothing else. If you are really heart-hearted, accept my request. Oh, God! Please, accept my request. Please save the life of my father. If you want, I can also give you an exam for the life of my father. I can give. Now I am ready. Tell me, what can I do for my father? I can die in place of him. Do you listen to me? His condition is serious." She said with pounding heart.

Suddenly, something stroke in her mind and quickly she moved towards the red light area. She went to meet Marten in the brothel. When she walked inside the bagnio, Marten surprised. She saw her cute face ashen and saw dark lines of tears on her rosy cheeks.

Quickly she turned to one separate room with her and asked the reason, "Why have you come here? Someone could see you while coming here and your future…"

"I have no tension of my future but now I have only one thing in my mind that how I can earn money. It is compulsory to me to earn money anyhow." She said before listening to her complete statement.

"Money!" She said wonderingly.

She said, "Marten, condition of my Uncle…Father is very serious. His operation is very compulsory and we have not enough money for the operation."

"Sorry to help you in this matter. I am also flat broke at present because I also have to give money to mafias." Modestly she said.

"I don't want to take your wealth. If you have any call of your client for a prostitute, I can join him for this."

"Shut up, an imprudent girl. You know what you are saying. Are you mad? He is not your real father then why are you going to destroy your future? This work is not for juvenile."

"I am not a selfish girl. He saved my future from prostitution and now I will save him by prostitution. It is my duty also. Don't worry; it is my first and last evil work. You don't know Marten last time when you demanded money for releasing me; he sold his kidney for taking out me from this hell." She ascribed while weeping.

"What?" She wondered.

"Yes. It is true."

She detracted herself, "One sin has added in my life."

Marten hugged her. Her heart was pounding.

"Now I am ready to sell my body for saving the life of my father."

"I am not complacent from you. You can think again."

"I have thought. I am half without him. Now, this is my turn."

"God, what type of a game are you playing with this cute girl?" She complained to god. She said further, "Let's come with me."

Marten called out Diana.

She was stunt seeing Olga there.

Marten said, "Diana, go to Allan Pearson's penthouse with her."

"With Olga. Why?" She said startlingly.

"He has asked me to send a Page three girl."

"Why should I go with Olga? Where is Roman?"

"It is her wish to get a client because she has need of money for the operation of Roman. I can send Olga with you to anyone but I believe Allan Pearson will give her chance in his upcoming movie after seeing her nonpareil beauty. I want to save Olga. He will not harm her chastity."

"But Olga…"

"It is my wish. Please, don't argue. Try to understand me. I have little time and have urgent need of money."

"Your wish." Hopelessly she said.

Then Marten told her everything clearly.

She said, "Olga why are spoiling your life. Dear, this work is on full of risk. It is marshier than the marsh."

"I can take every risk for my father."

Conceding defeat, Diana went to Allan Pearson's penthouse with her. Diana came back to brothel while her conscience was crushing the heart badly. Perhaps she did not want her in this profession by heart.

When Roman did not find Olga in the apartment, he worried about her. He thought, "Where can she go? I think she cannot go her friend's home leaving me in this condition. How can she leave me alone in this tough situation? She never goes any of her friends' houses so where can she go? Oh! Yes, she also knows the address of Marten. If I am right, she must be there with her. Perhaps she has known about my critical condition. I feel she has heard everything. In my opinion, she is about to reach there for earning money. I will have to stop her as soon as possible."

He had understood everything. Immediately he ignited the car and drove down the road to the brothel. He went inside and asked, "Did Olga come here?"

"Yes." Marten said.

"Where is she?"

"She is with Allan Pearson in his penthouse."

Hearing this, his heart shuddered. He asked, "Why?"

"She wants to earn money for your operation."

"I had understood that she would be here. She had said to me that anyhow she would not want my avulsion from her life. Oh! Marten, why did you not stop her?"

"My all the efforts were worthless but it is clear she is more faithful than dog while you are not her real father. I feel after this incident, nobody will say blood is thicker than water."

"Marten, she wants to return my gratitude. If I am unable to save her this time, I will not be able to complete my confession. I will not let her becoming a whore."

"Of course she is going to be a whore but VIRGIN WHORE OF RAW-AGE. This wrong work is divine because it is for saving the life of dear one. It means she always wants to see you as a father."

"Oh, my god."

His heart was beating fast and face was languid.

He saw Diana while coming near him.

She said angrily out of control, "Roman, what are doing here, and what type of a father you feel yourself?"

It seemed both Diana and Marten loved her very much.

"Sorry. I was unaware of this matter."

He quickly drove car with Diana towards his penthouse without wasting time.

———————◆———————

On the other hand, Olga was standing silently in front of Allan Pearson. She was suffering from fear and perspiring. She concentrated on Allan Pearson; he was masculine, handsome unmarried man of twenty nine. He was not only script writer but director also. Diana told her on the way.

He reviewed Olga from top to bottom as he had intension to pour her beauty in his snifter. Her beauty surprised him. He saw many beautiful actresses, beauty contest winners but all were insipid in front of her.

He poured Champaign in the snifter while asking her name.

"My name is Olga Rodionova."

Instantly it came through his mouth, "*Olga* **Radiation**, *plus* **nova**. *Obviously, you have nova figure and radiant beauty. Your name is Olga Radiation-nova.*"

She did not react on his words.

"Are you Russian?"

"Yes."

"I like Russian girls because the flag of their beauty hoists everywhere but *you are not of this world. You are heavenly.* I never…wait! Go to wash basin and wash your face. It is outside."

She went there. After washing her face, she came in front of Allan Pearson but her heart was throbbing fast.

He described her beauty, "*You are amazingly beautiful girl. I never saw such type of a reigning beauty but today I am seeing a prodigy of god. I feel one beauty Goddess has come in my hell making it heaven…*"

"Excuse…"

"Don't divert…Shit, my mind diverts. Well your age?" Obstruction of Olga made his mood bad.

"Fifteen years old."

"How many days have you wasted in this work?"

"I am not what you are understood."

"It is not my answer. My question was how many days you have wasted."

"Not even one but I will waste my some hours with you tonight."

"First time?"

"Yes."

"Be scared?"

"Yes."

"How will you cooperate with me?"

"It depends on you."

"Okay. So why are you standing like a statue? Make a peg for me." He ordered.

She made a peg for him with quivering hands.

She had been standing silently after making his peg but in parallel, she was fighting with her conscience. She was afraid.

He did not drink it and throw the Champaign on her face. Temper of Olga shot up but she put up thinking something.

"Now I make you Nereid and drops of Champaign on your face are increasing the inebriation of your beauty. Now it is a perfect combination of wine and the whore. Your appearance is like an angel in my penthouse. Nymph when you bathe in the river, bartender in bar, actress in my movie, and very beautiful princess in any beauty contest. You are a beautiful princess of inebriating eyes, healthy buttocks, and good projections. You are charming like an unripe rose bud." Further, he said, "Why are you not doffing your clothes?" He had smitten on her charm.

"What are you saying?" Her heart punched savagely.

"Then my hand will be tight. I will not give money to Marten and she will not give you your commission."

She remembered her father's condition then in a minute she took off her clothes. Now she was in lady vest and knickers. Her heart was not throbbing properly but running fast and she was quivering.

He took new bottle of Vodka and started drizzling on her body. Her chastity was dissolved. Tears came down on her cheeks. She felt her purity vanished.

Again, Allan saw her from top to bottom and went on further, *"Your glabrous figure is looking like a smooth slab of ice. You are cynosure of my eyes. I can say with bet that you are cynosure of all the eyes. Your platinum hair, lips, hips, breast, thighs, face, everything have a perfect symmetry and nobody can live without taking a dip in the blue sea of your eyes. In this dress you are able to make celibate lusty.* Man wants three things during sex from woman, first is beauty, second one is a well figure, and third one is a developed clitoris."

She was scared after hearing 'clitoris' from his mouth because the words of doctor started thundering in her mind. She recalled Light-minded, AIDS, Tears, Rape, sex, Clitoris, Vaginismus and Venereal diseases.

She said while weeping, "You can do everything with me but don't rape me."

He laughed as he could. "Do you understand me a rapist? Don't worry. I am not a rapist." He added while taking peg, "I asked you to take off the clothes so that I can use to inspect your figure."

Olga saw him unusually.

"Will you want to work in my movie?" He asked.

"No. I have no experience of facing cameras."

"Don't take tension of this. I will make you ready for this. However I want to tell you one thing- every struggling actress does sex many times with directors, actors, and producers to get a chance of playing a role in the movie but I am giving you an opportunity and you can trust me. I will never force you for a cheap work. Tomorrow I will provide you money and I request you to think on this subject. I can make you the most successful actress. You are a wonder girl."

"Sir, I cannot take ill gotten wealth."

"No. It is not an ill-legal wealth. You have spent half an hour with me and I will give you money of this work. You are not a prostitute but for me, you are an eye-candy. You are respected. If you really want that I should harm your virginity so come on the bed but it is not my wish. It will be yours."

"No. It is not my meaning."

"I don't want to exhaust the strength of your chastity."

"Thank you, sir."

"No need of it. Don't accept deplorable condition. You do not look quite good while crying. By the way, I did not want to take bed with you. *Seeing your very cute face, I have really decided that I will not muddy your holy spirit. I respect your wonderful beauty. You are a miracle of nature.* If someone were on my place, he had prepared himself for the couch because rose bud is superior to flower."

"So why did you throw Champaign on my face?"

"Sorry for that. But I wanted to test your patience. You are a very good girl."

"Could I wear my clothes?"

"Yes. Why not?"

"Thanks."

"One more thing is that I cascaded whiskey not for playing with you but for the recovery of my money. I am a diplomatic business man so I spend money where I get profit."

"Oh!"

"Well why did you join this work tonight?"

"Sir, I have much money but my granny…Leave it. We are flat broke now. I am helpless because the condition of my father is not good and we have urgent need of money for the operation that's why I am here. My father has not sufficient balance for operation."

"Does he allow?" He asked.

"No. I came here without giving him any information. Basically, he is not my real father. My father has died but he purveys me as a father."

Seeing her good spirit, he felt himself ashamed because real daughter could also not do that. Bowing the head he said, "Sorry."

"No. It is a business and in business, there is no place for emotions and I am very grateful that you understand me."

He had been seeing her delicately.

At last when Olga was about to wear the skirt, she found her father while gritting his teeth. She astonished while feeling half dead.

She concealed herself through shame. Her blood was frozen and heart pounced.

When he saw Olga putting the skirt on, he came inside angrily and said to Allan while clapping, "Well done! Have you had any daughter? I think, your answer will be no. Well! Can you harm the girlhood of your own blood? You could not think that she is a girl of fifteen. How can you spoil the life of an innocent girl?" He said angrily.

Olga put on her skirt quickly but she was quivering while standing aback of him. She ran to hide behind Diana and began to weep. She was afraid of his anger.

He was speaking in bemoaning voice. Allan said nothing. He had also known that Roman was in trouble. He bore his scold. He did his insult too much but Allan did not say anything.

Roman held the hand of Olga and returned home. He was scolding her. He smote, "Why did you go there? How dare you to go for doing social evil work? Why did you cross your limit without my permission? Do one thing. Go to court and give written command against me that I harass you. Up to when you live with me, you will have to live under my rules and regulations. You can take your decision only when you will complete your eighteen years. Now you have no right to take self decision. Is it clear? Tell me, are you a bad girl?"

"No."

"Then why did you go there?"

While wiping her tears unsteadily she said naively, "P...papa. You can beat me as well as kill me, I will not protest. I know it was wrong doings but I had no other choice. You have full authority to give me punishment. Please, excuse me. First, I lost my father, mother, brother, aunty, and uncle and now I do not want to see you dead. You saved my life after giving one kidney and now it is my turn to save your life anyhow and I could not think best way to earn dollars in bundles. I cannot live without you. You are everything for me.

You are my father, mother, brother; uncle, aunty, and friend and I cannot lose you. I heard your conversation when you were talking to doctor. I don't want requiem again. Please sorry. I will not go against you. Sorry. Intentionally I also did not want to do it."

Then he had a pity on. He said while cuddling her, "Dear, I have no tension of money for operation. Money plays importance in private sectors but I can get my operation in the government hospital. I already saved money for my health and don't forget Dr. Anton. Undoubtedly, he will help me. He sent me here for giving support to Oksana and you. You know he transfers money in my account for depositing her fee and hostel charges. And now she is living with Igor. Zinaida met him in Russia and discussed with him to purvey her in America even after he sends me money." Further, he said, "Let this not be happened in future. You are precious."

"Sorry." She said.

Tears were coming through the eyes of Diana seeing her sacrifice for unreal father.

Roman embraced her and Diana moved her hand on her forehead. He kissed her many times but his heart was weeping. He thought, "If my blood were in the place of Olga, she would not think to do that. Marten was right. She is more faithful than dog."

He reproached himself eternally, "Fie on me! I was a sinner. Why did I smite her? Oh! Why did I smite her? She did only for me and I smote her."

He wanted to say something to Olga but his words had stuck in his throat. He assuaged on her.

He mumbled, "Why did I not think that she is a child and it was her puerility. She changed one history. She wrongs this proverb that blood is thicker than water."

He was happy seeing her faithfulness. He was rubbing his hand slightly on her back. Diana also coaxed her.

He said to Olga for taking bath because he had understood what Allan has done with her. Smell of Vodka was smothering him.

Taking bath, she slept. Roman had been sitting beside her. He was weeping putting head on the shoulder of Diana because he could not complete his confession. Off course, he saved her life but Olga did reciprocal of his deed. She tried to indulge in prostitution for saving his life.

Kissing her, he walked into the room and fell on the bed. Diana sat next to him. His conscience was giving him solid shaking. Heart of Diana was not in a level to put up with that incident while it was his profession and she was a popular high class prostitute.

In the penthouse, Allan was also sad. He had also regret that he should not have done illicit armour with that cute girl. He had feeling of compassion; fully Bowelled. He confessed in great din of conscience. He could not sleep at night. He had mania for getting Olga and wanted her in his movie anyhow. He had sorrow of his misdeed and wanted to meet her at any cost.

CHAPTER 14

Next morning, he was admitted in the hospital. He phoned Dr. Anton and told his condition. He transferred money in his account. Olga did not go to school and doctors were doing his work. She was sitting with Diana outside the chamber of the doctor.

It was lunch time and Diana went to restaurant arranging lunch for Olga. After sometime, Olga found Allan Pearson. She stood and walked far from him.

When doctor came outside, Olga asked, "Is everything fine?"

"Now his condition is not worse but treatment will be long."

"Thank God! Thanks, doctor! Will operation…"

"No. Regular treatment can cure his problem."

"Thanks, doctor."

"Welcome. You should now manage these medicines."

"Yes doctor."

Then Allan said, "I can pay you money. Tell me your charge."

Doctor told him that money has been transferred. After talking with doctor, he sat beside Olga on the bench.

"Sorry." Olga said while avoiding him.

"Listen to me last time."

"Sorry but thanks for trying to deposit money."

"Oh! Leave it. It is in consideration of giving me your time."

"Please don't disturb me. And I do not have need of your money."

"Excuse me Olga." He said and further he asked, "Did I do anything wrong with you?"

"No."

"Did I call for you?"

"No, no, no. Please leave me otherwise I will have to use help line."

"I did not do anything wrong with you then why are you not talking to me?"

"My father will not bear it."

He is not your father but father-like."

"Shut up Mr. Allan. He is more superior father to my real father." She asked rudely.

"Sorry. My intension is not to hurt you but your parents had died and Roman is completing his confession because before two years he met you in Moscow and at that time he wanted to come in your contact but his nature changed suddenly after seeing your naive face and same thing also belongs to me. Truth is I did not want to destroy your virginity last night. Yesterday he scolded me and I did not feel bad but I want to help you by heart. I want to show your talent in front of the world. Olga only last time I want to talk to you."

"You do not want to show my talent but want to show my beauty to earn money."

"No. It is not so. I have seen your confidence last night. Olga if you understand me wrong, I like to tell you, in half an hour one can calm down one's passion twice times in a row but I did nothing except pouring Champaign on her face while your beauty is capable of increasing the peak of carnality. Did I?"

"No." She snarled out.

"Please, talk to me…"

"Okay."

"Why don't in restaurant we have coffee together?"

"By and by you are crossing your limits Mr. Allan Pearson."

"I am not crossing my limits and you can understand me your well-wisher."

She thought a little moment and said, "Okay."

Then she moved outside the hospital with him.

Diana saw her with Allan coming across them. She was coming after arranging lunch for Olga. Diana said, "Olga."

"I am going with him…"

"Are you mad? What will Roman think?"

"It is in your responsibility to make him understand."

"I can try only."

"Thank you."

Allan opened the door of car for Olga and after this; he sat on the driving seat and drove to a restaurant. They were in the restaurant within ten minutes.

He asked to Olga, "What would you like to take?"

"We come here only for coffee according to deal."

He ordered waitress two cups of coffee.

Olga started, "On what matter do you want to talk to me?"

"Olga, I want that you should apply in the beauty contest. This will make your future bright and you will have not been pinning for money. You will be the respectful personality of the world. If you can qualify the contest, you will brighten the name of your parents. Do you not want this?"

"Yes but my aim is different."

"Silly girl! It is a big opportunity and opportunity doesn't strike again and again."

"Due to popularity, I will not study properly because meddling of media in my life…"

"You are right but everything depends on you."

"I do not get your point."

"If you do nothing, what will media publish?"

"And my father."

"Don't worry. I will convince. You have not to take any tension. Now come to the point…You do not know I have never seen such *an incredible beauty* in my life. Your confidence is good and you can win the contest. *You have good symmetry and your perfect symmetry is your weapon.* Use it in front of the world. Do you know symmetry formula?"

"No."

"$V = \dfrac{(S+C) * (B+F)}{(T-V)}$. Scientist has discovered this formula.

This mathematical formula to pick out the perfect pair for the well buttocks, where 'V' denotes hip to waist ratio, 'S' denotes over all shape, 'C' represents how spherical the buttocks are, 'B' records the bounce, 'F' belongs to firmness and 'T' measures presence of cellulite. Professor David Holmes discovered it. You are a very beautiful girl and gifted by God and you can get your bum score checked. If you scores 80 for bum perfection so you can be contemporary to Kylie Minogue. Are you ready? One more thing is that last night I asked you to put off your clothes for examining your hip to waist ratio which is absolutely perfect."

"I should take time to think on this matter. It is not so easy to give you answer right now without discussing it with my father."

"Okay." He again described, "If your perfect posterior scores near to eighty, you will be popular ere time."

"Okay I will think it again."

They returned after finishing their coffee. Roman was waiting for her. When Olga went there, he raised his eyebrows. He had taken a look at Allan.

"It is not good." He cried.

"Cool down." Diana said.

She feared but after getting some courage, she went close to him and said, "I am sorry but he is not so bad. He wants to help us."

"Shut up. I saw you out of dress in front of him. He is lusty and cannot make me fool."

Bowing her head she said, "It is true I took off my clothes but he did not do anything wrong. You do not know he said to me putting on the skirt. He is not a bad personality. He also wanted to deposit money for your operation."

"I do not want his wealth and now stop your lecture. No more arguments now."

At last, Allan had to come chasing him, "Why can I not reform my nature? I know I was wrong but I did not call her for my amusement. You are also completing your confession. You cannot hide something because Marten has told me everything about you. If she is your daughter, I can also make the relation of guide with her. If I get success to make her popular, it will add pleasure."

Now Roman was in mum position.

He said further, "Can you secure bright future for her? But I can make her popular personality."

"She has no need of my help in making future. She is incarnation of success. Lames need the crutches."

"You are right but she has not a proper base and she will take lot of time to make her settle but I can give her the biggest podium before time."

He thought something and shook hand with Allan. He felt that Allan's help can push up Olga.

Now two hands were on Olga's head.

Allan had gone from there.

Roman mumbled, "Olga has something which alters people's ideas when they come into her sedate and innocent harmonization while the nature of man is like the tail of a dog."

Two weeks had spent. Roman was normal and started his routine life.

———————

One day Olga said to Roman, "I want to say something."

"Yes. What do you want to say?"

"I want that you will never take whiskey."

"Okay."

"Do promise with me."

"Yes. I promise you."

"Done."

"Yes, done."

Then she was happy. It was Olga who made him a gentle man and he also changed himself for Olga.

———————

Olga was spending her days normally. Her full concentration was on her studies. She was completing her syllabus of Eleventh class (K^{11}).

It was twentieth of July. She found her home decorated when she came back home after the practice of figure skating. This time Igor did not go to Russia. Again she started doing practice with Igor in the USA. She felt herself in Eden. She astonished why her father decorated it.

She changed her clothes and started studying after taking lunch. She had been studying for three hours.

In the evening, somebody knocked the door. Olga went there to open the door then she found her father.

"Good evening."

He accepted her wish.

"What were you doing?" Roman asked.

"I was completing my syllabus."

"O, my God! More than 40 days are left in taking admission. Change your clothes."

She saw him surprisingly.

"Why?" She asked.

"Follow my order."

"Please tell me, why?"

"I come straight here to celebrate your birthday." He said while passing bright smile.

"It means you were pre-planned for celebrating my birthday that's why you decorated home but how did you know about my date of birth?"

"As a father I would know this much."

"Okay but…"

"Yes. Say what you want to say."

"I want to invite Oksana and Igor. They gifted me birthday present. Amrit has also given me party on his birthday."

"Sure."

Then she invited all to come for celebrating her birthday by phone.

When she phoned Amrit, he could not believe that he was hearing her voice.

"Hello. Is it Olga?" Again he said.

"Yes. It is I."

"Are you speaking?"

"Yes. Friend, I am speaking."

"Yes. In fact, you are calling me first time and I do not expect it that you can call me."

"Oh! Leave it and listen to me first. As you know, today is my birthday so I heartily invite you to attend the party and you are to come."

"Okay, tell me your address."

"No. You tell me your address. I am coming to receive you."

"Is true?"

"Yes."

"Olga, Am I dreaming?"

"No."

Then he gave her his address.

He started jumping due to happiness. His heart beats quickened and he was taking deep breath.

Olga was now ready. She wore a yellow and while frock and *she was fully blossoming in this dress.*

She reached his home with her father. He did their hospitality very well. Then he came with her for celebrating her birthday. He looked at her face intently. Forthwith he whispered, *"Beautiful. Is Goddess of beauty with me*? You are *beautiful…absolutely stunning."*

"Leave it. Don't boast. I am not a beauty goddess." Olga interrogated him inauspiciously.

"Have you heard me?"

"Yes."

Then he laughed.

In her apartment, he celebrated that party and danced with her. Igor, Oksana, and Roman were celebrating her birthday while dancing. Igor gave another gift to Olga. She astonished. "Why are you giving me a gift one more time?"

"It is not a gift. It is my heart. Please, take it carefully." He said in her ears.

Amrit was deliriously happy and before going home he also gifted her one gift.

"Thanks." Olga said.

Now the party was over and this time Igor dropped Amrit at his house. Amrit was extremely very happy.

After the party, Olga was going to see the birthday presents then cell phone rang. Roman picked up the cell phone. It was Allan at the second end. He started talking with Roman on an important matter.

He said, "Roman, I am going to Britain with Olga."

"Why?"

"David Holmes has derived one figure formula and I want to know her bum perfection. Well! Do not need it. This is all nonsense but Olga has not done anything big in order that media can publish her. After doing this, I want to bring her among the media. She exemplifies wonderful beauty. Once media accord the most cordial welcome, all the work will be easy. I decide to make her perfect for fighting the beauty contest and I want to see her on ramp. Actually, it is her starting."

"Okay. As you wish."

"It does not depend on my wish. It depends on your stamp."

Roman laughed and said, "Yes. You can think better."

Next day, they had moved to Manchester, Britain.

After reaching there, they lived in the hotel that day but Igor had been waiting for her with Oksana for practice. Now Oksana was living with him. When he told his mom about Oksana, she accepted his proposal of her living in their apartment. Now she had been living under the shelter of Zinaida since a year. She was happy with them.

But now, Igor was sad. Oksana understood her feeling. She said, "Call her."

He phoned Olga but phone was picked by Roman. He told that Olga had gone to Britain.

He asked startlingly, "Why?"

"She is going to know her bum perfection."

"Oh!"

Then he returned without practice.

Next morning they were ready to go to Manchester Metropolitan University. He met the professor who was very pleased after seeing one of the best directors of Hollywood. Further he said, "Sir I want your help."

"Yes. What can I do for you, Mr. Pearson?"

He said, "Sir, she is my friend's daughter, name is Olga Rodionova and now I am making her prepare to join the Miss Universe contest. I want to know her bum score with full details. Actually, I want to bring her into the media."

That professor was also crazy after seeing *her figure and beauty*; *he never saw such a beautiful girl* in his whole life. He went inside the lab with her and asked, "Have you ever joined the gymnasium?"

"No."

"Dieting?"

"No."

"Do you use cosmetics?"

"No, I ever live simple."

"Liposuction?"

"No."

"Any surgery."

"No."

"Massage?"

"No."

After an hour, checking her symmetry he said to Allan, "I studied her three times but according to age her symmetry is perfect. She scores perfect points. No one could cross this score but she does it. She has perfect bum with well hip-to-waist ratio. I can say it with bet that *god made her in spare time. By the way, artistically. Her texture is perfect and she belongs to alphabetical symmetry. I think she is a wonder of the universe.* It is not my exaggeration. She has perfect hip-to-waist ratio."

"Could you provide me a certificate?"

"You can have to wait for it."

"Why?"

"First I have to give proof to media because I will also be censored."

"Yes. You are right."

Then he phoned media. Media took fifteen minutes in reaching there.

In front of media, he started describing about her bum score. He come straight to Media and started making them clear, "I think her posterior is hundred percent because external factors like temperature, weather, and other factors like tension, extra workmanship can affect the body texture. I think she is a gift of nature."

Allan met the professor when media left the University.

"You can meet me tomorrow."

"Okay. I will come tomorrow."

Next morning, the first news in the British newspapers was **EIGHTH WONDER OF THE WORLD.**

Now Olga became popular.

At the noon time Allan went to the college and took certificate from him. When he read the certificate, he asked, "Why did you write hundred percent perfect?"

"I have given proof to media and I think you have also read in the newspaper. Why are you taking tension, this will help her in the world of glamour. Members of governing body have also passed it. See! Little fiddling does not raise big issue when work is done for such a famous director. Truth is I wanted to promote her because she is an incarnation of beauty."

"Thanks professor."

"Welcome. Convey my best wishes to Olga."

They returned to New York and Roman was very happy seeing her with certificate. He thanked Allan exuberantly.

Olga was also very happy from her first success.

Next day that article had also published in New York. That news had spread all over the world.

Zinaida, Igor, Oksana, Amrit and Helen were very happy after reading that news. Her School mates had also read that news and wanted to meet her.

Amrit Phoned her, "Hi!"

"Hello! I am fine. How are you?"

"I am fine but will you forget me?"

"No. Why are you asking this?"

"You are achieving popularity and I am afraid you will forget me because big guns never think about small fries."

"What are you saying my dear? You should remove this illusion from your mind." She went on, "We are friends forever and it is very bad sad that you couldn't identify my nature."

"Sorry."

"Anyway, leave it. Don't take tension. I have some pending work so talk to you later. Okay?"

"Okay. Take care."

"You too." And then she disconnected the phone.

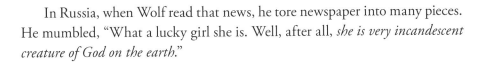

In Russia, when Wolf read that news, he tore newspaper into many pieces. He mumbled, "What a lucky girl she is. Well, after all, *she is very incandescent creature of God on the earth.*"

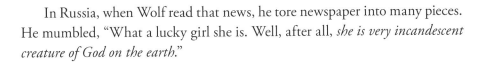

Tory was also shocked. She said to David while putting the newspaper in front of him, "What is this David? Olga is with Allan Pearson. He is one of the best directors of Hollywood and how did she get riddance from the pimps? Was she saved by him or panders set her free."

"Why are you taking tension?"

"She can tell my evil deeds to police."

"She will not do that."

"Why?"

"If she wanted to say that, she should have said but she did not then it is confirmed that she will not go for FIR. Don't worry."

"I have tension. She must be dangerous for us."

"You are taking tension of no rhyme. You need not to think much. She will not defame herself after telling this thing to police. After all, everyone loves his esteem."

"Yes. You are right."

CHAPTER 15

Allan helped her to bring her on ramp and started doing good efforts with Olga. He did not want to take any wrong chance with her.

Olga brought into play studying with ramping. Her teacher helped her but Allan did efforts more than any others did. Olga was doing practice on ramp heartily. *All were enamoured on her undulating hips when she had bundle of delusive mischievousness on her lips while smiling.* Now she was a model.

After coming back from Manchester, it was her second month. She was in the restaurant for taking coffee. She listened to voice of one person and she was astonished because she knew that voice.

She turned fast to see him. She could not acquaint his face because his face was burnt badly even if she understood he was Andrei Uncle. She saw him intently. She mumbled, "Andrei Uncle...but he had died. Is a g...G...Ghost?"

"Olga. How do you act? I am not a ghost. I am your uncle but my face has burnt."

"Are you my Andrei uncle?"

"Yes."

"Then who was he?"

"He was different one."

"What do you mean?"

"Can we not talk at different place?"

"Yes. Come with me."

Then she returned home with him.

Roman was also there. He asked, "Who is he?"

"Papa, he is my maternal uncle."

"What!"

"Yes papa."

"But he had died."

"Yes. You are absolutely right but it was not I." Andrei said.

"How can it possible? How did it happen?" Roman asked.

He went on, "What happened to me only I know. It was false news of my death. My mother got me kidnapped by one street gang after giving them money. You saw the dead body of another person but her face was same as my face and it was the magic of science. My mother gave dollar one million to doctor for changing his face with the help of plastic surgery. He made himself ready for it because he was needy. My mother gave him assurance that after the work done, she got his face as it was by doctor. She made him clear everything for this work. When I went to party, after sometime I got out from there to smoke. At that time, members of the street gang kidnapped me and they sent that person who was similar in look. He had drunk more because there was only voice problem at that time otherwise he looked ditto. Nobody could identify him that he was another one and the main problem was that he was novice in driving and his reckless drunk driving caused accident. I have no tension of losing money but I have sorrow of separation. I have lost my wife. My mother is responsible for it but I wonder how could she give wood-hind to police? I am surprised to the fury of one mother but now I have understood that greedy of money can do anything." Further he said to Olga, "I want to live with you again. I searched you everywhere. I also searched you in the school but I could not find you there. Although I did not feel right to meet the Head Master directly but today, I saw you coincidently."

Olga thanked God. It was the precious gift to her from God but again she lost in the love moments of Samantha Aunty. Again, avulsion grief of Samantha aunty started pinching her.

"She being a mother did so." Said Roman.

"Yes. I have already told you she is not a mother but avaricious of money."

"What is its guarantee that you are Andrei?"

"First thing is that my mother has run away after selling all my property. Think! What I can get from Olga and if I really wanted to grab her property, I could do it easily but I did not do that. The second thing is that you can ask anything which relates to Olga. I know her Samantha aunty and also know the address of her house in Russia. I also know her Director's name. As well as I know you while you know me. I met you in Russia at the time of my sister's death. I also know your name. You are Roman, personal assistant of Dr. Anton."

"Papa, he is telling right. My granny beat me for papers of my property but Andrei uncle never asked me for it." Olga said.

"If you do not believe in me, you can take the help of medical science. I am ready. You can call up the police also." Andrei said.

"I trust you but how could you save yourself from them?"

"It was the grace of God. After the death of that person, they changed their mood to kill me but they burnt me before dropping me in the sea but I was saved. Two dead bodies of same face could entrap them so they burnt my face."

"Now you can describe their physical feature to police."

"Please, use your common scene. The first thing is that they were in the masks and the second thing is that they wrapped ribbon around my eyes and I could not see anything except darkness. I cannot describe their physical feature as well as route of their halting place."

"Oh! What action do you want to take for your mother?"

"I want to see her in court and now I am going to the police station for getting the FIR registered. Now I have witness also."

Startlingly Olga said, "No. No Andrei uncle…"

He said seeing her worried face before hearing her complete statement, "Why?"

She did not say anything and kept standing silently.

"What happened?"

However, she was in mum position.

Then Roman said, "Olga, go and do your work."

She followed his instruction.

Roman started, "By the way, her granny sold her to one whore monger after your death, and now for the future sake she does not want to take risk because when you will be scribbling your mother to court, she can raise that matter and this matter can defame her. Think she will not be able to show her face in front of the society. They will treat her as a market girl."

"Oh!"

Roman said after some minutes, "What is your program with Olga?"

"It is not good for me to live here with Olga that's why I want to go to Canada with her."

"How can you purvey her? I mean, at present you don't have money and any job."

"I have $ 7 million in another account."

"Oh."

Roman called out Olga. She came near him then Andrei said, "Let's go."

She said nothing.

"Hurry up, Olga."

She saw Roman's face. He nodded then she moved into her room.

"I am very grateful to you that you purvey my daughter responsibly. You are very kind and I will never forget your gratitude."

"This is not a matter of kindness. It is humanity."

"It is your greatness."

"Don't make me ashamed. It is my duty."

"Please allow me to go."

"I request you to stay a little longer, please."

"But…"

"Please."

"As you like." Andrei said.

He could not stand in front of his insistence.

"Thanks." Roman said.

He did not want to leave the hand of Olga. He loved her very much. Olga was not his real daughter so he could not have expressed the direct authority.

Olga came back luggage but her face was long.

"Are you going?" Roman asked Olga.

"Yes."

Soon Roman made direction towards Andrei and said, "Let us enjoy the party."

"No."

"Please, today is a special day and you are my guest also then I wish to enjoy party with you."

"But…"

"Don't be prim."

"Okay."

"Good." Then Roman asked her, "Can I take whiskey today?"

"No. Not at all."

"Please. Last time. At least, it is the time of great happiness."

She said while passing charmed smile, "Okay. This permission is only for today."

That day they enjoyed party themselves.

He did not want to drink whiskey but for removing the grief of separateness, he took permission from Olga. His attachment with Olga was too much and he was not happy.

When party finished, Andrei asked, "Roman, Please allow me to go. I want to go to Canada with her. I know your emotions have added with her but she is in my responsibility. I have no great words to give you thanks and I cannot repay an obligation."

He could not say anything but disappointed.

Then Andrei said to Olga, "Be ready."

Olga said, "Uncle, what about my school?"

"Oh, this is a thinkable topic."

This matter gave one flash to Roman. He thought possibly Andrei could start living here with Olga.

"Don't worry. You will not have to join again same class. You can continue it as it is."

"How will it possible?" Olga said.

"Why do you take tension? Nothing is new under the sun."

"Okay." She said disappointedly.

Roman felt him again helpless and hapless. He was not late to understand that Andrei was talking about the transfer and conduct cases.

Some days, Andrei lived with her in the hotel of New York. In this period, he had completed all the important works.

It was the tenth day and they had taken flight for Canada. They started living in Canada. Andrei bought one flat and also applied for a job.

Here in New York, the condition of Roman was not good. Without Olga, he felt his life as a burden. He was half dead.

Not he, Amrit was also in very deep sorrow. He had known that Olga had gone. Igor and Oksana were on the same boat. Igor said, "At least she could have met me before going."

Oksana said, "Yes. You are right. Before going she should have met us. Perhaps it would be any problem or compulsion."

"Yes. You are right. Otherwise she obviously came to meet us. She cannot live without us." Igor said.

However, his heart was heavy and eyes were teary. Oksana wiped his tears. Amrit was also very sad.

———◆◆◆———

Allan was also disappointed because his big Ace had gone. He was full in mood to make a great empire of fame and money with the help of Olga. He was also a good director but he knew the significance of Olga in the world of glamour.

Here Roman had been suffering from heartbroken sorrow. Again, he was totally alone but he did not go to the brothels and not drowned in wine. He loved her too much. Olga was his soul, life, heart, heartbeats, and everything.

He did not go to the hospital and he was spending his days inside his apartment. Fifteen days had spent and he did not come outside from the room. His maid servant was also unhappy and in his room, he was spending all the days restlessly.

———◆◆◆———

In Canada, Olga lived some days happily but after a few weeks, she deeply recollected her moment with Roman uncle. Eagerness of Igor was making her fret. She again wanted to go in the lap of Roman and wanted to join her friend circle. She also loved Roman very much because after the death of father he was the person who gave hundredfold love.

She felt herself sapless in Canada. She had been living happily with him but mentally and heartily she was very sad. Her soul was listless. One day she said to uncle clearly that she wanted to live with her father again.

He made her understand but she was fully immovable on her statement.

After a week, Andrei again took a flight of New York and directly went to Roman's apartment. She knocked the door. Roman was on the bed and his eyelashes were wet. Hearing the sound of the door bell, he opened the door and found Olga in front. He being happy fondled her politely while kissing.

In the arms of Roman, she felt the felicity of father's love.

"Glad you are back, Olga." He said to Andrei, "Welcome, please."

Thank you. Take care of your child. She is dying to meet you. She cannot live without you."

He saw him cutely and said, "Same here."

Then Andrei moved to the airport for taking the flight.

Just he reached; he saw Tory and moved near her.

"My dear mom, hello! How are you?"

"Who are you?" She astonished. She said again seeing his burnt face, "Who are you?" Actually, she had known him.

"Recall please. I am your son."

"But my son has died. You are a burglar." She said with sharp tongue.

"Oh! I feel that it is an advent of an old age."

"No. My son has died."

"Are you unknown from this matter that you gave money for kidnapping me?"

Her face was white. She said unsteadily, "N…No. It is not right."

"Look, at present I am not going to call Police here. If you can tell me the right story, I can forgive you."

Her face was white and she wiped her sweat.

"Yes, tell me, Where is Olga? What did you do with her?" Andrei forced her.

She started seeing by the side of armpit but she was unaware that Andrei knew where Olga was living.

He said, "Don't try to be smart by hook or crook. You are inside the airport and something will happen wrong with you if you do anything wrong. Everything is in your hand. What do you want? Either prison or freedom."

"In fact, you know I am your mother and how I can do something wrong-dong with you. Actually, I want…"

"I am not in a mood of hearing about our relation. I have less time to spare. Don't talk with me in round about manner. Where is Olga?"

"Okay." She went on, "I hate Olga that's why I sold her to pimps. After that, I don't know anything about her."

"You are telling a lie."

"No. I am not but I read about her in many newspapers. She is alive. I think she is in Britain and living with Hollywood director Allan Pearson."

"When I have given you dollars thirty million, why did you get me kidnapped?"

"It was my order to kidnap you but the accident was not in my plan. His driving in drunkenness caused accident. With the help of Kris who died in the car accident, I wanted to get her departed. If he denied Samantha for purveying her, we could have sent her for living in orphanage. After completing my plan, they would set you free but after his accident, they could not set you free, so for the safety point of view, they killed you after making your face burnt but it is a great wonder to see you here."

"Why did you not stop them to do so? Even, I am your son."

"I had no other choice. They intimidated for killing me. You never treated me mother so I let them do. Well! Who saved you and what they did with you?"

"They burnt my face and dropped me in the sea. Cleverly they wanted to get success but God wanted something else."

"Well! However, Kris died. Without the help of David, I could not have acquired all your properties but as a lover, he is also my partner that's why I persuaded him to give 35 percent of the property and rest amount is safe in my hand. I was also afraid of him because he could black male me therefore I did not tell him about my plan. When Kris died, I felt that it was his work but he was not involved in this accident. He gave me a piece of advice to drop her at orphanage but I sold her to the dealer of women. I do not know about her condition but I left St. Louis with him and started living at Edmonton in Canada but I came here for some important work and it is my bad luck and your good luck that you find me here."

"Olga is safe now. She is with me and now she is living with her new father."

"With new father! Is Allan Pearson?"

"No. Roman. He was the only person who gave her good life. He sold his kidney for saving her life and she could not live in the brothel for prostitution. Weight your character with this person. You are very cheap grade woman and he is God for her."

"You are right. But where does she live?"

"She lives here in New York."

"They could have killed you but why did they choose this way?"

"As I understand, they did not want to take the risk after killing me because Police could understand the matter after seeing the dead bodies of same persons that's why they dropped me in the sea where I could be the meal of fishes but one ship captain saved me."

"Oh! For safety point of view they did so."

He said, "Yes but now tell me what I should do with you."

"Please, forgive me. I can give you all my bank balance. Please."

"This money is baseless for me. I have lost my lover, my wife and now I will have to call police for you."

"Please, no. I am your mother…"

"I am not your son. You did two sin. You sold my daughter to one whore-monger and due to your plan, my wife died in car accident and you are killer of my baby also. Sorry, I cannot help you."

She astonished. "Your baby?"

"Yes. My wife was pregnant and now I cannot leave you to live luxurious life. After that I am the last one of this property that I will give to Olga. And yes. Don't try for defence because Olga will bear testimony. She is a witness so it is good for you to accept your crime in front of Police."

Tory was helpless. He phoned police and told them everything then Inspector took her in police custody immediately and also gave him assurance to arrest all the gang members.

However, Andrei did not tell the incident of Olga to police because he didn't light the fire in her future.

Tory accepted her fault and then Police started searching for arresting David Weinberg.

Andrei changed her program and moved to Roman's apartment.

He knocked the door again.

Roman opened the door and found Andrei.

"You, please come in."

"Thanks." He added, "Where is Olga?"

"She is in her room."

"I want to meet her."

"Yes. Sure."

Then he called out her, "Olga. Come here. Andrei wants to meet you."

"I am just coming."

Olga was happy seeing Andrei uncle, "Did you plan to live here with us?"

"No. I am coming here to tell you that your granny is under the custody of police. She met me fortunately inside the airport and I phoned police for arresting her and now your granny is behind the cell. She has accepted her crime and now our revenge has fulfilled."

"Is right?"

"Yes."

She was very happy. She said, "She is only for this. It is her right place. She is a killer of my Samantha aunty." Then she went near him and said, "Do we not live together?"

"No, Olga. We cannot live together. It is not good to me to live here. In fact, David can give written command to court and I will have to do some work for fighting this case that's why I am sorry for not accepting your proposal but may be, I will feel need of your testimony."

"Don't worry. I will be ready. Last time, when I was silent to give you answer, my conscience felt that I am selfish but now I am ready."

"Thanks."

He stepped outside the room without saying anything more and Olga had been seeing him.

Andrei had gone from there but Olga remained standing silently.

Roman held her shoulder and said, "He has gone."

"Yes." She nodded.

"Will you go to meet Allan?" Andrei said.

"Yes. Well, wait a bit. I will not take long time to get ready."

They both were at the house of Allan after an hour.

Allan could not reckon on his eyes that he was seeing her next to him. His eyes were beaming with satisfaction.

He said rubbing his eyes, "Am I really seeing Olga?"

"Yes. I am Olga in front of you."

"I am very happy seeing you here. I was disappointed when you left New York because I did not want to skim the creamy part of my life. I did not want to lose my great ace."

"It is my pleasure you understand me a great ace but actually, you have been a great helper to me and you are a big ace."

"Everybody should learn from you how to give an answer."

"Why do you make my every little work praiseworthy?"

"It is for your encouragement."

She laughed charmingly and Allan had been seeing her intently how *incredibly she laughed.* He said, *"You enchant surprisingly when you laugh."*

"I think it is too much."

After spending some hours with Allan, Olga had come home.

Next morning, Olga was ready to go to school. Her father dropped her there. She moved not to her own class and sat on the bench stepping inside another class. She was waiting for Igor. When she saw him while going to his class, she went behind him silently as like a cat and closed his eyes while putting palms.

He said suddenly, "Olga."

"............"

"My guess is right. You are Olga."

".........."

"You are wasting time because I can feel the *smoothness of your palm* in trillions. *You are the only princess over the world that has everything incredible.*"

Igor held her hand and kissed her while taking round. She kissed him also.

"I felt that you have left me alone."

"No. How can I leave you alone? I come straight here to meet you and now again I start to study here in this school."

"Is true?"

"Yes. Trust me, dear. Again I am with you forever and with all."

When Amrit, in school, knew that Olga was again with them, he started sloganeering, "Olga! Olga! Olga has come. Our Olga has come and now again she is in our friend circle. Our first wonder of this school is again with us."

Oksana was also happy and Olga's class mates were offering ovation to her. She felt first time that how much she was popular among class mates. How much they loved her while she would not talk to them.

Her class mates absconded and arranged party for Olga. They were making the festivity of her return. Olga was very happy after seeing their pure love.

Father was also happy that Olga joined his school again. Olga changed her behaviour after seeing their insanity and started talking to every student.

———————◆◆◆———————

Days were rolling. Tory and David were inside the cell. Andrei was the legal representative of all the property. He was happy and made Olga the owner of his property.

Olga denied but he said, "It is yours. Your mother handed over me 37 million dollars in which she made Tory heir of 30 million dollars but now it is yours. You are the owner of this property."

"Thanks."

"No thanks. Allow me to go."

"No. How can I have let you go? We will live together and you have to accept my request."

"Please." He said.

"No. We will live together."

"Okay."

Olga bought a duplex and started living with Roman and Andrei uncle. They were happy now. Olga felt herself a lucky girl on the earth. That delicate figure was diving deeply in the sea of happiness. There was no description of her rejoicing days.

CHAPTER 16

Olga was now a show stopper and counted in top ranked models. Her attitude and confidence were increasing her popularity and wealth. Her estimated earning was more than $ 21 million in the first year of her career. Oksana was also in the modelling world but her endorsement income was more than that of Olga. She was a brand ambassador of five international companies. These two beautiful Russians were hoisting their flags of beauty all over the world.

Olga passed eleventh class with top rank but this time Amrit could not maintain his rank.

Olga became disappointed seeing his percentage. She had the burden of Modelling with studies but after this, she took his responsibility also for making his fundamentals clear. Now Amrit started living with Olga in her duplex after taking permission from his parents. They denied first but allowed later.

Olga was very busy but she would teach him in free time. She could not bear his downfall in the rank.

Her tension was increasing day by day because she had the burden of the syllabus of K^{12} class and another responsibility of ramping was also on her shoulder but she made her mood with pledge to do both the works consistently.

Seeing her demand in market, thirteen companies wanted to do agreement with her but she denied. She was also the brand Ambassador of two companies. Allan Pearson used to guide her in every way.

One day, Olga was coming home then she found John Bullock. Olga said to driver for applying brake of the car. She came out from the car and met John.

John understood that she had forgotten him but she treated him in well manner.

She said very politely, "John uncle."

"Yes Olga. I come here to meet you."

"Yes. Come with me."

He followed her and sat inside the car with her.

She said to driver, "Go."

Driver screeched the car in front of the gate and she stepped inside her room with him.

She ordered her servant two cups of coffee.

While taking coffee, she said, "It's been a long time since we met."

"Olga, when Igor killed the members of my gang, I got freedom from their hold then I decided not to do such type of bad business. Now I am here to become your bodyguard if you can allow me because I am jobless."

"Sorry. But you are criminal."

"But I have no criminal record in any police station of New York. My presence with you will never defame you. Could you choose me your private body guard?"

"First of all, I have to give your name to police department for satisfying them about my private security. I want time to think."

"Okay."

They completed coffee then John said, "Okay, I will meet you after two days."

"Okay."

Then he went back from there.

Olga put that matter to Allan and her father then they gave assurance. Allan did all the essential work to make him private body guard of Olga.

Now John was her body guard.

———◆◆◆———

One day, Allan went her home for some important work. At that time she was studying with Amrit.

"Hello, Olga. Sorry to disturb you."

"I am fine. Please sit down."

"Thanks. Olga, I want to discuss with you on the business matter."

"Business matter! I don't understand."

"By the way, I am going to make a movie and want you as an actress."

"What about my studies? I have Intermediate exam and also burden of modelling. I am sorry. I cannot sail three boats simultaneously in a row."

"Don't take a quick decision. You can think on this matter. Even, you cannot deny me like this. I know you will pass out the exam easily."

Olga thought about his obligation and said, "Well, what is the title of your picture?"

"Sapphic Vice."

"Sorry. I cannot work in this movie."

"In my views, you can give good expressions because…"

"Just wait." She had understood his aspect so she requested Amrit to go outside from the room. She went on, "Carry on."

"You are perfect for this movie because in this movie you have to do lesbianism with prostitutes. According to story, you do not find partner for sexual satisfaction so you choose the way of the brothels for girls. Your struggle belongs from social evil that's why I found you suitable for my movie."

She squelched, "I feel vulgarity in it and for your kind information; my struggle did not start from social evil. It was just a bad part of my life. I would like to forget it. I did it only for saving the life of my father. Please, don't shove me in the past life."

"Hey! Sorry. Don't fret and fume. There is no vulgarity in this movie. You will play your role with a lady partner and making an understanding with her while developing the genuine face expressions and emotions during the time of shooting. You can give perfect expressions with good body language. You can make people emotional."

"I don't want sexuality in this film."

"Don't take tension. I can use duplicate. You may trust."

"What message story has?"

"No message. It is totally entertaining."

"Sorry."

"It will be my pleasure if you…"

"The words I say mean it. I don't want to expose myself but I cannot dismay you."

"What does it mean?"

Olga said, "I can also give you the best script."

"Okay, tell me."

Then she told him story briefly. Allan gave satisfaction. "Exciting and diplomatic story but I have to add the dialogues for making it more interesting." Allan said, "Could you write down this script?"

She nodded, "Yes. After a week, you can take it from me."

"Thanks." Allan said.

"When will you start shooting of your movie?"

"I will tell you after estimating the script."

"Okay."

"Your fees?"

"What are you saying? I have no need of money."

"I am in full business mood. I sit next to one of the most popular celebrities of the world therefore I am totally professional here. I could have sent my Personal Assistant but I come here straight to meet you and I always come to meet you alone."

"Yes, I know but how can I deal with you for this? I am very obliged to you. I am very grateful to you. You support me every time and without your help, I could not be at the top of the world. You are a very kind personality."

"Not at all. This is not a matter of kindness. Truth is I am a selfish man. After seeing your beauty, I had mania to get you anyhow. If you remember, I had proposed you for my film in our first meeting. I did not want to lose. I helped Roman only for winning over you."

Olga laughed and said, "Yes. You offered me a movie."

"You are really a Universe class beauty. You have marmoreal figure and I bet you will be a history of beauty. You can fascinate anyone."

"Okay. Okay. Leave it. It is too much. You can mention my total amount in my contract and I will sign."

"Okay. Well! Allow me to go."

"Why?"

"I have an appointment with someone."

"Okay."

When Allan got out from the room, Amrit came near Olga. He said, "Why did you say me to go outside from the room?"

"Amrit, he started talking on personal matter that's why I said to go."

"Oh!"

She was busy writing down the script. Olga had tension to complete the script so she took help of Igor for completing it.

Now she had got success. She reached Allan's office and gave him script. Allan read it while understanding the every aspect.

"Good but I want some changes in it."

"Yes, you can change this script according to your suitability."

Allan gave her contract paper and Olga signed after reading it properly.

"Well, my per day effort." She said.

"Do you afraid?"

"No. Not at all."

"240 to 250 meters film per day."

"Okay, I am ready but also nervous because it is my first chance to work in a movie."

"Don't be afraid. Take this experience also." He said.

"Yes." And she left for the house.

Olga was going to start double efforts. However, she was conscious about studies because her aim was to join the Russian army.

Olga was busy. Her movie had completed but she acquired second position in class assignments. Seeing her result, she was not happy and came in tension. She cancelled out all the contracts of Modelling and she had to lose her $ 63 million wealth. Now she was busy in studies and completing the movie.

Her movie beat all the records. Now she was the demand of Hollywood. Allan was very happy because it was his first movie which did great business.

Olga was the cynosure star of all eyes and one of the most popular personalities in the world.

Igor was happy seeing her success but sometime he thought would she forget him. Oksana told him that Olga had been also in his love so he had no need to worry but other side, every step of her popularity was increasing the rage of Wolf. He burnt completely in the fire of revenge.

Again the beauty contest in her school had started. She also participated in the contest.

One day Olga was studying in the class room. One girl, Helen Taylor met her. She said, "Hello Olga."

"I am fine. And you?"

"I am also fine."

"Is any important work?"

"No but I want to say something to you." She said.

"Don't say anything. I know you want that I should take my name back from this contest."

"Yes. Yes. You are a dream girl for all people. I am not your friend but as a class mate, I hope you will not fight this contest."

"Don't worry, be happy. I did not want to take participation in this contest but Amrit forced me to do so. For his heart sake, I gave my name but don't worry, I will not appear."

"Thanks Olga."

"It's okay and best of luck."

"Thanks."

———————————

Now her final stage of qualifying the exam was near. Olga had immersed in studies forgetting all the things. First time she was in tension but she did work firmly with peace of mind. Her will power was strong.

Her movie nominated for Oscar and had the chance to bag awards.

'We are the soldiers of the world' movie won the Oscar award. Allan received the award of Best Director. Olga did not get any award but she had the satisfaction that she was the actress of Oscar winning movie. Even after, she was the polar star on the earth.

Olga did her exams consistently and got highest grade. Again she was encircled by media. She brightened the names of her parents. The struggle and desire of her mother had been completed because she was on the top of the world and also got the highest grade in the final stage of the academic education.

CHAPTER 17

After a week, she went to Allan for making another movie.

"Have you decided any title and script for the movie?"

"Yes. This movie is based on my life. And the title is 'Virgin Whore of Raw-age'. This is my last movie and after that I will take permanent leave from the world of glamour."

He astonished and said, "Why?"

"Zinaida aunty says to leave this fashion world and I think to do so."

"Why?"

"She does not want me in the world of glamour after marriage with Igor and I am going to Russia after completing this movie. I think to take admission in Lomonsov Moscow University."

"You can take admission here in Harvard University."

"I want to join the Russian Army. It is my first and last aim."

Allan was shocked. He said, "I think you should think again on this matter."

"I am pre planed. Let me be free from this work. Don't worry."

"Hollywood is similar to the desert without you."

"Oh! What a great exaggeration."

"No. It is true."

"No. I come after many actresses. Forget me. You know the talented actresses of Hollywood. Make movies with them. You can take Oksana in your movie. She is also one of the popular personalities."

"But she works for Russian Models Agency. She will not accept my offer. I know she hates Americans and pure Russian by blood."

"What are you saying? I think it is not right." She said wonderingly.

"Many directors have given her offer but she kicked all of them."

"It is a puzzle to me why she did it. Well! Don't worry. She will accede."

"Could you try for this?"

"Sure."

"Well! Why do you select this title?"

"It is because whore cannot be a virgin and this story is based on my life as I told you earlier. It is the reason to decide this title. I will represent one whore as a virgin."

"Oh! I understood that you chose this title seeing the demand of people. They want hotness in everything so you're going to give them a hot scene."

"It is not an adult movie. It is full of emotions, sacrifice and based on the struggle of a juvenile."

"Okay. I am ready to make this film with you."

"Thanks. Well! I am going to meet Igor. Please allow me to go."

"Go. Go."

"Okay. Bye."

"Good bye."

She went to meet Igor at his apartment. He was happy seeing her there. He said, "Hey! Come in."

She sat on Sofa. Igor ordered two cups of coffee.

Olga said, "Igor, come here to sit with me."

"Yes."

"I want to share something with you."

"Yes. Sure."

She cohered while sliding her fingers on his face. She said holding his arm tightly, "Igor."

"Yes. Tell me."

"Will you like to know my past life?"

"I know your past life. Your struggle is really appreciable."

"No. I am telling you that part of my life which you cannot believe."

"Tell me."

"I hope that you will not transpiring this secret. There is no doubt you are leaky but…"

"Don't worry. Believe in me."

"Igor, when you left me after passing out the final exam of class eighth for going to meet your father in Russia, my life filled with sorrows. My granny made my life stained after the death of my uncle and aunty. She gave me many injurious marks on my body and sold me to pimps and further I was sold by the master of the gang to Marten. She is a prostitute but a very kind woman. She did not want me in this cheap work and also ready to give me healthy surroundings but at that time Roman uncle, now my father, coincidently came across me and saved me from that hell. Truth is that, he bought me from Marten after selling his kidney to anyone for saving my life. John Bullock, my private body guard, helped me too much. He was one of the members in that gang. He phoned you but phone was out of reach. He could not make contact through phone but he helped me from my gang rape. Due to him, nobody could touch me and beat me."

Face of Igor became red. He said, "Did granny inflict punishment?"

"She is inside the cell. Leave it Igor but I want your help."

"Yes tell me. Is anyone black mailing you?"

"No."

"Do you want to see that racket in police custody?"

"You killed all the members of that racket."

"Oh! Then what type of help do you want?"

"I want to establish two restaurants for Marten and her members. I must do something for them. We should make them free from filthy life."

"It is your very good spirit. Okay. First, I talk to Engineers for this project."

"I want these two restaurants in Colorado."

"Why?"

"Marten is a popular high class prostitute and works under some Mafias. Colorado will be safe place for them. Everybody knows her here that's why I select Colorado a safe place for Marten and her members."

"Good. You are very kind for others."

"Thanks. And one more thing is that I am going to Russia for taking admission in Lomonsov Moscow University."

Igor was shocked. He could not believe ears. He said holding her, "What are you saying. How can I live without you? Can you live without me?"

"I miss you but I am going there for further studies. Please understand me."

"You can take admission here."

"No, Igor. I have taken my decision. I don't like this place."

"It is tough to me to spend one year without you while I cannot spend one second."

"Try to understand me. No doubt I cannot live without you. I love you so much and loneliness stings me in your absence. Please try to understand. You know I am after studies."

"Okay." Hopelessly he said.

"Don't worry. I will remain in your contact by mail and phone."

"Okay."

"And yes. Amrit is now your responsibility."

"Don't worry. I know Amrit is your ideal friend. By the way, he is a good guy."

"Yes. You are right. He is a good person. He does my care too. I am proud to be his friend. He is totally different than others. He is naive like you."

"His morality is also appreciable." He added.

"Yes but why are you so sad?"

"Your departure news makes me sad."

"Come with me." She said while pulling him.

"Where?"

"We are going to the restaurant."

"Okay. Let me wear executive dress."

"Okay. Be fast."

Igor moved inside one room and Olga remained sitting on sofa. She was also sad. She loved Igor so much. Her eyes pooled with tears but she wiped when Igor said, "Let's come."

She was in the restaurant with him. They were talking while taking junk food. Igor was not happy and Olga was doing fun with her. She stood to pay bill. He said while putting his hand on her hip, "You pay always but now this time let me pay this bill."

"Okay."

He paid the bill and returned home with her. Olga started talking with Zinaida aunty. At the time of evening, she took permission for going back.

They both had lost in their work. They wanted to get maximum output in minimum input. Olga directed the movie with Allan 300 to 350 meters films per day and got success to complete it within a month. It was she who did it soon.

She was giving regular time to Igor and her aunty. She did not want to go to Russia but she had mania to fulfil the desire of her father that's why she was firmly fixed on her decision.

She was in news. Her picture was doing good business all over the world. Restaurants were also about to complete.

She gave grand party to all her friends to enjoy happy moment with them because she was about to leave for Russia.

She was again in news. When she did any work, media enclosed her as a clique of bees covered the flower. Obviously, she was the centre of attraction for all the eyes.

One day she called up to Marten and Diana. When they came to meet her, she said, "Marten and Diana, now you are free from this work. Today I am giving you charge of my restaurants and your duty is to help feeble people. Now you both are the owners of my two restaurants."

"Why are you doing this for us?" Marten said.

"Why did you want to save my life from this social evil work?"

"It is not for children and a bad job for the helpless."

"I am making you owner not for earning money but for helping helpless children for bearing the charges of their studies."

"And what does about your money? We cannot return your debt."

"I am not a bank or I do not give you loan. It is a gift by me and you are the holders of these restaurants. It is a matter of thinking how one person can tolerate the weight of many businesses? I have your need that's why I want your help."

"Thanks but we can come in trouble. Mafias of this field will not leave us." She said.

"Don't take tension. The first thing is that my both the restaurants are in Colorado and the second thing is that Igor will help you to send there. So, don't take tension."

"Thanks."

They were happy.

Olga Rodionova

Special day had come, now Olga was ready to go to Russia but before going, she put an august party. She invited all the present relatives, actresses, actors, directors, players, writers, big business personalities, some royal personalities, and her fans. She shared that moment happily with them. She come directly in the circle of fans after celebrating the party with other celebrities and gave them autograph hundreds in number and she could not sleep whole night.

Igor was there but he was sad. Olga did not leave him alone for a single moment. She knew the condition of his heart. The face of Amrit was also down. Andrei and Roman had a sinking feeling. After all, they loved her so much but Oksana was in full mood to enjoy the party. She had no tension of her departure because she was happy in her work.

Next day, she was at airport with Igor, Amrit, Oksana, Zinaida aunty, Roman, Allan and Andrei uncle. Fans were seeing her last time in New York. Fans and media had enclosed her. Before sitting inside the plane, she said to fans taking mike, "My dear friends, it is my pleasure that you love me lot and come here to see me off. I am again thankful to you and I want to tell you one thing. I have been living in New York for four years and I saw mostly here divorce, murder and rape cases. It is very shameful to us that we live in unhealthy surroundings. Today's people want to spend a separate life. I question you why do we spend a separate life? Why do we increase our ego? Why do we give divorce to partner? Why do we rape others? Why do we plunder others? Why? Why? My friends, you all are social animals not animals. You have mind and you have power of thinking. You have a good gift of thinking from God to think better for better life. You can understand easily what right and what wrong is. If we are really on the right path, why social evils are increasing in our society, country, and in our world? I know we are not The Supreme Being but we are super beings then why we behave like an animal? Why passion has overtaken love? Why we are forgetting the language of love? Why do we rape girls for quenching the fire of passion? Could you tell me the answer of my question? Why our desires become negative? Have you had any answer? Why our body language, thinking, and etiquettes are negative? Why? Your attributes are degrading you in the eyes of the world and destroy the future of your children because they learn directly from the society. You have to make a healthy and peaceful atmosphere for the world because we directly or indirectly commonly depend on others and we cannot ignore them anyhow. Sorry, if I hurt you anywhere but it is the universal truth. If you really love Olga Rodionova, if you are good fans of Olga Rodionova, so please change your habits. Accept mutual understanding, platonic love, positive thinking, positive bonding, and positive language to create a positive society. Create love and do mercy on others. Remember it, world is like a mirror. If you laugh, you will find world laughing. If you weep, you will find world weeping. If you give something to world, world will give you everything. That is all my brethren." She added, "I hope that you will understand my feelings. May God give me strength to bear this terrible blow? I do not want to leave you. Heartily I want to live in the shower of your love but my mother land is calling me. Thank you my friends. If I am wrong here, I can feel sorry for it."

Everybody started clapping and they bid her adieu.

Before taking entry inside the airport, she kissed Igor. He said, "Take care."

"You too. I hope we will be soon together."

"I hope so."

She said this time to Amrit while ruffling his hair, "I hope you will give proper time to studies. You are a careless person."

"Don't worry and have a happy journey."

"Thanks."

She turned to talk with John and said, "You know I am going to Russia and I have cancelled out my security. Take this cheque of $ 60 thousand. If you will want more money, you can say to my father and now security of my father is in your hand."

"Olga, I have no need of money. You can take it back."

"Please, take it. It will help you."

Then he took cheque and put it inside his pocket.

Then she moved inside the airport while waving her hand. Her eyes filled with tears. Her plane started taking off to Russia. She sat inside the plane after receiving the regards and love of fans.

Inside the plane, she thought about the last four years and about the unforgettable prosaically efficient memories and her eyes were wet.

CHAPTER 18

At the airport, there was no description of her happiness. Obviously, she was on her motherland after four years. When she got out from the aeroplane, she took a round to see the airport. Nothing was changed during four years.

When she made for her home, she came across Wolf co-incidentally. Once she thought to talk with him but suddenly she cut him dead.

"Hey! Olga, where have you been so long? How are you? I am glad to see you."

She saw him strangely that she was unknown from him. "Who are you? I do not know you."

"Hey! It is too much. Don't be innocent. I am Wolf, your old friend. Why do you ignore me?"

"Sorry. I had no truck with the person whose name is Wolf."

"Oh, Olga, come in reality and leave to avoid me. I know I was defaulter. Sorry for that. Olga, you wanted one topper in your life that's why I did it. I wanted to remove Igor from your life. Please sorry. If you do not forgive me so who will forgive me."

"Sorry. I cannot help you in this matter."

"Olga you cannot give me a big punishment for little mistake. First flaw should be forgiven. I cannot live without you. If you do not forgive me, what will be the aim of my life to live?"

"Sorry, now you are late. I love Igor."

"It means you are a jilt."

"Shut up. Mind your language."

"Then why are you going far from my life?"

"I have closed your chapter because you are fraud. Sorry but infatuation is not love. You should understand."

"Leave it Olga. I am not fraud. It was my mistake, I accept it but I am not fraud. It was my blunder and at least it was my childhood. If you want, we can start new life again."

"Excuse me. I say that you have late."

"Please Olga. Exculpate me. We again …"

"How you can think that I will make you clear from imputation?"

"Why do you contradict me? If I was a defaulter, you were also. It was your felony that you broke his heart. You played from his holy feelings. Now tell me what your punishment is."

"My punishment is I love him."

"What he wants! He has given you punishment and now he loves Oksana."

"Again you are making me fool. Oksana is his fast friend." She did not tell him that Oksana and Igor lived together.

"You are so much innocent Olga. Well! Would you like to come with me in my house?"

"No."

"Please, only one time. At least I lived without you many years as a dead person."

She said while coming from the world of thoughts, "Okay."

She slid inside the car with him and he drove car towards his house.

"Does Igor love you?"

"Yes. He loves me by heart."

"Will you marry him?"

"Yes. He is my perfect life partner."

"Have you forgotten our relation? You are my first love. I love you so much."

"Sorry Wolf. It is too late."

"I think we can proceed..."

"Sorry."

"Please Olga. Don't give me this severe punishment."

"Don't force me Wolf. You had been my fast friend that's why I am here with you."

He did not say anything. He drove car silently. He reached home with her. When she entered the room, she found her many posters and photos on the wall. Once she thought, "Does Wolf really love me?" Other side, Wolf was drawing the old newspapers from the store room.

After sometime, he said, "See all the newspapers in which their affairs have published with photos."

Olga was normal after seeing snapshots and reading news. She said, "It is rumours nothing else. I believe in him firmly because petrified is not in his habit."

"You do not accept it because you love him." After a sudden moment, Wolf leaned over her and said, "Why do you not understand my feelings? *Bland beauty*, I love you. I love you more than my life. Now you cannot see past Wolf in me." He locked her in his arms and went on, "Look glows of love in my eyes. Are you not feeling that my eyes are thirsty to see you? Listen to my heart beats; do you not listen to the panic voice of my heart? Olga, I love you. If you are not a jilt, why are you leaving me alone? I will die without you. I know how I spent four years without you."

She had been standing silently like a statue.

He said further, "I like what you have liked Olga. I ever got top position and I did so only for you. Remember your words, you ever used to say that your first love is last love. And now you also cheat me."

"No. It is not a cheating but tit for tat."

"When I play fraud, you gave me slaps in front of everyone and that's all. Now…now you are going to do fraud with me. Tell me before going near him, what will be your punishment?"

She was puzzled and she could not say anything.

He started saying, "All this while I waited for you, and I know that truth triumph in the long run. If you leave my company, I will understand that there is no God in the universe. It is a wicked world of frailers. I make you judge and now ball is in your court. You have to announce your judgment. I make you equal to Jesus because to err is human and to forgive is divine. Rest assured after your judgment, I will leave you because love lies in sacrifice. Tell me, do you love me or not?"

"You had let me down. You had betrayed me but you make me judge. I think I must come out with truth. When I slapped you I broke my relation with you. You pretend to be innocent yet holy now. My conscience permits me that I should tell you the truth but I am in dilemma. I have seen your honesty but truth is that I have drowned deeply, madly and badly in the love ocean of Igor. Wait…I can solve this problem however typical it may be. By and by, I believe in you but I can treat you as a friend but cannot get back. I am committed."

"Now you can go Olga but remember it, tomorrow news will be that Wolf has died in the love of one *beauty queen*."

"Don't behave like a child. Life is not to die."

"Leave it Olga. You break my heart. You do not understand my feelings. You cannot understand what love is because you are a jilt."

Listening to his words, she came in the madness of emotion. She started, "No, I am not a jilt. It is true I used to love you but I want time. It is not easy to me to do so. Please. Give me chance to comprehend you."

"Okay. I can understand your situation. One cannot change oneself suddenly. I know it takes time to settle."

"Yes."

Tears ran down on her cheeks. There was thundering on her heart for Igor. He effaced her tears. He held her hand and moved to slide inside the car. He drove to 'Kalitnikovskoe Cemetery'. Olga noticed nothing was changed but her parents' graves were covered with rose flowers. Olga understood that it had been his work but it was get it done by Igor. He phoned his father to do so. Igor knew that Olga would move directly to cemetery for consecrating. However, she was happy from Wolf seeing this. When wolf moved near her after getting out from the car, he was astonished after seeing graves covered with flowers. However, his fortune was imposing height.

"Who did it?" He mumbled.

But she saw him greatly. Going beside him, she put her hand on his shoulder and said, "Thanks Wolf for doing so."

"Hey! No thanks."

"But you are changed. I feel you are not sticky and arrogant that you used to be."

Perhaps her hidden love had come out.

She sat near her mother's grave with him and drops of tears fell on the grave. Suddenly dense, gloomy, and bellowing clouds enveloped the sky, fierce wind started blowing and lightening thunder. Possibly, her mother soul wanted to tell through nature that you adopted straight way of hell. She told her indirectly that he was playing fraud with her, be alert! But it was baseless. How could Olga understand the typical language of nature?"

Wolf went to the car, took two rose flowers, and gave to Olga for paying the homage.

With reverence, she put the rose flower on mother's grave while closing the eyes. She remembered mother's love and tears started flowing. After this, it was her requiem for father.

Wolf said, "You brightened your guardians' name. I am proud of you."

"Thanks."

In his house, Olga said to Wolf, "Allow me to go."

"Why?"

"I am going to live in my house."

"Why are you going there? You can live here."

"Thanks."

"You have changed, Olga. Before leaving for America, you wanted to spend every second with me and now when I am giving you offer again and again, you are creating a gap between our relations. *My Dear Angel*, if you heartily love Igor, I can back my hand."

"No. It is not my meaning but truth is I love him."

"Do you want to judge me?"

"Yes."

"So why are you not living with me? If you live with me, it will easy to you to judge me easily. I am not going to force you. As a friend, I request you. I don't want to leave you alone for a single moment."

Her heart pounced and she hesitatingly said, "Okay."

For changing the mood, she asked from Wolf, "What are you doing nowadays?"

"I am going to choose Veneriology."

"Why? Why? Your dream was to become an economist."

"Not now. My mood had changed from this field. Well, don't use your mind for it. In fact, you cannot understand my nature."

"It may be."

"I think you are going to join the army."

"Yes."

"Good."

"Wolf your nature is changed but you could not change your ridding and stubborn behaviour but you are better than before."

"Oh! Thanks. It was my childhood."

Olga stepped into the bathroom and made her brain cool under the shower. When she came back in a wrapped towel for putting on the clothes, Wolf said, "You can take rest in my bedroom."

"And you."

"Don't take any tension because I am going to do some important work but *you are beautiful than before. You have a clot's tooth.* I think hyperbole or exaggeration can shy in front of you. *You are a rhythmically diction poem of God.* I think y*our beauty is increasing day by day and you are a Goddess of immortal beauty…*"

"Stop! Stop! You are doing great buttering."

"Okay. Well! I am going for completing an important work and now you can take rest here."

He had gone. Olga was on the bed and while thinking she was taking tossing and turning. She was disturbed but at present she could not do anything.

Wolf returned in the evening and proposed Olga for a long drive.

"This time! It is night!" She exclaimed while frowning. "Not at all. I am not ready for it."

"Why?"

"I don't know. I am tired and feel myself abnormal in normality. I have severe attack of headache."

"Is your condition well?"

"My condition is fine but I am unable to understand something."

"Hey! Dear, leave it. I think you need some change. Let's come. We enjoy ourselves this night while driving. Come on."

"Please Wolf."

"Why do you not want to enjoy with me?"

"What should I tell? My mood is not good."

"It is too much. We are meeting after many years and you ruin happiness. Let's come."

Then she moved with him. He ignited car and drove it towards an unknown place. "I think you want to meet Igor." He started talking.

"Yes."

"By nature, he is a good boy."

"Yes." Olga changed topic, "Where are we going?"

"Resort."

He had been raising many questions and she bore his nonsense quietly. After four hours, he stopped the car inside the garage of one Motel. It was the lonely place and population was negligible.

"Are we in Moscow?"

"No."

"This place is fearful."

"Why?"

"See! It is too desolately quiet place, totally nook."

"Dear, follow me."

He went to reception and said to book one master room. Receptionist gave a key to one servant and said, "Show him his room."

Olga soon fell on the bed and what she thought, she moved to the bathroom. She was going to take off her clothes then Wolf said, "Can I give you company under the shower?"

"Shut up."

"I selected this lonely place for loving you but…can't say anything taking you. When will we love each other?"

"Wolf I am not your love. Do you not understand? I treat you a friend. Just a friend. At present, I have a tension to complete the expressed wish of my parents. How can I think for love and marriage?"

"Okay. Don't be red. I know you are in the age of completing aim. By the way, I feel you are mad. Study! Study! Study! Aim! Aim! Aim! I say shoot them. Come in another world. There is another study…"

"Just shut up Wolf. Go to bedroom and wait for me." She said while giving him slight push.

"Okay."

Inside the room, he angrily said, "Am I her servant? Continuously she is giving me orders…Well! I should not lose my patience because that right time has not come."

Having tub bath, she went inside the room. She was drying her hair then Wolf came near to lift her in arms.

Seeing his intention, Olga said, "Stop. You flirt! You are not in a level to touch me. Control your emotions."

"What a nonsense question are you asking? I am cascading my love."

"Stop at all." She said ruminatively.

"*I really need to drink the peg of your vinaceously sensuous lips. I want to take deep dip in the ocean of your alluring eyes.* I want to create superposition. Dear, you are coming from America and Americans love near to sex."

"Oh Wolf! First of all, I am not American and I did not go there to study the sex practical and now you are creating a problem. I cannot forget my morals. I cannot transgress my limits. I am refined. You are not changed."

"I am changed but I am doing so for changing your mood."

"No one can beat you in talking but being a good friend, please, calm down your passion. It is my request."

"I want to feel the bliss of amatory night."

"Wolf, it is not a love. I am feeling that you are much too romantic. Are you libidinous?"

"What an absurd question are you asking? Naturally, lover feels romance with partner and it is not lustiness. It creates intimacy."

"I cannot keep intimacy with you. My intimate partner is Igor. And don't compel me for this. I have not any interest in living with you. It seems I should break friendship. You are not my lover. I am living with you only to judge your habits. Is right it?"

"*You are fire*, Olga. Now come on and start lighting my fire. You will see what type of masculinity I have."

"Oh, shut up. You are really very cheap. You are provoking me. You are crossing your limits. Please, do some mercy on me. Otherwise I will have to take a legal action against you." While saying, she gave him tight jerk. On the bed, Wolf gazed her in peculiar condition and she tried to control on her temper.

After drawing the comb in hair, she sat beside him and said, "Wolf, you never understand the situation of others. You are a person of high enthusiasm. I am not yours. Is it clear?"

"All clear." He said rudely.

"Are you treating me friend only to fulfil the desire of sex. Can you not understand my feelings?"

"It is not my meaning."

"Then why are you trying to stimulate me for it?"

"Sorry but everybody wants to do romance with friends and lovers."

"Friends and Lovers…Yes, it was given by Igor." She mumbled and recalled her memories with him. "I did not read that novel. Sorry Igor. I will read it."

"Where are you?" Wolf asked.

She unsteadily said coming from dreamland, "Y…Yes."

"What are you thinking?"

"Leave it."

"At least, you can share…"

"Don't puzzle your mind."

"I think you do not treat me friend."

"Obviously I treat you friend. Therefore, I am here with you. Well, is it less I am with you?"

"No. Something is better than nothing."

They spent a nonentity night. She slept after taking dinner.

Next day they checked out from there.

Olga took the newspaper and started reading headlines. She was astonished after seeing her snapshots with Wolf and she was nescient at airport. Media claimed him childhood friend of Olga in small column.

Olga was worried. She thought with the lament heart, "What will Igor feel after reading this news? I should phone him."

Other side, Igor had seen her photo with Wolf then he could not tolerate it. He lacerated the newspaper into thousands of pieces. Oksana saw him silently dumb as a dog.

"Why are you angry?"

"I love her very much and she did not even nominally think about my condition."

"She is not with Wolf and she did not go to meet him. If you see this photo carefully, it is the snapshot of area near the airport. It means Wolf was there to receive her. He received Olga at airport that's why she is with him."

"Oksana, you don't know he is a ribald ruffian and can do anything wrong with her."

"He will not take a big risk because she is a high profile personality as well as government property and she is also in the range of media. If he wants to give her mortal wound immediately he will be in the custody of police."

"If something happens wrong with her, what will be my life? I will die. You are talking about her mortal wound while I cannot see a lacerated wound on her body."

"One point is striking again and again in my mind why security was not there for her? Without crossing security he could not meet her."

"As I understand, it was her order not for giving security. She forbade."

"Why did she choose this way?" Oksana said.

"As you know, she lives reserved...I mean private. She does not show her interest in others. As I know her since childhood, she never talked with others except me and Wolf. She is like a lioness and devours her prey alone."

"Is she fighter or animal?"

"I said idiom. She works alone and does not want helps of others in her work."

"You are right. It was just like a joke to change your mood."

"I am not in a joking mood. Does she love Wolf?"

"No. I have seen love in her eyes for you. She loves you. You can phone Olga."

"No. I am not going to ask this thing. If my love is pious, Olga will call me to tell everything. If not, I can spend whole life without her."

"I can take the place of Olga in your heart. Try to testify me. I will be out of out."

"Just shut up. I am not in a mood of joking."

"I am serious."

Then his mother went on, "Oksana, don't tease him. He cannot think to cheat her. He can do what he is saying."

"Sorry Igor." She said further to him, "Aim of love is always full of quest. We can..."

"No. Now it is her turn to pass out this love quest. I don't care whether she dials my number or not."

"Even if..."

"I don't want arguments in this matter. Isn't it?"

"Well, don't be red."

Igor sat in the chair while putting hands on his forehead.

———————◆—◆————————

Olga shouted, "Why media works like a police?"

She swallowed that nonsense. She was livid with rage.

"Why does tiger work like a lion?"

"Oh! You are really unbeatable. Will you mind keeping your mouth shut, please?"

She held her head tightly and leaned on the table.

At last Wolf broke silent, "Will you join the Russian film industry?"

"No. I come here to take admission in Moscow University"

"Good spirit. Good work."

"Thanks. And don't lick my mind."

"Okay." Then Wolf sat on the sofa.

She felt an acute headache. She stood hopelessly with long face. Low in spirit with totally lament heart she lay on the bed. Her conscience was impatient.

Closing her eyes, she made the face of Igor and heartily started looking him intently.

Her *sensuous lips were pining for kissing him*. She was, even if, with Wolf but her soul had overlapped the soul of Igor. She was dying to meet him.

Wolf locked her in arms tightly as he could.

"My God, don't do that!" Gruffly she said.

"Why?" Dispiritedly he said.

"I am in a spun condition. I have tired and you are indulging in frolicsome behaviour."

"I think you should take complete bed rest."

Then he went outside from the room.

She again lay on the bed but her mind was disturbed. She took many sides. After sometime, she phoned Amrit.

"Hello! Is Amrit speaking?"

"Yes."

"Olga is speaking."

"Are you all right?" Happily he said.

"I am not fine, Amrit."

"Is something wrong there?"

"Amrit, Wolf received me at airport and now I am living with him but my heart forces me to fall in the arms of Igor. What should I do?"

"It is very simple, listen to the voice of your heart. Conscience never shows wrong way."

"It is easy to say but difficult to do. If I leave the company of Wolf, I am girl who capriciously discards the old lover because he is my first love. Amrit, I love Igor eternally. I cannot live without him. Wolf questions me to know about my intension. I gave clear cut refusal. I am on the two boats, one is of Igor and another is of old love."

"Olga according to American proverb- One who chases two frogs at a time will catch neither. I know only one thing, heart never tells a lie. Igor is good for you because man cannot change his character."

"Amrit. I feel here myself very helpless. He does things very well and he is putting me in dilemma. I am enduring his nonsense while I still do not like him, not knowing why I am unable to convince my real thoughts frankly."

"Could you not understand his nature?"

"His nature has changed and he looks like a good adult but it seems he wants to change my heart theory while giving lip services. I feel that he wants to get me after making sexual relation."

"Are you peril from him?"

"No but he is lusty than before. I feel that he wants me for sex only. He forced me for it but I got success to save my virginity."

"Look before you leap. There is one safe way; Start living with security. You are also a silly girl. Why did you cancel out your security? At least, you should leave America with John uncle."

"I did not understand the need of security."

"You are not an ordinary person. You are high profile and it is dangerous to you to live alone without security."

"I feel like a prisoner with bodyguards."

"Allow me, what can I do for you?"

"When you will ring me up, it will enough."

"Okay Olga, bye."

"Good bye."

Then she disconnected the phone while breathing gruffly.

Two days later, early in the morning, the phone of Olga was ringing but she was sleeping.

While waking her up, Wolf picked up her mobile. "Hello!"

"It's Amrit. Could I talk to Olga?"

"Yes."

Then she aroused her while giving her phone. "Your phone."

"Hello." Olga said.

"Amrit is speaking at this end."

"Yes Amrit."

"Olga, was Wolf speaking?"

"Yes."

"Well, I want to say that you should apply for SAT. Come back here for applying in college for the graduation."

"You are right Amrit. Now I do not want to take admission here. I have changed my mood. Well! What are you doing nowadays?"

"I am doing preparation for SAT."

"Okay, let me make plan for coming back to America."

"Good."

"How many days are left?"

"Where are your mind Olga? Are you all right?"

"Yes, I am."

"SAT is conducted seven times in a year from October to June. More than one month is left. You can take the test as many times as you want. You must get Scholastic Aptitude test registration done at least three weeks in advance. You can search…"

"Okay. I know this thing. I think www.collegeboard.com is a website."

"Yes."

"Okay. Let me search."

"Okay bye."

"Good bye."

After a minute, Amrit phoned her again. "Hello."

"What make you calling me soon?"

"You can register yourself by mail, phone or online."

"Oh, Thanks."

"Mention not." He laughed while giving her answer."

"Bye."

"Wait. Talk to me Olga."

"Yes. You can continue."

"No matter of talking. Life is sapless without you and no words to explain. Life is totally blue, blind, and black."

"Don't try to find me; try to feel me because friendship dwells in heart."

"Your words make me happy. Well! Did you phone Igor?"

"No."

"He is angry seeing your snapshot in the newspaper. It is not good. Seeing your photo with Wolf, he was totally diffused. This thing can't rouse warm emotions in his heart."

"I know but don't tell him that I am coming. I want to give him surprise."

"Okay."

"Can I end the call if you want?"

"Sure. Bye. But book your flight for Mississippi."

"Why?"

"I am making picnic here. We will enjoy together."

"Okay."

She switched off her phone. Later half an hour, she was ready to go. When she was going, Wolf interrogated inauspiciously, "Where are you going?"

"I have some important work."

"Okay. Where do you want to go? I can drop you there."

"Thanks."

"No thanks. I can drop you there."

"No. No need at all."

"Obey me. I can drop you there."

She busted, "Enough is enough. It is too much. Don't afflict me. Please, don't afflict me. I cannot live under your pressure. I want my freedom and I like freedom. You cannot order me around like that. I don't like to dance to one's pipe. Don't seize my freedom. I am feeling myself as a seized bird. Please live as a friend with me. Don't try to become holder of my life."

"To help someone is a sin; I will not help anyone. You can go. I am not seizing your freedom. You are free."

"Thanks."

She was mentally disturbed. She moved to the Moscow River with laptop. She was surfing on net. She downloaded prospectus and form on the desktop. Now she was reading the prospectus.

She phoned Amrit.

"How are you, dear?" Amrit said.

"Not fine."

"Why?"

"I am feeling a prisoner of Wolf. I decide not to take admission here because I cannot fulfil his expectations. He can make my life hell. He will not let me live."

"Your decision is good. I am waiting for you. What is your flight number?"

"I will tell you."

"Okay." She cut off phone.

She worked out for taking ticket of her flight. After four days, she told Amrit by phone before reaching the airport that she was coming to Mississippi and also made him clear about the flight number.

"Okay. I will receive you."

Olga made her luggage and reached the airport immediately. Wolf was also there.

Plane had left for New York. He disappointed while seeing his plan dead. Wolf cried, "*Sukindoch*. I have lost my chance. I cannot forget that insult. I could not prepare good prologue for spoiling her life. It is good that I subdued her."

Inside the plane, she was feeling easy. Now she was free from him at least up to four-five years. She was thinking about the condition of Igor. She closed her eyes and fell in those days in which she used to spend time with him.

CHAPTER 19

Amrit received her at airport and gave her welcome kiss.

"Where are you living here?" Olga said.

"I am with my uncle."

"Oh! Where can I live here?"

"You can live with us. You're Welcome."

"No."

"Why, my dear?"

"You know my nature. I will stay in the hotel."

"Why are you going to lodge in the hotel? You will feel at home here in my uncle's house."

"I cannot live there. Don't give me a baseless suggestion. Try to understand me."

"Do you not treat me a friend?"

"Bring it to notice that I do not treat you friend but you are really my fast friend. Please."

"Okay."

He dropped her at the hotel. Olga booked one luxurious room and fell on the bed. Amrit put her luggage on the table.

She said, "I have tired. Now I will relax for a while."

Servant served her water.

"Thanks and go."

They were making plan for going to India. After an hour, Amrit said, "Well, take rest. Allow me to go. I start preparation for this picnic."

"Okay. I think I should take bath."

"Of course. Your journey is quite tiring."

"Yes."

Amrit has gone. She went inside the bathroom. She doffed her clothes and stepped under the shower. She felt water a good coolant for cooling her head. She was feeling fresh.

After putting on her clothes, she sat on sofa. She picked up her phone and dialled number of Igor.

"How are you, my sweetheart?"

"Fine. I am angry."

"Oh! My dear, why are you angry with me?"

"You phone me today. Why did you not call me when you reached Russia? I think, after getting the company of old lover, you forgot me."

"No. How can I forget you? You are my supreme, my world and your love is everything."

"I don't know Olga but my heart was burnt to ashes after reading that news. I hate him. Your presence with Wolf offends me."

"I am sorry and can understand your feeling. I could not live well without you but he received me at airport and he caught me up in his talks. It is true, I lived with him but fairly speaking, I was not happy. I was living with him in the same house but not to get together with him. He confessed that's why I had to forgive him. I treat him a friend. Well! Leave this matter, and here is good news for you."

"Yes."

"I am in Mississippi with Amrit for making plan to visit India."

"Is right?"

"Yes. Now I am going to take admission here in New York after qualifying SAT."

"This is indeed good news."

"Yes, my dear. I come here for giving you company."

"Thanks."

"Make Oksana ready for this trip. We will enjoy."

"Okay."

"I will meet you soon."

"Sure."

She was happy after talking with Igor. She came out from the hotel and enjoyed herself the surroundings of Mississippi. She was feeling relaxed from the terrific life with Wolf. She spent many hours in strolling and after that she decided to see one movie. She was tension free after seeing one romantic movie.

Before going to bed, she phoned Amrit.

"What are you doing?"

"I am preparing for the trip."

"Okay. Meet me tomorrow. We are going to New York tomorrow."

"Will you manage for tickets?"

"Why are you taking tension? Leave this for me."

"Okay. Sweet dream."

"Same to you."

She fell on the bed. She was about to switch off the lamp, her phone had rung. It was Igor's phone. She picked up the phone and said, "Hey! How are you?"

"Fine, darling. What are you doing?"

"I am going to sleep."

"Oh! Sorry to disturb you."

"No. No. What are you saying? Have you informed Oksana and Helen for this trip?"

"Yes. They are happy."

"I am coming New York Tomorrow. Okay?"

"You are welcome." He took some seconds and said, "It is very difficult to pass a single second being away from you. Life becomes prosaic. It is totally insipid in your absence. I am addicted to you. Your absence is responsible for the mental agitation, inadequate sleeping, loss of willingness, palpitation and loss of appetite. Olga, I love you. I love you so much. I want to talk to you every time. I want to live with you every second. I don't want to leave you alone for a second. Your absence creates irritation. I don't know what it is but, you are beats of my heart, blood of my vein, soul of my body, thoughts of my mind, and prop of my life."

Her heart swelled. She said, "I know I give you little time while you care me so much. I know you love me more than your life and it is true you are the only one to whom I love by heart but at present, I cannot think anything else until unless I will not complete the desire of my parents. After that, I will strive to spend more time with you."

"I know and I also want to see you in the Russian army. My heartiest wishes are with you. I am happy that you are hoisting flags of success."

"Thanks."

"Okay. Sweet dream. We will talk later."

"Okay. Take care and good night."

"Good night once again."

Aeroplane had taken off. They went directly at the apartment of Igor. Olga wished Zinaida aunty. Oksana and Helen were happy seeing Olga there. Zinaida ordered six cups of tea. They made a schedule of visiting India. Oksana said, "My Personal Assistant will manage everything. I send him there before going."

Olga said, "I have decided the schedule of this trip. We will alight from the plane in IGI airport. That day we will take rest. Next two days, we will see the Jantar Mantar, the Red Fort, Qutab Minar, Akshardham, India Gate and the National Museum. Fourth day, after taking proper rest, we will go to Agra for seeing Sikandra, Eitmad-ud-daula, the Taj Mahal, and the Agra Fort. We will stay at Amar Villas in Agra and Radisson in Delhi. Then after we will go to Goa."

"Okay."

"It is confirmed program from my side and we have five days for reformation. If anybody wants some changes, we can consult it again. And you, Oksana, send your assistant as soon as possible for the good arrangement in India."

"What does about security?"

"You manage it."

"Now let me do for this."

"You can take my help." Igor said.

"Thanks."

Olga moved to her home and met father. Roman was happy.

He hugged her while saying, "Oh! My daughter. Here you are. Welcome. When did you come?"

"Yesterday. I was in Mississippi. How are you? Is everything fine?"

"Yes but I was sapless without you."

"You talk really very sweet."

"No. You are dearer and more precious than others."

"It is my pleasure. But good news is that I have come here for my graduation. I will live with you."

"Oh! Really."

"Yes."

"It is an occasion of joy."

Olga smiled magnificently. She said, "I want to take rest so please, let me sleep. I will talk to you later."

"Okay. You can take rest. I can understand."

"Thanks."

Olga moved inside the room for taking rest.

———————◆◆◆———————

Time was 10:30 pm. Andrei stirred her up from sleeping for taking dinner. She wake up and said, "Please. Let me sleep. I am not feeling hungry."

"Why?"

"I don't know." Hardly she could say these three words and again lost in sleep. She was too much tired and he left her room.

After half an hour, Roman came inside her room with food and placed that plate on the table. He sat beside her and put her head in his lap. He was rubbing her forehead gently. Again he said, "Come on. Take dinner."

"No Papa. You can take."

He fed her one morsel. She took while sleeping. He fed her fitfully and she had been eating during sleeping in his lap and at last he was satisfied that she had taken much enough. He left her room and fell on the bed after taking dinner.

———————◆◆◆———————

Next day, when she woke up early in the morning, she felt herself fresh as a fresh rose bud. Her mind was cool and the most important thing was that she was tension free. She got out from the bed and moved into the bathroom.

She was ready for breakfast. She went to meet Allan Pearson after taking breakfast with her father.

She met Allan. He was also happy.

"How are you?"

"Fine and here is good news for you."

"Yes."

"I will spend my five years here in America with my friends and relatives and I hope Zinaida aunty can permit me for working in the movies."

"It is really very good news."

"Yes and now I am going to India with Igor, Oksana Amrit and Helen."

"It means you have made program of going aboard."

"Yes."

"Dear, if you had included me, it would be my pleasure."

"Sorry. I want this trip only with my friends but you are most welcome. You can join us."

"Thanks. I said solely this way."

"No. You are Welcome." Full mellowness in her voice made Allan melt.

"Hey! Darling of my heart, it is your days to enjoy tours with friends. Enjoy, enjoy yourself."

"Thanks."

She immersed in talking to him for discussing on the project of the next movie but she placed her proposal for taking Amrit in the movie for the side role. She had tension taking his future. She wanted to do something for him.

Allan nodded but he had tension inside any corner of his mind. He did not want to take risk of Amrit taking him in his movie. Olga reached home and had been busying for the preparation.

———◆◆◆———

They all were ready. Assistant did his duty well in India for them. Their flight to Delhi took off. Olga wanted to enjoy some special moments with friends that's why she decided this trip. Indian Newspapers had promulgated that news. All fans of Olga and Oksana were crazy to see them in India.

Igor, Amrit and Helen reached the baggage carousel. They found Personal Assistant of Oksana standing nearby. He helped her for picking up luggage. He said, "CAB driver is waiting outside for you."

"Okay."

When Olga came outside from the airport with Oksana, all fans did their welcome heartly. Seeing the hospitality of Indian people, heart of Olga and Oksana became swell. Many people offered rosary chaplet to all. Olga and Oksana gave them autographs and moved to the car.

———————◆◆————————

They set luggage in a specified position of the back of the car and glided inside. Driver dropped them at Radisson Hotel, near Mahipalpur. Inside the room, Olga dropped off to sleep after taking bath and Amrit had been playing cards with Oksana, Helen and Igor.

In the night, they were taking dinner and after that Olga stepped out from there. She took many rounds of lobby. Seeing chagrin on her forehead, Igor said, "What happened?"

"Matter of Wolf is giving me tension."

"See! If you want to marry Wolf, you can. Don't take tension of my life. I am happy in your happiness."

"Why do you not understand my problem? I am not going to marry him. I feel some suspiciousness in his behaviour. As I feel, he wants to subdue me. I have scrupulous distress taking him. As you know, I used to love him and he was my first love. He wants to arouse that hidden love which I had buried inside any corner of my heart. He wants to take me away from you. He is a master of talking and capable to wash my mind that's why I decide to marry with you. Will you marry me Igor?"

"Yes but you have to think again with cool mind. Don't be in haste. Your success is on the peak. I cannot see downfall of your career after marriage. I will marry you but not now. Olga, I have to get my own success for you. Please, give me time to make my backbone strong."

"Okay." She said while kissing him.

He moved into the room with her and locked door and windows. He fell on the bed and Olga too while putting head on his chest. He started bestowing caress on her. She felt pure heaven in his arms and lost in sound sleep within a minute.

***

Next day, they visited Jantar Mantar, India gate and the National Museum. After that day, they visited Akshardham, the Red fort, Qutab Minar. They were happy now. Their trip was good and they took departure from there to Agra. He stayed in Amar Villas and saw the Taj Mahal, the great symbol of love. They moved to Eitmad-ud-daula.

They enjoyed their picnic in the Agra fort and Sikandra before going to Goa. They were happy after seeing the culture of India.

They took flight of New York and immersed in daily routine life. Olga was preparing for SAT exam with Amrit. She has passed out the Ist paper of SAT and now she was preparing for qualifying Optional test. She chose mathematics from the entire list for displaying skill in a particular subject. Amrit also passed out his SAT exam.

Now they were able to take admission in any college of the USA. They took admission in New York University.

Igor and Oksana were preparing for the exam of Intermediate and Helen was taking Bachelor Degree in Economics. Igor was busy in his studies to get good Marks but Oksana was taking it lightly. She had been busying in her movie and for getting the market value. She did not want downfall of her popularity and wealth like Olga.

***

Day before joining the University, Amrit said, "Will you demand for taking security?

"No. No need of it."

"We are going to take admission in the college and you know American ragging is popular all over the world."

"I cannot enter the college campus with security. I do not want to show off and we are not the special students. We will enjoy the college life with mates. Don't worry. In fact, no one have much courage to take my ragging. After all, I am a high profile personality. How can they do wrong with me?"

"When we have source, why should we not use it? We should live according with the way of present power."

"You talk like a child. It will show our princely glamour while we will be on the same platform and we will have to create common understanding with all. Tell me, why do we wear uniform during school time?"

"I could not think this matter."

"We wear uniform to reduce the gap between lower and middle class students. Uniform gives same flavour and colour to all."

"I am agreed on this matter. You talk to the point."

"Don't worry about ragging whenever I am with you."

"Thanks."

"But I want promise from your side."

"Promise!" He said startlingly.

"Yes."

"Okay. Tell me your demand."

"You will not take ragging in sophomore."

"Okay. Done."

"And I hope you will study properly. It is not only for taking degree. Percentage is must. Is Okay?"

"Yes. If you leave me, I cannot say anything what my result will be."

"What type of a silly person you are. Why are you spoiling your life for me? I am not your future. Being a good friend I suggest you that your knowledge, your effort, your workmanship, your percentage, your concept will help you to pass out the campus."

"Leave it. It is a very big lecture. Why do you not think extra except studies?"

"Gabby, as soldiers want to fight a war so toppers want to study."

"It is not fair. I am not gabby."

"Sorry. Don't take it to heart."

"Leave it. Let's come."

"Where?"

"Restaurant."

"Okay."

Amrit was happy with Olga. Obviously, he was again with her and restlessness of his life had removed. He was studying perfectly because most of the time Olga taught him when he was not able to understand the concepts of any subject. She made him clear every problem.

Roman, Andrei, Amrit, and Olga were living happily together but Olga could not find out the end of her happiness. Wolf was not with her so she was not under his force. She was free. How she could live under the instructions of others while her father, mother, Igor, Zinaida aunty, Roman, teachers, Amrit, and Allan uncle loved her very much beyond her expectations.

Everybody was excited seeing Olga in the university. All the students wanted her company in their groups. There was a gang, named 'ROCKY'. Boss of this gang wanted her in his group but Olga was a reserved personality. As Olga was the high profile celebrity so he could not get courage to tell his intention.

Once, Rocky came to convince Amrit and he denied rudely. In fact, Amrit was harassed by others and he was mentally disturbed that's why he treated him insolently. He did not know the nature of that boy while Rocky was a boy of combative nature. He beat Amrit badly. If Amrit wanted, he could rout him easily but he didn't want to create an undesirable fun.

When Olga knew that incident, she met Amrit and asked about that matter.

He told her everything clearly then immediately she met Dean and told him that problem. Dean took hard steps for all and rusticated him for two weeks.

———◆◆◆———

One year had gone and Olga could not judge the speed of time. The truth is that she could not judge the best and precious time of her life. Igor passed out his Intermediate exams.

Olga arrived at his home. She met him and said, "I want to consult something."

"Yes."

"Igor, I want that you should leave America. You have time to apply in any University of the Moscow."

"But why, my dear?"

"You are one class behind me. When I leave America after completing my graduation, you will be applying in the third year. And you know, I cannot wait for you till a year and I cannot tolerate the expectations of Wolf in Russia so please, leave America for my sake. You can give time to your father that is important to you. You can share his load while living with him. Do you understand what I am striving to make you make out about my imbroglio? You should be there to receive me when I will reach. I will not be able to handle coercions of Wolf in your absence. He is a man of high enthusiasm and can plunder my pleasant life."

"It is impossible to live without you…"

"Why don't you understand?"

"No. cannot possible. You should understand condition of my heart."

"Oh! He can steal your Olga. Do you like this thing?"

"No."

"So please. It is a matter of only three years."

"Okay."

"I will wait for you."

"Thanks."

Igor took admission in Lomonsov Moscow University. His father was happy because after five years he was going to live together. He loved his son so much that's why he had been ready to fulfil the desires of his son. Now, he was happy but Igor was not feeling well without Olga. Zinaida was taking his care too much.

Oksana was happy with her father. He could not give her time when she used to live in America but he reached there to meet her from time to time. Now she was permanently with her. Her father also met Zinaida when she was purveying her in America. He was ready to give her expenses of Oksana but she denied. Now, his relation with Zinaida was good and he knew her from that incident when he met her at the time of Irina's death. Oksana felt mother's love in the lap of Zinaida aunty. It was Olga who made Igor ready for this. She also discussed on this matter with Zinaida aunty and she persuaded but Helen shifted to Olga's house because she was completing her graduation.

Olga was not happy but Amrit was with her for making her mood normal.

Time was rolling; Olga was busy studying and working in the movies. Now Amrit was also a side hero. Olga did three films with him. She gave him a platform of an international level. Allan was happy after seeing the return of the *beauty bomb*. Her demand in the market was too much.

Three years of her life spent happily. She enjoyed every moment heartily with Amrit, Helen, father and Andrei uncle. When her heart skipped a beat for Igor, she phoned him immediately for pleasant diversion. In fact, she felt those three years are like three centuries without him. She remained topper in every year of her graduation. During this period, Oksana participated in Miss Russia contest and she was successful in wearing the crown. Olga sent her many wishes. And that year, in the month of November, she applied for the Miss World contest but unfortunately she could secure the place of second runner up.

Now Olga had a Bachelor Degree. She hoisted the flags of ability in her stream.

After convocation, eyes of Amrit were wet. Olga wiped his tears and said, "Why are you weeping? Hey, don't weep."

"My heart is heavy. I miss you. I know I cannot get you but I love you. I know, you are love of Igor and I don't want myself a wall between you and him. Perhaps now we may never meet."

"Why are you saying like this? Don't try to find me; try to feel me. I am everywhere in your mind. Dear, you are my ideal friend. How can you think it? I will come to meet you here."

"Olga, I cannot forget those days that I spent with you. It was my precious time. I spent eight years with the celestial beauty. You are the beauty whom I love and respect blindly."

"Leave it. Leave it. It is too much."

"No. I will not forget you. I am living with you at least more than five years but you did not feel my burden but I could not do anything for you."

"Oh! Leave it. Let's come home."

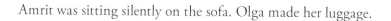

Amrit was sitting silently on the sofa. Olga made her luggage.

He asked, "Do you need my help?"

"No."

But Roman helped her. Olga said, "Why are you taking tension? You can write me mail. I will give you response. You can phone me. I will talk to you. I am going to Russia not to heaven."

"Hey! Shut up. Don't say like this otherwise I will not talk with you."

"Okay sorry. I will invite you in my marriage."

"I will come."

"Thanks!"

Roman, Andrei, Helen and Amrit see her off. Before moving inside the airport, she said to Amrit, "Take care of your parents. Is it clear?"

"Yes. Don't worry."

"You can call me anytime when you feel problem."

"Okay."

Then she moved to hug her father and said, "Take care. We will meet soon."

"Okay. You too."

Further she said to Helen, "You take care too."

"You too."

She met Andrei uncle and after wishing him, she sat inside the aeroplane and she left America for Russia. Roman and Andrei were not happy.

CHAPTER 20

The plane landed at last. Immediately she was let out and walking out to find out the taxi. She scrambled into the taxi and sat on the front seat.

She said to Chauffer, "Please drop me at Kutafya tower."

"Yes madam."

He said after a minute, "I am astonished seeing you alone."

"Can I not live alone?"

"It is not my meaning but…"

"Most of the time, I like to live in peace."

"Could you give me an autograph?"

"Of course. Paper please."

"I don't have a pen or paper."

"I feel for you." Sadly she said.

After sometime, she ordered him to stop the taxi.

"Madam, Kutafya tower is almost two kilometres far."

"Wait for ten minutes."

"Okay Madam."

Olga came out from the car and moved towards the stationery shop to buy a permanent marker.

When she came back, she gave an autograph on his front mirror of the car. Chauffer was very gleeful from her behaviour.

"Such I am feeling as you cannot see your fans unhappy."

"Yes. I know I can never be a high profile personality without my fans. My standard, my popularity, and my wealth belong to my fans. The more my fans, the more I maintain the status of celebrity so I love my fans heartily and it is my duty to make them happy. They give me respect so my duty is to love them. Wealth and fame of great personalities depend upon the fans more than luck and efforts."

"It is our pleasure madam."

"Don't say me madam. I am your daughter-like and it is my pleasure that I live in the world of trillion hearts."

"You are great. First time I saw a heart-hearted personality. Often others don't give time to their fans while they have sufficient time to spend with their pets."

"It also makes me wonder why people love their pets more than human beings and partners. Husband and wife give divorce each other but never leave pets. In present era, people create relations with humans for selfishness. What a wonderful nature of human beings we see!"

"You are fifty percent right but the universal truth is that they also cash the animals for money. They cash cows, buffaloes, goats, horses and kill elephants, rhino, rabbits only for fulfil the daily requirements. Here I want to say that to cash is a nature of human beings which make them selfish."

"Yes, it is a hundred folds view."

"Thanks."

Chauffer dropped her at Kutafya Tower. She gave him money and moved to meet Dr. Anton Turbin.

He was happy seeing her in front. "How are you Olga?"

"I am fine. What about you?"

"Fine."

"How is your work?"

"Good."

"Where is Oksana?"

"She is with Igor."

"Oh! Okay, I will meet you later."

"Okay."

She went to meet Igor at his house but he was not there. There were only servants. One told her that family had gone out of city to attend a marriage party.

"What a bad luck?" She said.

She was about to return then one servant said, "Autograph please."

She passed best condescending smile. "Yes."

She gave him an autograph. Out of six servants, two were old. She knew them.

They had also identified her. One said, "Had you come here once before?"

"Yes. When Zinaida aunty fed me food."

"I acquaint you, Miss Olga."

"Same here."

"What would you like to take?"

"Nothing but I want to go."

"Please. Take something."

"Thanks. Well! When will they come?"

"You can meet them in the evening."

"Okay. I think it is right to meet tomorrow."

———— ✦ ————

She went directly to the Hotel and moved towards reception. She got one room booked and took complete rest.

Next day she was walking on the footpath, coincidently Wolf saw her. He stopped short near her and said, "When do you come here?"

"Before seven days." She told him a lie.

"Why did you not come to meet me?"

"Why should I come to meet you?"

"Why are you rude? Where are you living now?"

"I am rude because you are sticky."

"Why are you so angry?"

"Sorry. I feel irritation."

"Okay. Be calm. Well! What will be your next program?"

"I cannot say anything."

"Tell me what can I do for you?"

"Don't lick my mind. I am upset. Just leave me alone."

"I am trying to make your mood change and you are saying don't lick my mind."

"Sorry. Please leave me alone."

Actually, she was unhappy when she did not find Igor at his house.

"Would you like to come at my house in the evening?"

"As far as I understand, it will depend on condition and time."

"Do you love Amrit?"

"No." She said while making a bad face, "He is my friend. Why do ask a wrong question? And don't irritate me."

"Why are you avoiding me? Why are you not coming in the evening? I want to make one evening with you in Russia."

"Okay. I will come but leave me alone this time."

"That's the way, I like you." He moved to hospital and suddenly took a round while saying, "Give me your mobile number."

"Is compulsory?"

"Yes."

She gave him mobile number and he moved to hospital and she turned round to meet Igor at his home. Igor was very happy and he hugged her without wasting a moment. She asked, "Where is Zinaida aunty?"

"She is in her room. Is any important work?"

"Yes."

"Okay."

They stepped into her room. Olga said after wishing her politely, "Aunty, please give me the keys of my house."

"Oh! Yes. She stood to move towards the Almirah. She picked out the bunch of keys to hand over her.

Igor said, "You can live here with us."

"I will live here with all. Don't worry. Right now, I am going to make my accommodation clean."

"Oh! You can take one servant." Zinaida said.

"Thanks."

Zinaida gave order to driver for dropping her. Servant was with her.

When she entered home, she found it as a junk house, sophisticated and suffocated dirty place. She set all the things on its place with servant, removed dust from the goods and made her house cleaned. She was feeling tired and wanted to take bath while she worked little bit. When servant got success to clean her house properly, she ordered him to go and servant immediately moved to the destination.

She, without wasting time, moved under the shower.

———————

On the other side Wolf met one person, who was the M.O.I/c of semen bank.

"Hello sir."

"I am fine. Yes, what can I help you?"

"Please, issue me the phial of semen of any HIV positive person for testing and making a report on it."

"Show me the permission letter and fill up these entries in this register."

"Could I not take without signature?"

"Don't talk foolish. Are you new here? First of all you should know every rule of this hospital."

"No. I have no permission and want to do some tests."

"Go and get permission of Dr. Turbin."

"Yes."

Then he returned doctor's room. "May I come in sir?"

"Yes."

When Wolf came inside the room, Oksana astonished. She said, "Is he working here?"

"No. He is completing his report on Sexual transmitted disease. He is good at Venereology…but how do you know him?"

"I saw him in the newspaper with my friend Olga."

"Oh! I also know you." Wolf said.

"Is she your friend?" Oksana asked.

"Yes."

Then he said excuse me to Oksana.

He requested him to write the permission letter for him.

"Okay." He said while turning towards his face.

He wrote permission letter for him.

"Thank you to give me permission for taking the semen phial. I want to do some tests on it."

"Good. But do it under supervision of Dr. Yulia Poklanskaya and also show me the report."

"Yes sir."

He moved fast to semen bank and after sometime, Oksana also left the company of her father.

Wolf took phial and moved to the laboratory.

———————

Olga sprawled on the bed after taking bath. She thought to do rest of work next day. She had tired therefore she slept in a minute.

In the evening, her phone was ringing. She picked up late. "Hello."

"Olga, Wolf is speaking at this end. Dear, where were you? It is my second call."

"Actually I was sleeping that's why I couldn't pick up the phone."

"When will you come?"

"Sorry. I cannot give you company. I am tired."

"Please. I will make you fresh."

"Don't joke. I feel myself abnormal mentally as well as physically."

"Oh! Come on. I am waiting for you. How much will I have to wait for you?"

"Okay. I am coming. I will be with you after two hours."

"Why? I feel distance can be covered in thirty minutes."

"In fact I have some pending work."

"Leave it and come soon."

"But…"

"Please come immediately." He said before she could speak.

"I am coming."

She disconnected the phone and moved to the bathroom, came back for changing the clothes.

After putting on the clothes, she reached to meet him. It was the time of eight o' clock and Wolf was alone inside the house.

Olga broke silence, "Hello Wolf."

"Fantastic. How are you, my dear *Matryoshka*?"

"I am fine."

"Olga!"

"Yes."

"I want to ask one thing again."

"Yes. You can ask."

"Do you love Igor?"

She was silent but said firmly, "Yes. I love my yearning man."

"If you love Igor, you are free to marry him. I think you are nubile now. I can live without you but I love you. It will be my sacrifice for my love."

"Wolf it is true I am in dilemma and my heart warms for him but I also know, you are my first love and you have regretted your fault but it is too late that's why I can accept your friendship proposal only. I am steady on my words either anyone condemn me to death or trample underfoot because what is to happen must happen, we cannot do something extra or anything less."

"What is to happen must happen!" He said while frowning.

"Yes. You can unfaltering faith in me. You are my friend; it means you are my friend."

He sniggered mysteriously but Olga could not understand. He said, "I miss you that you cannot imagine."

"And he loves me eternally and you can never think."

"Will you marry him?"

"Yes. Of course."

"Sorry. Well, what would you like to take?"

"I want nothing."

"Champaign or Vodka."

"*Nyet. Spaciba.*"

"Well, I think coffee will do."

"Yes. I can take it."

"When will you grow up?"

"I think there is no relation between whisky and age."

"Leave it and take it." He said while handing over her coffee mug.

He said, "As I think you have decided to join the Russian Army."

"Yes."

"Are you sure about success?"

"Yes. I am sure."

"Well! Take it."

"Thank you."

She took it sip by sip and her memory temporarily vanished with misted eyes.

Next morning she was astonished when she found herself in unmanaged dress on the bed and again more astonished when she did not find Wolf. She managed her clothes immediately as she could.

Now she had understood all the things what he did with her. Quickly she searched something but she could not find that. Her heart rate was fast.

With pounding heart she said, "Am I pregnant? Did he rape me?" Suddenly she gave herself answer, "No. It can't happen." And suddenly her thinking changed. *Yes. It can happen. Oh! What will be my life? Oh! No. He is capable of doing such things. Why did I believe in him? Oh, God! How can I live with this unexpected baby?*

She immersed again in finding out the used condom but she felt herself hopeless. She was totally disappointed. Her eyes dazed when she found one letter. Her palpitation was fast and her hands were numbed. She unfolded that paper while quivering.

OLGA,

Now you are mother of any unknown person. I have completed my revenge. Since starting I am not your friend but it was compulsory to me to take you in confidence that's why I played this drama. I could have done this earlier when you came last time in Russia but at that time my plan fell through. With the use of **'ARTIFICIAL INSEMINATION'**, I have inserted semen inside you last night. I want to tell you something that this semen is of unknown person and it indicates that you and your child are in the contact of HIV disease. Now you have no name of father for your child. Either you can accept it as a rape or revenge; I have no tension or regret.

I want to make you clear that if you want to go to court I am also ready to fight the case because I never take any tension of future. If you go to court, you will be responsible for your ill-fame. Today, I am very happy that I have completed my revenge. I am not Igor who can bear the insult.

Yours enemy.

"How fool I am?" She said weeping convulsively on bed.

"Her heart and mind were pounding. It was more dreadful than either condemn to death or stone to death.

"Wolf, your nature is like a wolf. You are really a wolf. You are a werewolf."

She was abusing him as well as herself. She thought, "I am a very popular personality and it is a sin or unexpected ill-legal pregnancy. When this issue will open in front of the world, what will be my life? No. No. I will not be able to face all the questions of media. It will not be easy to stand among crew of my fans. God, why did you make me ominous?"

She died half and lost her energy. Her face had parched out completely. She was stunt and unable to understand something.

"In my views death is the last way." Suddenly, something stroke in her mind, "I think abortion is fine but there is no way to make the fame safe and what about AIDS? Nobody can cure it. This will show my haplessness. Many fingers will be pointing out to me. Oh, god!"

She returned home thinking deeply. *What should I do? Can I take the life of one child who is inside me even if he is suffering from AIDS?*

CHAPTER 21

She was weeping badly in her room on the bed. Repeatedly she was remembering her future with the unexpected pregnancy. She was scared of her ill fame.

Wolf had tormented her. She had been sitting tacitly in her room and unable to put up with the highhandedness of Wolf.

She was feeling her demolished life weeping sobbingly. She had totally hanged in despair.

"Alas! Woe is me. How stupid I am. He raped me and I could not do anything. What could I do in the condition of swooning? It is hard to believe in his temerity but I have to." While saying, she angrily moved her hand fast on her study table. Four-five books fell on the floor. Her eyes settled on one book, name was 'FRIENDS AND LOVERS'. It was on her study table with some books. It was the keepsake given by the Igor.

She wiped her tears and picked up it quickly. She read first its title after removing the thick layer of dust. She mumbled, "I have totally forgotten this book."

Again, her eyes brimming with blood and she kissed that book. "Igor I am really sorry. I could not judge your love at that time correctly but I know how much you would love me. You are my real love and I cannot forget cascading your care on me. Really, you did my care too much. After all, I hurt you every time. I love you Igor. I love you very much. This sentence by Wolf is not wrong. It is my punishment and I am for this."

Then she opened the book and found one folded paper in it. She opened to read it; it was the letter of her mom. Her curiosity increased for reading it.

Dear Olga,

My blessings are with you. My dear child I have no words to narrate about my life. Olga, doctor has left the hope that I will survive and it is time to tell you everything. Before dying, I want to clear about the truth that I could not get the courage to tell you in the hospital. I was afraid of telling the truth because I did not want to damp your feelings after listening to the name of Wolf that's why I am writing you all the things in this letter. Olga, somehow Wolf cannot be your love because you have proximity of blood and now you cannot think to marry with him. He is your brother. I know your age is not proper to tell you right as it were but conditions sometime make us slave. You don't know Olga; my father did second marriage and nature of my step mother was not good. She wanted to grab all the properties of my father. Therefore, she did my marriage forcefully with one person name is Joy Kotzwinkle and Wolf is his son.

When I knew, he was also involved in the trick of my step mother I decided to give him divorce. You don't know Olga, he had given divorce to one other woman, and he had his relation with someone else at the time when I did marriage with him. He cheated me and how I could bear it. I gave him divorce because one wife can never bear the presence of another woman in the life of her husband.

Soon I gave him divorce but I handed over him the responsibility of Wolf because I did not want to live with a sin of a sinner. I did marriage with Sergei, your father.

My little girl! As I have introduced you with my brother, he will bring you up. He is a very gentle person and able to give secure life because he loves me lot when I used to live with him.

May be, your granny can do wrong with you because she will not want any heir of the remaining property but you will have to cope with difficulties and you will have to make good future. I hope that being a good daughter you will fulfil the last desire of your parents. Now your aim is to stand up on the top of the world.

Sorry but you have to forget your love. If you want Igor as a life partner, I have no problem. My eyes weigh him a good boy and he is gullible. He loves you and can die for you.

What I am making you clear you can understand. If by god grace! My health will be good; I will represent myself before you for confession for this because I have no right to break your heart.

Situation is tough and our condition says to conduct with it properly.

I know very well you will read this novel after the exam is over because I know every inch of you. It is also your exam in which you will have to pass out. I can hope that you will perform the task of my desires successfully.

I hope that God will help you at every step and at every sharp turn of your life and rest of the things depends upon your efforts because not everything depends on destiny. I cannot dedicate you love but my lots of blessings are with you forever. I will ever miss you after death and Take Care.

Your accursed mom,
Irina Rodionova.

She was shocked after reading the letter. Her face stained with tears. She mumbled, "Wolf is my brother. Oh! No. This is the reason we both are the toppers."

Her disappointed face had shown that she had lost everything, her life, her fame, love, friends, fans, kith and kin, and wealth. She was feeling herself mom of an unexpected baby who will not get the name of his father.

She was weeping virulently. Her life was full of Tsunami. Her soul, heart and world were going to sink in murk. She felt herself not in the wicked world but in the jerry-built hell. She shook her head in disbelief. She thought. *I am drinking as I am brewed.*

She said herself, "Suicide is better than ill-fame. My character has been assassinated by the sly man and last safe way is death, only death can save me from this blunder."

She went inside the store room and started finding one rope. She took a rope and moved inside her room. Now she had given sentence herself to hang till death. She made a halter and made another knot with hook. When she was going to hang herself, one person cried, "Stupid, what nonsense are you doing? Are you mad?"

"Igor!" She said while weeping. She busted into tears.

She stood next to him and locked him tightly, wept badly putting her head on his chest. "Igor I am helpless. My all the things have destroyed. I have a child of unknown HIV positive person. My life is not for surviving on this earth. Hell is a good place."

"Who told you that you have an unexpected baby?"

"Wolf wrote me in a letter. Again he played fraud with me."

"I made you understand many times but you did not. Well! Leave it and don't take tension. I am father of your child. I will give my name to your child."

"No. No Igor. What are you saying? How can you spoil your life for a frail girl? I did frailty with you. You should not help me this time."

"You are not frail and in love everything is fair. His scintillation on your principle made you ready to follow him."

"No! No! Tis sin."

"No, it is the exam of love. I love you really by heart. I am able to accept you with child."

"No. I am HIV positive. I am not a puritan. I am leavings of Wolf."

"So what? In fact, I don't want puritan, I want my lover, *my scenic Olga*, and good lovers are those who never leave their partners in bad situation."

"Igor, are you in consciousness? I think you are blind in my love. I am a frail girl. You should not spend life with leavings. I am a rejected piece."

"Yes. True love makes every lover blind and I will live with you. Why are you taking tension?"

"There is much difference between you and Wolf. What type of a girl I am! I could not judge the right person but I cannot spoil your life. I know I am leavings of Wolf. He is a very good prevaricator and I could not save myself from him. Once you told me that I would feel the pangs of remorse and now I am feeling. I am a victim of his coercive measure but I am obliged to you for your kindness and humility."

"You are not leavings and to err is human. Don't worry you have my full support and you are not frail. I know, you love me lot but the force of Wolf made you to come under his pressure. Whenever I am with you it means no problem with you. You are salt of the earth."

"It is not a time of joking. It is a serious condition. Why are you spoiling your life for me?"

"Don't worry Olga. You are not suffering from AIDS." Oksana said while coming into the room through the door.

"How is it possible?"

"Wolf did it possible."

"What!"

"By artificial insemination he inserted semen of Igor."

Listening to the words of Oksana, Igor saw him confusedly.

"I am confused. It is Greek to me. Tell me clearly." Olga said.

"Listen to me, Wolf is a student of Venereology and works under the supervision of my father, Dr. Anton Turbin."

"Oh!" She said startlingly.

"Yes. I could know his intension yesterday. He came to meet my father for the purpose of taking the permission for issuing the phial of semen of any HIV positive person from the semen bank for making a report on it but I did not know that he wanted it for inserting inside you to spoil your life. When I was going to meet Igor from the hospital, I listened to his words. He said that how would you save your life from him. He said that he would spoil your life through artificial insemination. He had made his mood to use this process to embezzle your life. I told him everything and then after I phoned my father for sending him to Kremlin. My father gave one work to Wolf and he had to go to Kremlin. In this period, I went to the hospital with Igor and with the help of Doctor, Igor gave him his semen and I replaced the semen phial from his lab. First, I read the name of a person from the phial and stuck the name slip of ex-person on the semen phial of Igor. This thing made him fool. Actually, Igor wanted to tell you everything but I forced him not to tell you. I made him understand if we would tell you the truth so Wolf can change the trick to spoil your life and maybe he could show us wrong in front of you that we are provoking you against him. Although, we wanted to make you realize your fault therefore I decided this wrong way. Igor was against this but I could handle him hardly. Now you are safe and safe from ill-fame and I apologize for my mistaken attribute. If you want, you can call police for me."

"What are you saying Oksana? You did nothing wrong and this is the right way to make me understand. You did a right job. Thanks."

"I know, I did wrong, so, you can give me any type of punishment. I am very sorry for it but it was compulsory to me to do this. We did only for showing you the actual face of Wolf. What he actually is. I am sorry for this."

"No. Again I say that you did right. I am for this. I am very thankful to you and I am proud of you. I cannot reciprocate your obligation. Whenever you want my life, I will give it to you without any hesitation. You saved my fame and my life."

Now Olga was very happy and looking like a youthful daisy. She flung her arms around him and nestled him tightly giving kisses.

Oksana stated, "I don't want your life; I want you forever with him. He lives like a dead man without you every second. He loves you lot and I want to see you with him forever. He enthrones you in his heart."

Then Oksana moved to leave the room. Olga said, "Where are you going?"

"My work has over and I do not want myself as a wall between your relations."

"No Oksana, I will be his wife but you have full freedom to live with him. I am not cheap minded. In fact, you are a very good friend of Igor."

Igor returned home with Oksana after consoling her. He said to Oksana, "Why did you tell her a wrong story? When I gave my semen for preservation? When Olga will know about the truth, who can face her?"

"It is the part of future. What I thought right at that time to calm down her I did. It was necessary to make her normal. She is very sensitive and can attempt suicide. My father is one of the best gynaecologists of Russia. I will talk to my father. He will guide us properly."

"Okay. Now phone your father and get the address of Wolf. I want to meet him."

Oksana phoned her father to get the address of Wolf.

He said, "I do not know where he lives. But wait a minute. I call you back after talking to him."

"But don't tell him that I want to know her address."

"Okay."

He phoned Wolf. He picked up the phone and said, "Who are you?"

"Wolf, I am Dr. Anton Turbin. Where are you?"

"Sir, I am in the laboratory."

"Okay. Have you completed your report?"

"No, sir. I am working on it."

"Okay." Then he disconnected the phone.

Wolf's heart was pumping fast. He thought why Dr. Turbin phoned him. He mumbled wiping sweat, "Have not Olga told him everything? My career will ruin."

He poured water in the glass and drank it to make him normal. Other side, Anton phoned to tell her daughter that he was in the hospital. Oksana conveyed that message to Igor and he, without wasting time, went to meet him in the hospital.

Wolf was perplexed while seeing him coming into the laboratory. Igor grabbed his collar tightly and dragged him outside from the room. All the members were stunt after seeing his courage. In the ground, first he beat him badly and then asked, "Why did you deflower Olga?"

"I wanted to take retaliation of my insult."

"It means you will spoil her life. Stupid! God will never forgive you. She is your sister."

"Sister! How can it possible?" Startlingly he said.

"Yes." And then after Igor told him everything what Irina wrote in the letter.

He was shameful. He said bowing his head, "Sorry! Really, I am a sinner but I did not do anything wrong with Olga. Your Olga is virgin. I wanted to take revenge of my insult that's why I chose that wrong work for doing. I did nothing but mismanaged her clothes. I had one last card to play to find out whether it was an ace or just a joker to make her fool writing a totally false letter. I cooked up a concocted story. I knew that after reading it either she would make her alone from the world or want to knock the door of the court. In both the cases, indirectly my revenge would fulfil. If she goes to court, judge will want to see medical report and medical report will declare her clear so I can sue her and after this she obviously lose her dignity in front of the world. If she decides to live alone, so many months she cannot live carefree life. That's all. It was my plan. Truth is I did not touch her."

"You played a very good game sarcastically. Wonderful! You did not think she is a sensitive girl. She was going to die. You could be responsible for her death." He asked, "Wolf! How did you think that you would spoil the life of Olga through this technology? I think a vermin can also not do such type of an odious work. How did you decide to do so?"

"In fact I did not want to take her life and also want to save myself because I know she is a government property and police will catch me somehow. She insulted me too much so I wanted only tit for tat. I loved her also but not now and also aware that she is a pride of Russia. I could not have seen her with you but now my relation is different with her. I did not use my genuine hand writing to write the letter and I also not write my name in the letter. I did not want to leave any evidence."

"Either you accept it or not but you did a very cheap grade work. You are really a slovenly person."

"Yes, I agree. However, past never returns but writes future. Your Olga is pious. It is right I mismanaged her clothes but I did not do anything wrong. She is virgin."

Then he went off from there with numbed eyes. How could he talk firmly in front of him?

Igor arrived home and moved to beach with Oksana. He spent a whole day with her and she was also trying to make him happy. On the beach, he told her what Wolf told him. Okasana was happy and said, "We can convey this to Olga and she will feel happy."

"Yes."

"And now we will make out her to participate in the Miss Russia beauty Contest. Now she is not pregnant and eligible for applying in the contest."

"Yes. And you could not win the Miss World contest but see this time in the month of February; Olga will win the Miss Universe contest."

"It also hurts me that I could not get the crown."

"No problem baby. A girl who wore the crown is not more beautiful than you. You are beautiful, my friend." He said.

Igor went to meet Olga. When she opened the door, he said. "Why are you so sad?"

"That matter pinches me so deeply. I am much tensed."

"Here is good news for you. Wolf did not do anything with you except mismatching your clothes. There is no truthfulness in his letter. You are not a victim of artificial insemination. First I am sorry that Oksana told you a lie that she replaced the semen phial. We did not do anything like that. Only for consoling you she made a false story."

Now Olga got relief. She said, "Is it right?"

"Yes. Believe in me. You are virgin."

"Thanks God! Now my chest is not heavy. I am happy that he did not sully my chastity."

"I am also tension free. I beat him badly."

"He is for this."

"Well! Leave the chapter of Wolf. He will not disturb you in future. Now I want that you should participate in the Miss Russia beauty contest. Now you are not pregnant and also honourable so you can apply."

"Yes. I will grant your wish. I will apply in the beauty contest."

"And in coming February, you will have to participate in The Miss Universe contest because I bet with Oksana that you will wear the crown."

"Ha ha. Okay. But I cannot say that I will be able to wear both the crowns."

"I know you will win both the contests because you are an incarnation of success."

"Thanks but I will try my level best."

"You have to win otherwise Oksana will tease me."

"Okay. Don't take tension. And I have one request."

"Yes."

"Now I want to live with you. I do not want to live far from you. Loneliness stings me. Just hold me in your arms tightly. Hug me tightly as no one can separate us."

"Don't worry. No one can separate us." He said while hugging her warmly.

Olga left for his house and now they were living together.

Olga participated in the Miss Russia beauty contest. She was confident, beautiful, respected, charismatic and potential contestant. Finally she won the contest and wore the crown to beautify her beauty.

Next year, in the month of February, she participated in the Miss Universe contest. Ninety countries sent a candidate to compete but only sixteen contestants could qualify Preliminary round.

When she updated Igor through phone, he was very happy. He wished her for the next round. She also talked to Amrit and he was also very happy. He also wished her and complained her why she did not meet him. She said, "If I win this contest, I will live one year during my reign and then we will live together."

He said, "Good. And best of luck."

"Thank you." She said before disconnecting her phone.

When she won the evening gown segment with a large margin, she threw cold water on all the contestants' enthusiasm. Her starting was very good.

It was the final day of the contest. In America, Allan, Amrit, Roman, Andrei, Helen, John, Marten and Diana were very curious to know about the final declaration. In Russia, Igor, Zinaida, Oksana, Anatolye and Wolf had eagerness of knowing the final result after personality Interview. Everyone was praying for her success. Igor and Oksana were in excitement and praying to God for her victory. Igor, being very earnest, sat to watch live telecast.

Olga acquired maximum points. She was a devastatingly charming, pretty, well curving, enthusiastic, confident and brainy girl of 5.9 feet. Confidently she qualified the last round and judges declared her winner. First Runner up was Susana Crispens Nosek from Argentina and second runner up was Aliya Kudryashova from Belarus.

Igor and Okasana gave high five and all her relatives were happy. Olga was also very happy. She thanked God. She was glad that she had brightened the name of her country and parents. Next day, One Russian newspaper printed the news 'Tsarina of Russia'.

It was her good luck but bad luck was that she could not have gone to Russia for a year. She gave a very grand party on her success. She invited all her class mates, popular personalities and her relatives.

After the party, when she was going to the Trump Place apartment, unfortunately Olga's car collided with truck and she had severe injuries. When Amrit, Roman, Allan and Andrei got information of her accident, they immediately moved to the hospital.

Doctor declared, "Olga has urgent need of blood."

Amrit came forward for giving blood to Olga because his blood group was 'O positive' and doctor was successful in the Operation. Olga was safe now. When she knew about his sacrosanct dedication, she felt his friendship ideal. She thanked Amrit.

When Igor got news of Olga's accident, he took a flight for America and went to meet her. He asked, "Are you all right? How did it happen?"

"A truck ran over and I got deep cut on my head. I was in danger stage due to severe bleeding."

"Oh!" He said further, "I am very thankful to Igor that he gave you blood in a hard time."

"Yes. He is a very good friend."

"No doubt in this."

Igor lived with her in America till her recovery. And when she was able to make multiple appearances at media outlets, events, network and charitable organisations, Igor left for Russia.

During her reign, she went overseas to spread messages about the public awareness and control of AIDS. She also raised fund for the poor children.

After completing her reign, she went to Russia and applied for joining the Russian military. She was selected and could fulfil the desire of her parents. After a year, she married with Igor. Igor Invited big wheels of Russia and Olga invited father, Andrei uncle, Allan, Amrit, Helen, Marten, Diana and other international personalities. Marten was a Magdalene now.

Igor accepted her wife in front of all. That party was a very grand party. Her fans came thousands in number. Workers of Igor's company were also there to celebrate the party.

Everybody was celebrating that party heartily. Igor was happy after accepting her wife. Her love was with her. He gave her welcome kiss in front of all and all were clapping for celebrating it. Olga and Oksana came between her fans with him and gave autographs to all.

It was the time after mid night. Olga was inside the bedroom with Igor. She felt bedroom totally Eden. Olga was happy and locked him tightly as she could. She was in full mood of joyous temperament. She had made herself totally gay tempered.

"It is a day of rejoicing. Now I have completed all the wishes and expectations of my parents and now I want to complete your wish." She said while smiling.

He looked at her a moment and kissed her forehead softly.

She started kissing him and rolled on the bed with him. "Igor, today I am eager for your love. I want you to stimulate my sweet fantasies. Love me. Igor, love me. Let me bathe in your love rain. Start yourself for melting over me seeing my endearment." She said taking his finger in her mouth. Her mischievous lips were dancing on his lips.

He tugged her closer gently and looked straight into the *blue diamonds of her eyes.*

She said again, "Don't see me intently but love me deeply."

He held her in his arms and came in face to face position. "I feel that my understanding power is going away. *You are a respectful, reigning, and touchy beauty* and I do not want to destroy your beauty. *You have crossed your limits of beauty and looked beyond beautiful as you are the princess of great Angels of heaven.* I want to make a beautiful picture of your face on the wall of my soul."

"Why do you ever describe my beauty? I am not as beautiful as you ever say. If you do not love me, I will start to make you romantic. I spent eleven years without your love and you are saying not to love me. You also want to cross the limit but your respect for me do not give you permission for it. Now I want to complete my world. I have vehement desire of your love. I am going on hankering after love."

"Beautiful as you are, you are not proud. You are right." He said giving her a white rose which was gifted by her in childhood.

"So nice! You keep it very carefully."

"Yes. I can keep all your things carefully."

This time, Olga gave him a red rose which was gifted by Igor in the room of Olga. Igor smiled and said, "You also keep my rose very carefully."

"It is just a rose but I can keep you very carefully with lots of love. Now I want to read 'Friends and Lovers' with you."

"Now, there is no need to read this book because 'you' and 'I' are going to become 'we'."

When he leaned over her, she switched off the light.

By and by, time was rolling. Olga was in the blandishment of Igor, mother-in-law, father-in-law, and Oksana. After nine months, she was mother of one daughter but after all, day by day *she was becoming more and more beautiful. Her beauty remained glimpsing on her face.*

Olga put her daughter's name Katya Levina. Soon she decided giving her child to Okasana for purveying because she rejoined the Russian Army. Oksana was very happy and that child had two mothers, one was Olga and second was Oksana.

Now Olga Levina was the captain in the Russian army. She had been doing social services whole life for the country. She did her job perfectly by heart. She was awarded by *Albert Medal* and *Lenin peace prize*. She also won

Medal of Pushkein. After marriage with Igor, she lived happily with him and her marriage life was successful because fast relation in earth never dies. No ominous, no helplessness, no haplessness, and no hopelessness were with her. Her peachy days had started.

Amrit became a software engineer. Olga and Oksana helped for making him actor.

One day he asked Olga, "Why are you forcing me for acting?"

"If you become popular, I will suggest your name to Oksana for marriage."

"Is it right?"

"Yes. She also likes you."

Allan Pearson signed him in his two movies. A few financers were not ready to spend money on the immature actor than Olga spent $ 80 million for completing his movies. He could not be popular in this profession but he was in the contact of media. He tried to make his level best for Oksana.

Two years had gone by and now Amrit had the satisfactory followers. Olga talked to Oksana for doing marriage with Amrit. She gave her answer in a positive manner after thinking so much. She also liked him because of his very caring nature. She married with Amrit and started living happy life with him. He took her care too much and she was happy in his love. Olga had completed her promise.

Olga also immersed into her work. Themis was also happy from her work, devotion, and loyalty. After ten years, she had the rank of Colonel.

It felt that she had a boon of five goddesses Venus, Hebe, Juno, Psyche, and Themis. This belle was '*the rose of*' when she was about to cross her age of thirty six.

Olga took retirement and made an association, WFRC- 'Work for Russian children' with Igor, Oksana, Helen, Amrit and with other political members. She started working for the Russian children who were the victims of violation as well as to increase the women empowerment. She made four headquarters at different places. Her main headquarter in Chelyabinsk. Three more headquarters were in Yakutsk, Nyanga, and Perm.

However, great wonder was that whole world did not accept her name Olga Levina. Everybody *likes* to call her Olga Rodionova while she married with prince of Levin dynasty. *This 'beauty, brain, and brawn' remained popular by her genuine name.*

ACKNOWLEDGEMENT

I am happy that after 15 years, this book is now in your hand and I hope you will enjoy this story. I wrote this novel when I was 13 years old but my family did not help me because they are philistine. My father does not like literature and wants to see me in the stream of engineering so forcefully; he got my admission in Technical College while I wanted to take degree of Bachelor of Art. Finally, the credit goes to my father who helps me this time. The pain which will never go from my heart is that I could break the record of Marry Shelly who wrote her first novel at the age of fifteen but I could not break the record. Maybe, it was not in my destiny.

Moreover, my focus while writing this novel was to make the most beautiful character in the world of literature so I represent you the most beautiful character who is above Cinderella, Snow white, Alice and Barbie.

Now it depends on you how you feel the sensation of this beauty.

Furthermore, I dedicate this story to those Russian women who struggled for bread and butter when soviet lost tragically twenty eight million people at the time of World War 2nd and to Maria Arbatova, Russian feminist and writer, whose works inspire me lot.

I dedicate this book to my adorable brother, Mohit Srivastava, who died on August 17, 2014.

I dedicate this book to my god-daughters Sherlie Benjamin, Tanu Sharma and Asha Tomar.

I also dedicate this novel to my teacher Ritu Bansal madam, Rakhi Parashar madam and Jitendra Raghuvanshi Sir.

I also dedicate this novel to my god-sisters, Deepti didi, Asha didi, and Gunjan Sharma.

Printed in the United States
By Bookmasters

This is a story of a nonpareil juvenile who saw many ups and downs in her childhood life and struggled for her education. Her mother brought her up after her father's death. She lived a very short period of life with mother but before dying, her mother handed over her to her cousin who lived in America. She continued her studies there but she came in trouble when her granny sold her to pimps. Further, that gang of pimps sold her to Marten, who was a high class Prostitute, for sending her to Dubai.

However, one Russian man saved her from the prostitution. He bought her from Marten and purveyed her like a daughter and Olga was happy with him.

Once again a strange anomaly happened; she was kidnapped by that gang of pimps but this time she was saved by her boyfriend.

Fate changed its side and again she adopted prostitution for saving the life of her father-like. Diana, one of the members under Marten served her in front of Allan Pearson who was a Hollywood Director. He was astonished seeing her beauty. He helped her and offered her film to play a lead role.

She denied but when he made her understand, she accepted his proposal after discussing with her father-like. He gave her an international podium and then she was a popular personality.

Again she took a U-turn. She left America after completing her studies. When she reached Russia, she came across her second childhood friend. He deflowered her and Olga tried to attempt suicide but Igor stopped her and gave her full support.

Finally, she joined Russian Army after leaving the world of glamour and fulfilled the dream of her parents. She married with Igor and kept living a very happy life with him.

. . . .

DEEPAK SHRIVASTAVA was an engineer, but he left his job. Now he is a proprietor of LMC Electronics Company and also teaches those students who prepare for the government job. He writes in both the languages, Hindi and English. He has been attending Hindi poetic session in Agra for twelve years.

ISBN 978-1-4828-5115-1

9 781482 851151

9000

PARTRIDGE
A Penguin Random House Company